RISE OF A PIRATE

ALSO BY NELLIE H. STEELE

Cate Kensie Mysteries

Shadow Slayers Stories

Lily & Cassie by the Sea Mysteries

Pearl Party Mysteries

Middle Age is Murder Cozy Mysteries

Duchess of Blackmoore Mysteries

Maggie Edwards Adventures

Clif & Ri on the Sea Adventures

RISE OF A PIRATE

A CLIF & RI ON THE SEA ADVENTURE

NELLIE H. STEELE

A Novel Idea Publishing

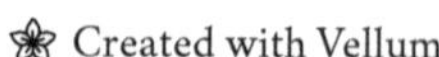 Created with Vellum

For Mark and Lori!

ACKNOWLEDGMENTS

A HUGE thank you to everyone who helped get this book published! Special shout outs to: Stephanie Sovak, Paul Sovak, Michelle Cheplic, Mark D'Angelo and Lori D'Angelo.

Finally, a HUGE thank you to you, the reader!

PROLOGUE

1802

 ind whipped across the violent sea. Dark clouds raced up the coast, bringing with them an impending storm. Lightning tore through the night sky as thunder boomed overhead.

Hidden in the house's secret chamber, one meager flame fought to keep the darkness at bay. The hurricane lamp's light danced off the gold bars scattered on the floor. More gold glinted in the scant light as Henrietta pulled open a wooden chest. She snatched one of the bejeweled necklaces from the pile and shoved it into her dress pocket. She'd need it for the task that lay ahead of her. She'd need more, of course, but one was enough for now.

The chest slammed shut as she released the lid from her grasp. She climbed to her feet and dusted off her dress. Reaching down, she grasped the hurricane lamp and spun to leave the chamber. A chill passed through her and she shivered. She squared her shoulders and strode from the room.

Henrietta navigated through the tight corridors to the end of the passage. She located the trigger to open the hidden corridor. The bookcase swung open and away, and she stepped into the library of her home.

Whispering Manor sat seaside in the small northern town of Hideaway Bay. Henrietta had moved here after marrying Captain William Blanchard. The man flitted through her mind as she shoved the bookcase closed, masking the hidden corridor behind it.

She glanced at the clock on the mantel, ticking the time away. She had hours before her task.

Henrietta stepped into the manor's ample foyer. She grasped hold of the intricately carved wooden banister gracing the stairs leading to the second floor.

"Jane!" Henrietta called. "Jane!" She huffed when the woman failed to appear. "Jane!" she shouted again.

A mouse of a girl appeared at the rear of the foyer. Her blonde hair was tucked into a bun at the nape of her neck. She folded her hands in front of her apron which covered her black uniform. "Yes, Mrs. Blanchard?"

"Where have you been? I've called three times."

"My apologies, Mrs. Blanchard, I was scrubbing in the kitchen. With Elsie sick, I..."

"I do not wish to hear your excuses. Tea, please."

"Yes, ma'am. Will you take it in the sitting room?"

"No, in my bedroom. I must write. I feel a case of depression coming on, and it will be all I can do to stave it off. I must pour out my emotions onto the page."

Jane nodded at her and spun to retrieve the tea. Henrietta climbed the large staircase. She veered left at the top and entered her bedroom. Seating herself at her writing desk which overlooked a window facing the ocean, she gazed outside. The ocean's waves churned and roiled, crashing against the beach with all the fury of the building storm.

Her mind, too, roiled, but not with the depression she'd confessed to Jane. No, she mused, that was merely a distraction. An act. She had fooled them all. And she would continue to do so.

With a half-smile, she focused her attention on her brown leather journal. It sat open to a blank page. She dipped her quill in ink and began to pen a journal entry.

She finished the entry, penning the last words

Tonight, I shall take the first steps in cementing my destiny.

As she set the quill down, a knock sounded at her door. Jane entered after she called to her.

"I am leaving for my walk before the storm hits, Mrs. Blanchard. Unless you need something," Jane said.

Henrietta arched an eyebrow, and a smirk formed on her lips. Before she faced the girl, she let her features fall and slumped her shoulders. "Nothing else."

Jane nodded and departed from the room, pulling the door closed behind her. Henrietta stood and gazed at the stormy sea again. It was time. Time for death.

CHAPTER 1

1785

The hot summer sun beat down on the city of Savannah, Georgia. Henrietta lay under an oak tree, feeling the coolness of the grass beneath her, shaded by the massive tree's heavy foliage. Her book lay discarded next to her. It held no interest for her. Instead, she watched the blue clouds float by and daydreamed of her future.

A smile formed on her delicate features as she imagined leaving the city. She climbed aboard a carriage with her handsome and wealthy husband and waved goodbye to the small but stately townhome where her physician father had chosen to settle.

Although she was only a child of nine, the day could not be too far off. She'd overheard her mother discuss it with her friends when they assumed she wasn't listening.

"It will not be long, Miriam," Mrs. Caster would whisper. "My own Mary is already receiving male suitors. It seems like only yesterday that she was in the nursery."

"Already?" her mother answered.

"Why, yes. She is already eighteen!" Mrs. Caster said. "And not a moment too soon! I should be happy to have her settled."

"Undoubtedly," Mrs. Winston agreed. "Elizabeth has been married six months already."

"Has she settled into her household yet?" Mrs. Caster inquired.

"More or less. She is still sorting servants. Apparently, her maids haven't been working out. She's having a terrible time finding a girl with a good work ethic. She's dismissed three already. She married Jericho Roberts, you know," Mrs. Winston said to her mother.

"He owns the large cotton plantation outside of town, doesn't he?" Mrs. Caster asked.

"Yes. And the business is flourishing."

"She has settled well," Mrs. Caster said with a vigorous nod. "I hope Mary can make as fine a match."

"Before you know it," Mrs. Winston said, "you will be planning for Henrietta to be introduced to society and accept her first suitor."

"As a girl of nine, it still seems so far away," Henrietta's mother admitted.

"It is never too young to begin grooming her," Mrs. Winston said. "Henrietta is a pretty child. She can make a good match, but she must be groomed toward it. And you must have the appropriate connections."

Mother raised her eyebrows, and Mrs. Winston continued. "She should be clever, but never too clever. Men do not appreciate a woman who shows she is smarter than they are. She must possess her manners. She must show interest, but not too much. That sort of thing."

"Courting seemed so much simpler when John and I began."

"This is why I am so insistent that you join the ladies' flower club. This is where you will meet the right people and make the right connections."

"I shall speak to John about it," Mother said, "though I cannot imagine he would disagree."

"Put your foot down," Mrs. Winston said. "You must be firm. The trick, though, is to make them believe it was their own idea. Then they cannot argue!"

The women all cackled with laughter.

The memory faded from Henrietta's mind, but not the lessons. She could make a good match. She was a pretty girl. She would grow into a pretty woman. And she would make a fine match. A match like Elizabeth had made. Not a match like Mary would make.

A smirk crossed her features as she recalled Mrs. Winston's comments after Mrs. Caster had departed from the tea. "I fear for Mary's match-making. She isn't a very attractive girl."

"She seems to have a kind personality," Mother countered.

Mrs. Winston's eyebrows raised and she shrugged. "Men do not seek out kind personalities. Though, with Sarah's connections in Savannah, I dare say she'll scrape by."

Henrietta's mother, Miriam, had joined the flower club as directed by Mrs. Winston. Henrietta was sure, then, she could make a fine match. As she stared at the clouds, she daydreamed of her handsome future husband. He handed her a rose in the back garden. He gazed into her eyes on a starry night. He fell to one knee and proposed marriage to her. She closed her eyes, allowing herself to be swept away in the moment. Mrs. Winston's second daughter, Eliza, had supplied enough details gained from her sister about how men should behave when in love and when seeking a wife that she could imagine exactly how it would happen with her.

Certainly, though, she mused, her courting would be more romantic than Elizabeth's since she would be the prettier of the two of them. Mrs. Winston often admired her porcelain complexion framed by her dark curls.

The leaves rustled above her, and a thud sounded. The sun peeking through the foliage darkened. Even with her eyes closed, Henrietta realized someone stood over her. She snapped her eyes open.

Her eight-year-old brother, Clifton, hovered above her. His dark, unruly hair hung onto his forehead, framing his boyish face. His chocolate brown eyes narrowed at her and he thrust a stick at her, jabbing her in the chest.

"Ouch!" Henrietta shouted. "What are you doing?"

"I've killed you, Ri!" he shouted.

"What a terrible thing to say!" He retreated a few steps away, swinging and thrusting the stick as though it was a sword. "You've made a mark on my dress, you dolt."

Clifton danced across the lawn, jabbing and twirling his pointy branch. "Stop that!" Henrietta shouted at him.

"I cannot," he claimed. He continued his wild waltz.

"Why not?" Henrietta demanded, propping herself on her elbows.

He lunged forward and poked the twig at Henrietta, landing inches from her face. "I must practice."

"Practice what? Dancing about like a fool?"

He parried and thrust the stick again before he darted in another direction, swinging it wildly. "Sword fighting!"

"You are not sword fighting, Clifton, you are swinging a branch around like a madman."

"One must begin somewhere!" he gasped as he continued his antics.

"Whatever do you need to learn sword fighting for?" Henrietta inquired.

"Because, Ri," he answered, swinging the stick to graze her just under her chin again, "I am going to be a pirate one day!"

* * *

1785

"What ridiculous nonsense," Henrietta said.

Clifton allowed his arm to drop to his side and he thrust out his lower lip at her. "It's not!" he insisted. "Father says I can take on anything! And I wish to take on being a pirate!"

She rolled her eyes at him. "Oh, Clif, you are such a child. I suppose I should allow your babyish behavior. Though you'll have to grow up someday."

"And when I do," he said, lifting his chin and raising his eyebrows, "I will be a pirate!"

"No, you will not be," Henrietta said, sitting up from her reclined position and pulling on her shoes.

"Says who?" Clifton demanded.

"Says society."

"Who's that? I shall fight him myself," Clifton said. He swung the sword fiercely and growled.

"Not a person," Henrietta retorted with a sigh. "People in general. Pirates are not considered proper by any means. You would be shunned by society."

Clifton shrugged. "And I should care why?"

"Because society is everything."

"But I shall be a pirate! With a large treasure! I shall be fearsome, and men shall quake when they hear my name."

"Yes, I am certain Clifton Nichols will strike fear into the hearts of many," Henrietta jested.

"I shall be called Blackbeard."

"Blackbeard?" Henrietta asked with a roll of her eyes. "There is already a pirate named Blackbeard."

"Then I shall be the second! I shall make my own way in life, and no one will tell me what I can or cannot do!"

Henrietta shook her head at the boy. She gathered her book from the grass and climbed to her feet. "You are still a child. You shall see when you grow older."

Clifton snorted in laughter at her. "You are but one year older than me, Ri."

"But years more advanced in maturity," she contended. "And stop calling me Ri."

"Why?" he whined.

"Because I am soon to be a woman, not a girl. I shall not like to be called Ri, it sounds childish. I should not like to be thought a child. Soon, I shall seek a husband." She raised her chin and squared her shoulders.

The dark-haired boy burst into laughter. He dropped to the ground, rolling and kicking his feet as he continued his chortling. Henrietta stepped toward him and hovered over him. He sobered as she frowned down at him.

"Laugh all you want," she chided. "You shall see!"

She stormed toward the house, leaving him lying in the grass. He rolled onto his belly and stared after her.

"Ri, wait!"

She did not respond and continued her march to their home.

"Ri! Don't you want to be more? Don't you want to be your own person?"

His calls garnered no reaction.

As Henrietta entered the house, her eyes adjusted to the dimmer light. As she stood in the foyer, her mother descended the stairs. She carried her baby sister, Carolina, with her. Nearly eight years her junior, Carolina was the latest and last addition to the Nichols family. After her delivery, the doctor told her father that Mrs. Nichols would deliver no more children in his opinion. Her father and mother grieved the news, but Henrietta was overjoyed by it. One brother and one sister proved two too many. Mary Caster had no siblings and her parents doted on her.

"Ah, Henrietta!" her mother said with a wide smile. "Out enjoying the sunshine?"

"I was, though Clif's childish behavior has ruined my afternoon."

"Oh?" Miriam inquired as she furrowed her brow and glanced outside. Henrietta twisted to gaze through the thick glass. Clifton continued his imaginary swordplay. "It seems he is having a lovely time."

Henrietta held back rolling her eyes for fear of being told her face would stay that way.

Her mother continued, "Mrs. Winston is paying me a call this afternoon. I hoped to count on you to help with Carolina."

Henrietta's shoulders sagged and a grimace formed on her lips. A whine escaped her. "Oh, Mother, must I?"

"Now, Henrietta," Miriam said as she fussed with Carolina's dress. "Mother has asked you to do something."

"Why must I do it, though? I wanted to read!"

"You had time to read outside."

"But Clif distracted me and I couldn't."

"Clifton distracted you or your daydreaming distracted you? I watched from the window, and you did not pick up your book once. Now, I do not mind your wandering mind, but at this moment I need you."

Henrietta grabbed hold of Carolina, balancing the child on her hip. "Why do you never ask Clifton?"

"That would be most inappropriate," Miriam answered. "As a boy, Clifton does not need to learn how to tend a baby or rear a child. Do you not wish to prepare yourself for domestic life?"

"What if I do not?" Henrietta questioned, Clifton's earlier statements echoing in her mind.

Miriam's eyebrows raised high. She placed her hands on her hips and gave Henrietta a hard stare. "What are you saying?"

"Father told Clifton he can do what he likes in life. Make his own way in the world. Does the same not apply to me?"

"Of course it does, dear. As long as what you like is making a good match and raising a family. But the man you choose to do that with is entirely up to you." Her mother smiled sweetly at her, but the answer did not satisfy Henrietta.

"Suppose I wish to be a pirate or a plantation owner and not raise a family?"

"Henrietta!" Miriam exclaimed.

"What?" the child contended.

"You're speaking nonsense. Now, go upstairs with Carolina. I do not have time for this. Mrs. Winston is to arrive at any moment, and I am certain I've forgotten something vital."

"But, Mother..." Henrietta began.

"No, Henrietta!" Miriam said. "Go!"

Her mother shooed her up the stairs then spun on her heel and disappeared toward the kitchen. With a final glance at Clifton outside, Henrietta set her jaw in a frown and stamped up the stairs. The sound of her feet slapping against the wooden stair treads caused the tot in her arms to wail.

Henrietta set the child on the floor in their bedroom. "Oh, stop your howling," she said to the child. Tears streamed down the child's face. With a huff and a roll of her eyes, Henrietta pulled Carolina onto her lap as she plopped onto the window seat. Below her, Clifton climbed the oak tree and leapt from a low branch. He whooped as he wiggled the stick in the air at his fanciful opponent.

"It isn't fair, Carolina," Henrietta said. "My fate must be decided by a man. Clifton's can be decided by himself."

"That's very true, Henrietta," her mother said.

Henrietta spun to face the door. Her mother stood with her hand on the frame and an understanding smile on her face. "But I think you shall find that while life for a woman can be unfair, it can also be rewarding."

"But you cannot decide your own life!"

"No, you cannot in one sense, but you can in another. Let me tell you a secret. Behind every good man is a strong woman, Henrietta." She stroked Henrietta's dark hair, tucking a curl behind her ear.

"I don't want to be behind him!" Henrietta protested.

"Oh, I know it must seem terribly unfair, dear, but you shall come to accept it." Miriam leaned forward and kissed her head.

Henrietta harrumphed and set her gaze out the window. Mrs. Winston came up the walk. "Oh! I must run!"

Miriam flitted from the bedroom and down the stairs. Henrietta watched as Clifton leapt from the tree again and greeted Mrs. Winston. She stopped for a moment and said something to him. He approached her and spoke. A wide smile crossed her face. He spoke a few more words and waved his stick around. After his speech, he thrust it high in the air. Mrs. Winston clapped her hands and laughed before she waved and continued up the path.

Henrietta narrowed her eyes at the scene. Why could Clifton say and do as he pleased but she could not? Tears welled in her eyes.

CHAPTER 2

1785

Henrietta bit her lower lip as she blinked them back. She stared at the child sitting in her lap. Her mother's words echoed in her head. "You must learn to tend a baby. You must learn to rear a child. You must learn to be domestic. It is your lot in life."

Henrietta frowned. She did not wish it to be her lot in life. She wished to be free. One day, she would be, she vowed. If she could make a fine match, she would then be free.

Mrs. Winston departed an hour later. "Henrietta!" Miriam called up the stairs. "Henrietta, dear! Please come down and bring Carolina."

"Yes, Mother!"

Henrietta gathered the baby into her arms and proceeded down the stairs. Her mother stood at the door calling Clifton inside as well. "Come in, dear, and please go to the sitting room all of you. I have arranged some tea and we shall have a chat."

Henrietta entered the sitting room and sat on the settee. Clifton joined her, taking a place in an armchair. He still clutched his toy stick. Henrietta frowned at him as he offered a silly grin at her, bearing all his teeth.

Miriam entered and poured the tea from the set on the table. She set a cup out for each child before she pulled Carolina into her arms. "Hello, little darling," she said as she cooed over the child.

Henrietta sipped at her tea.

"Henrietta, dear, sit up straight, do not slouch."

Henrietta grimaced. "And do not scowl! Your face is most unattractive that way."

Henrietta glanced to Clifton. He sagged in the armchair, his legs dangling and flailing. He balanced the teacup on his stomach and blew bubbles into it.

"I only frown because you only corrected me, not Clifton! His behavior is far worse!"

"Do not be a tattletale, dear," her mother said. "Clifton, darling, do not play with your food, please. Now, I've called you both here because I have news."

Clifton scooched higher in his chair and set his teacup aside. "Are you to have another baby, Mum?" he questioned.

Henrietta held in a groan. "The doctor said she couldn't, stupid."

"The doctor does not know everything, Ri."

"Children, enough!" Miriam said with a clap of her hands. "Henrietta, do not call your brother stupid. And no, darling, Mother is not going to have another baby."

Clifton groaned. "Ohhh, Mummy, why not? I want another playmate. Ri is not very fun."

Miriam smiled at the boy. "Dear, if Mother had another baby now, he or she would be far too young to play with you. Younger than Carolina and Carolina isn't very much fun for you, is she?"

Clifton shook his head. "Now," Miriam continued, "Mrs. Winston has told me some wonderful news. She has engaged a French tutor for Edwina. And she has offered to allow you to join her in lessons. You shall begin tomorrow afternoon!"

Henrietta raised her eyebrows. "Why would I want to learn to speak French?" Clifton moaned. "Couldn't I learn sword fighting?"

"No, you will learn French. It is important to provide you with as genteel an upbringing as we can manage."

"Fine," Clifton said with a sigh.

Henrietta sipped at her tea. "Will I make a better match if I speak French?"

Her mother snapped her head in her direction. "That's a long way off, dear. Do not worry about it yet."

"But I heard Mrs. Winston say it wouldn't be far off."

"It is only a figure of speech, darling."

"But will it?" Henrietta persisted.

"Yes, I am certain when the time comes it will," Miriam said. "Which is why I took her up on the offer."

"Then I should be very happy to learn French," Henrietta said. She shimmied back on the settee and raised her chin as she sipped her tea.

Miriam dismissed them to their rooms before their dinner. Henrietta floated to her room on a cloud. She imagined her handsome husband, very impressed by her language skills. While all the other girls only spoke English, Henrietta stood out.

She strode into her room and sat at her small writing desk. Papers lay scattered across the top. Her mother despised her messy habit and often scolded her for it, but when she wrote stories, she could not find the time to organize. She did not see the harm in it.

She stared at her papers for a moment before pulling a fresh sheet and dipping her quill into the ink. Her writing instrument hovered above the page as a scene formed in her mind. The quill flicked across the paper as she made her first strokes before her arm shuddered.

Her jaw unhinged and she twisted to face the source that caused her arm to flail. Clifton stood at her side.

"Why did you do that? Now I've ruined the sheet."

The child glanced at the paper. "'Tis only a stray mark."

Henrietta narrowed her eyes at him. "What do you want? I am busy."

"Why did you ask Mum if you could make a better match if you could speak French?"

"None of your business." Henrietta turned back to her work. Another poke stopped her.

"Why, Ri?"

"I told you not to call me that."

"I shall always call you Ri," he said with a grin. "Even when we are old and gray. And I shall hobble in on my cane and say 'Hello, Ri!' and you shall laugh." He pretended to hobble about the room.

"I shall not!" Henrietta insisted though a chuckle escaped her.

"Yes, you shall. You laugh even now!"

Henrietta shook her head but chuckled again. "So, why did you ask mum about making a match? You are too young to marry a man, Henrietta. Girls have to be much older than you."

"But girls must start at a young age so they can marry the right man. Mrs. Winston says so."

"Must I start at a young age, too? So I can marry the right girl?"

"No, it is different for boys."

"Good," Clifton said with a nod. "I am glad to not need to begin so soon. I am not certain I wish to be married."

"You will change your mind," Henrietta assured him.

Clifton shook his head. He narrowed his eyes and gazed into the distance. "Pirates do not have wives, I do not think," he said after a moment.

"You cannot be a pirate," Henrietta insisted.

"Why not? Father says I can be whatever I wish."

"Pirates are criminals. You do not wish to be a criminal, do you?"

"Perhaps I do," he said with a mischievous grin. Henrietta rolled her eyes. "Are you writing, sis?"

"No, because someone continues to interrupt me."

He shrugged. "I cannot help it. I still do not understand why you wish to marry the right man. Do you not wish to do what you want? To have your own life?"

"That is impossible for girls. I should have to remain in Father's house until such time as I marry. Mother said. So, my best hope is to make a smart match. Then I shall have the freedom I want."

"Will you not just have a husband to listen to instead of a father?"

"You do not need to listen to your husband like a father."

He crinkled his forehead. "Mother listens to Father and does what he says. When she wants something, she asks. She does not do anything without Father's permission."

"It is different."

"How?"

"You must make them believe the things you want are their own ideas and then they will let you do them."

The boy frowned as he considered the statement.

"Oh, never mind, you are too young to understand."

"Will you tell me a story later?" he questioned.

"Not if I have none written!"

"Tell me one you already wrote."

"I've already told you those stories, Clif."

He shrugged. "It does not matter. I shall be happy to listen again." He darted to the door but spun to wait for her answer.

"Fine, I shall tell you a story."

Clifton punched his fist in the air. "Hurrah!" he shouted. He raced down the hall. Within seconds, footsteps raced back toward her room. Clifton skidded to a halt, grasping at the doorjamb to stay upright. "You know, Ri, you're the reason I want to become a pirate! So, I shall request the Blackbeard story again if you have not written another."

Before she could answer, he scampered away. Henrietta smiled in spite of herself.

* * *

Clifton clapped his hands from his cross-legged perch on his bed. In her nightgown, Henrietta danced around the room as she mimicked a sword fight between the dreaded pirate Blackbeard and his enemy. While she had written a new story, it remained unfinished, so at his request, she had begun the retelling of her fanciful adventures of Blackbeard the pirate. Based on the real man, her embellishments kept her younger brother thoroughly entertained.

"Hurrah!" the small boy cheered. "Strike him down with your sword, Blackbeard!"

In a dramatic display, Henrietta pointed her imaginary sword at an unseen enemy now relegated to the floor. "You shall never pilfer my treasure!" she shouted as she thrust a fatal blow.

Clifton rolled in his bed and giggled, tickled by the tale. Henrietta straightened and stiffened her posture before leaning forward in a bow.

"Tell another!" Clifton cried.

"I think not," Miriam said as she strode into the room.

"Awww," Clifton groaned. "But, Mummy, we only had one battle!"

"And one battle is quite enough. It is time for you both to be abed."

Miriam pulled the covers around the boy and kissed his forehead. "Come along, Henrietta. I shall tuck you in, too."

Henrietta grasped her mother's outstretched hand.

"Good night, Ri!" Clifton called from his bed. "I shall look forward to more adventures tomorrow."

"Good night, Clif," Henrietta answered with a wave.

Miriam led Henrietta to her own room down the hall. "Must I go to bed, Mother?"

"Yes, dear. It is time to go to sleep."

"I hoped to write more. May I please stay awake for another hour to write?"

"No, dear," Miriam answered. "Now, into bed with you."

Henrietta climbed into her bed and her mother adjusted the covers around her. "Good night, Henrietta." She pressed her lips against the girl's forehead.

As she turned to leave the room, she caught sight of Henrietta's desk. Papers covered the top. She twirled to face the child. "Henrietta, what is the meaning of this?" she asked as she motioned to the writing desk.

Henrietta slouched in her bed. "I… I had hoped to continue writing after I finished with Clif's story. I did not tidy my things because I meant to continue work."

"You should not be so careless, Henrietta! How many times must I tell you? You must always remain tidy in your house and your appearance." The woman scurried to the desk and began to push the papers together into a clump.

"No, wait!" Henrietta shouted as she leapt from the bed.

"Henrietta, get back into bed this instant!"

"No, you'll ruin them, Mother!" Henrietta exclaimed, hurrying to the desk.

"How will I ruin them?" Miriam questioned, her voice filling with exasperation.

"They must be ordered," Henrietta answered. She ripped the papers from her mother's hands and began to adjust their order. With a click of her tongue, she said, "You've shuffled them out of order."

"If you had tidied them to start, I would not have," Miriam argued.

"Why must I tidy them when I remain in the midst of working?"

"It is important to be neat. Cleanliness is next to godliness, Henrietta."

"Does God not understand I am still working on them?"

Miriam narrowed her eyes at the girl as Henrietta neatened the stack of papers and placed them under the desk's top. "Even if God does understand, your husband will not."

"Why not? Will he not understand how I am when I write?"

"Your husband may prefer you not to spend your time with writing."

Henrietta paused in her straightening of papers. Her brow furrowed as she considered the statement. "Lucky, then, that I do not yet have one," she answered.

"With these poor habits, you shall never have one." Miriam adjusted the covers again after Henrietta returned to her bed.

"Perhaps that is best," Henrietta said. "I should like to be on my own and make rules for myself. Such as leaving my papers sprawled while working."

"People will not like you if you remain unmarried, dear. They will find you odd. Do you wish to be found odd?"

Henrietta considered the statement. "Perhaps. Perhaps I am odd."

Her mother raised her eyebrows at her. "People will not be very kind to you if they find you odd. You will have no friends, no one to depend on."

"So?"

"So, you will have nothing, Henrietta. A woman cannot live on her own!" Miriam pressed her hand to her forehead and closed her eyes for a moment before continuing. "Please, Henrietta, listen to me. I am only attempting to provide the best life I can for you. And that is to make a good match where you will be well provided for. Is that not what you wish?"

Henrietta narrowed her eyes as she contemplated. "Yes, it is," she answered.

"Then you must do as I say. You must learn to behave like a lady, how to keep house, how to be a good mother. Your future husband will require all of these things of you. He will require that you be a loving and devoted wife."

"And what shall I require of him?"

"You shall not require anything of your husband. However, I pray every evening that your husband will provide well for you. That you shall have a comfortable life."

"Is that what I should search for in a husband?"

"Let's not discuss that now," Miriam said. "Go to sleep, Henrietta. Good night, dear." After another kiss on her forehead, Miriam departed and the room fell into darkness.

Henrietta considered the conversation. While she longed to be free, to write her stories, she had no desire to be an outcast. She must marry well, she decided.

She spun onto her side, her eyes falling to her writing desk. She would give up her writing if she had to. She would marry well.

Henrietta closed her eyes and settled into the pillow when her body shuddered. Her eyes shot open. The bed shook again. "Ri!" a small voice whispered. "Wake up, Riri!"

Henrietta spiraled to face her brother. "What are you doing in here? We are meant to be abed."

"Tell me another story."

"No," she said with a roll of her eyes. She turned away from him. "Go to sleep, Clif."

"Please, Riri!" he entreated. "Tell me another of your stories."

"I have no others."

"What of the one you were writing earlier?"

"I did not finish it."

"When will you?"

"Never. I will not finish."

"Why?" Clifton whined.

"Mother says I must not focus on these things, but rather making a good match."

"You are too young to make a match, Ri."

"But Mother says I must not write and become caught up in my work if I am to make a good match. She says my husband will not wish me to write but to be a devoted wife. And if I am to find a good husband, I must learn how to behave now."

"That's rubbish!"

"It is not!"

"It is, Ri!

Henrietta twisted to face him again. "I do not wish to be an outcast, Clif! I must make a good match! Now go back to bed!"

She huffed and pulled the covers up to her chin.

"Ri!" Clifton whined again, poking at her back. Henrietta refused to look at him.

He poked her again but received no response. "Fine," he groaned and shuffled away from her room.

Henrietta snapped her eyes open. A tear rolled down her cheek as she felt the weight of what she would give up. But she had to. If she wanted to live a comfortable life, she had to give up on her dreams.

CHAPTER 3

1785

Henrietta stretched and yawned as she climbed from her bed. The sun had not yet peeked over the horizon, but she'd awoken with a start. An idea propelled her from her bed and to her writing desk. As her characters danced in her mind, she hurriedly lit a lamp. She scurried to find paper and ink her quill. She scrawled words across the page as the players played out the scene in her head.

A smile crossed her face as the page filled. She bit her lower lip as the quill zipped across the page. She's written five pages before the sun crept over the horizon. After finishing her idea, she leaned back in her chair and studied her work. Her fingers found her chin and she rubbed it while she read over what she'd written. Satisfied, she grinned and set the pages with the others that were part of her new story. She stared at the page on top. *Across Land and Sea* was her latest pirate adventure tale. Clifton would surely enjoy this one, she mused.

Henrietta glanced out the window. The pink sky was streaked with red as the sun fought the night back. She set the stack of papers on her desk and stood from her chair. From the wardrobe, Henrietta grabbed her black and white striped dress. After changing her clothes, she splashed water on her face from the washbasin and toweled off before sinking into her chair to brush her hair.

As she stroked the brush through her long dark curls, her mind turned to her story. What would her pirate do next? Would he return to the beautiful maiden a changed man or continue to roam the seas in search of an even greater fortune? Her mind parsed through various scenarios as she searched for her story's direction. She became lost in the tangle of her thoughts and did not hear her mother approach.

"Ready for the day, dear?" Miriam questioned as she strode into the room. Henrietta's brush clattered to the floor as it slipped from her startled fingers.

"Yes, Mum," Henrietta said. She retrieved the brush from the floor and stood, spinning to face her mother.

Her mother ceased walking, a curious expression on her face. She narrowed her eyes and her jaw dropped open. She rushed to Henrietta. "What is this?" She squished Henrietta's chin between her thumb and forefinger as she tilted her head. "Have you been writing?"

Henrietta nodded without a verbal response.

Her mother squeezed her lips together and shook her head. "You've got your face dirty with ink! And on today of all days, when you shall begin your French lessons. Oh, Henrietta!" She whipped a handkerchief from her sleeve and drenched it in the washbasin. She scrubbed at the child's face as she glanced past her to the desk. "At least you have tidied your work."

"Ouch, Mum, that hurts!" Henrietta complained after a moment.

"I am sorry, dear, but I must remove the mark! You do not wish to arrive at Mr. and Mrs. Winston's home looking like a ragamuffin, do you?"

"No," Henrietta admitted.

"No, of course not. Oh, there is still a stray mark." She handed the handkerchief to Henrietta. "Continue to scrub at it whilst I rouse Clifton."

Henrietta nodded and scrubbed at her face with the damp cloth. A few moments later her mother returned. "Let me see," she prompted.

Henrietta tilted her head to show the spot she'd cleaned. "I can still see it. Well, there is nothing to be done now. Come along for your breakfast."

Henrietta surrendered the damp handkerchief and followed her mother to the dining room. Her father already sat at the head of the table with a bowl of grits. Henrietta took her seat to his left.

"Good morn…" he began before his voice trailed off. "Whatever is on your face?"

Miriam's shoulders sagged as she sat down with Carolina on her lap. "Ink," she answered. "Henrietta has been at her writing again. You know it always makes her careless."

"I wasn't careless," Henrietta insisted. "I must have smudged the ink as I read over my work."

Clifton popped into the room a moment later. He tore around the table in a circle.

"Clifton Henry Nichols!" his mother exclaimed. "Do not run in the dining room."

The boy bounded to his father and leapt up. John caught him mid-jump and set the boy on his knee. "Good morning, son."

"Good morning, Father!" Clifton said.

"Did you have a good sleep?"

"I did! I dreamt of pirates all night."

"I hope they did not capture you!"

"Not me! I fought them all off and stole their treasure!"

"Yo-ho! You must be the best pirate of them all!"

"Yes, I am!" he declared as he hopped to his feet and made a menacing face. He took his seat at the table.

"Pirate or not, you should still remember your table manners!"

Clifton offered a coy glance at his mother with puckered lips as he discreetly pulled his napkin onto his lap. She smiled at him and continued to feed Carolina as he dug into his breakfast. He glanced across the table at Henrietta and his eyes shot wide.

"Ewwww!" he shouted. "What happened to your face?"

"Clifton!" John corrected, his eyebrows high as he glanced sideways at the boy.

"But, Father, there is something on her face! Can you not see it?"

"Yes, I can see it perfectly well. However, you should not call attention to something that may embarrass another."

"But she looks ridiculous."

"My chin became stained with ink whilst I was working on my story FOR YOU." Henrietta poked her finger in Clifton's direction.

"Did you finish it?" he asked with an expectant grin on his face.

"No, I have not. I…"

"Clif," Miriam said, interrupting Henrietta, "you mustn't continue to ask Henrietta for stories. She has other things she must begin to focus on."

Henrietta's brow furrowed as she snapped her head in her mother's direction. She set her jaw and glared at her.

"But, Mummy, I like Henrietta's stories."

"Yes, I know you do, but she cannot spend all her days writing them for you."

"Why? What must she do instead?"

"Many things. It is time she learned to manage the house a bit. Learn how to behave like a lady when greeting company. What to discuss when paying calls. That sort of thing."

Clifton wrinkled his nose.

"I will write before breakfast," Henrietta promised Clifton.

He clapped his hands.

"No, you shall not," Miriam countered. "I do not wish you to come to breakfast with a stained face daily."

"I promise to be careful."

"Henrietta…" Miriam began.

"Mother!" Henrietta shouted. She tossed her spoon to the floor then grasped the bowl of grits. "I shall throw the bowl onto the floor unless you shall allow me to write."

"You'll do no such thing!"

Henrietta raised her eyebrows and waved the bowl.

"Put that bowl down at once!"

John raised his hand. "Henrietta, put the bowl down." Henrietta spun to face her father. "You shall be permitted to write," he assured her.

Henrietta placed the bowl onto her placemat and fluttered her eyelashes.

"John, is that wise?" Miriam whispered.

John shook his head and signaled for Miriam to hush. "Only if you promise to be more careful. If you present yourself for breakfast with another ink stain on your face, you shall not be permitted to write. Do you understand?"

"Yes, Father," Henrietta said.

"And you must obey your mother, dear. It is time you

begin to learn how a household runs. You are growing away from your childhood and into adulthood."

"Yes, Father."

"She only wants the best for you and aims to have you grown into a fine lady. And she is the best instructor, you see. She has made a fine match in me, hasn't she? And has three beautiful children." Her father beamed at his own tongue-in-cheek humor.

"Is that why you married Mum, Father? Because she was an instigator?" Clifton asked.

"Instructor, dear," Miriam corrected.

"I did not know you were a teacher, Mum," he said.

"No, dear, I was not."

"Then why did Father say you were a good instructor?"

"I meant in how ladies should behave, run a household and be a fine wife, Clif."

"Oh." His brow wrinkled. "Must I learn how to be a fine husband?"

"You must learn how to provide a stable household for your family, yes."

"Is that being a fine husband?"

John nodded to the boy and Clifton pursed his lips as he considered it. "Must I marry?"

"No," John answered. "Though you may find you prefer the companionship."

"I should think not."

"Really?" John asked with his eyebrows raised high.

The child thought a moment. "No," he said, "I will be away at sea often, so I shall not see her much anyway."

"Oh? So you will be a sea-faring man?"

Clifton nodded. "A pirate."

John roared with laughter. He slapped his thigh and said, "Oh, Clif, you are quite the character."

Clifton burst into giggles, and Miriam grinned at him.

Only Henrietta narrowed her eyes at him as she considered the unfairness of the situation. While her dreams must be quashed, Clifton's world knew no bounds. Frustration built inside her, and she bit her lower lip until it hurt.

* * *

Henrietta marched along the sidewalk under the early afternoon sun. The frown on her face suggested in a glance the frustration she felt toward her brother, Clifton.

"Stop dawdling!" she called over her shoulder.

Behind her, the boy darted back and forth on the sidewalk. Carrying his stick-sword, he thrust it between the wrought-iron fence spindles before dancing a few steps backward and lunging toward the fence again.

"I am not dawdling," he contended, "I am fighting pirates!"

Henrietta rolled her eyes. "We must not be late for our French lesson."

"We will not be," he assured her as he caught up to her side.

"If we are, it is I who will be punished, not you," she lamented.

"I would never tell," he assured her.

"Mrs. Winston would tell, you foolish boy."

"Oh, right," he said. "Still, we should not be late even with my battles."

He spun behind her and thrust the sword through the fencing again with a loud cry. He stumbled back a step as a large dog raced toward him, barking ferociously as it pounded against the fence.

"Ah!" Clifton cried as he staggered back. His foot caught on a divot in the ground and wobbled. His arms flailed as he attempted to regain his balance. He lost the battle and sprawled into the street in a heap. "Oof," he said as the wind was knocked out of him.

Clif!" Henrietta shouted. Her eyes widened as she witnessed the scene. A horse-drawn carriage barreled toward them, two chestnut horses running at full speed. Clifton lay in its path. "Clif, look out!"

The ground rumbled under Clifton's head. He twisted his neck toward the beating sound pounding through his ears. His eyes shot wide, his forehead wrinkled, and his mouth gaped open as he witnessed the scene. Large hooves beat the ground in front of him. The carriage driver waved his arms wildly. "Get out!" he hollered as he attempted to pull the horses to a stop. They did not stop, though. They barreled straight toward him.

Henrietta lunged toward Clifton. Grasping his foot, she hauled him backward and out of the carriage's path. They collapsed in a dusty tangle next to the gate as the carriage rumbled past.

Henrietta breathed a short-lived sigh of relief before her breath caught in her throat again as the dog pounded against the fence and let out a loud yip.

Henrietta shook her head as she inched away from the fence. "Are you all right?" she questioned Clifton.

"I...I think so," he moaned as he pulled himself to sitting.

Henrietta climbed to her feet and did her best to dust herself off and tame her hair. "Some pirate you are," she teased.

He stuck his tongue out at her before he pulled himself to standing. "And now you are a mess. Dust off your clothes before we continue," Henrietta insisted.

"Yes, Mother," he answered.

Henrietta stuck her tongue out at Clifton before darting ahead of him.

"I suppose it is good for your training," he teased as he hurried to catch up to her.

Henrietta rolled her eyes at him. "Is that what you want?" Clifton inquired.

"What?"

"To be a mum like Mum?"

"I suppose it is inevitable," Henrietta said.

"Huh?"

"It will happen no matter what I want. I cannot escape it," Henrietta answered.

Clifton considered it. "But do you want it?"

"Yes," Henrietta said with a sharp nod.

"Really?" Clifton inquired.

"Why shouldn't I? It is what is expected of me. What is normal."

"So? I do not wish to be a father."

"You are a child, you do not know."

"I do so, Ri. As a pirate, I will be too busy collecting treasure to smoke a pipe and read by the fire in the evening. Or carry a child around on my shoulders on a summer's day."

Henrietta sighed as they pushed open the gate leading to the Winstons' home. "And besides," Clifton continued, "I wish to be free. I do not wish to support a family and provide a home."

"Some of us cannot be free," Henrietta spat.

Clifton stopped dead at the words.

"Come along," Henrietta called to him as she climbed the steps to the large, stately home.

He hurried up the remaining path and clamored up the steps as Henrietta slammed the door knocker against the plate.

They were ushered inside and to the schoolroom. Edwina, three years older than Henrietta, sat with another boy of the same age. Thomas Cranston, son of prominent businessman Robert and Julia Cranston, joined them. Henrietta had met him on one occasion before. She hadn't recalled how mesmerizing his blue eyes were. Her stomach fluttered and she felt her cheeks flush as he greeted her.

Thomas Cranston would provide a fine life for her, she considered as they took their seats. Thomas sat catty-corner in front of her. She stole several glances at him during their lesson. His straight, dirty blonde hair framed his peach complexion. A few freckles dotted his nose. Henrietta found them adorable.

Miss Franks, their tutor, began by teaching them several French words such as man and woman, girl and boy. They practiced pronouncing the words several times before she moved on to numbers. She began teaching them the numbers one through ten. Henrietta knew the French words for these numbers. She used them in her stories and had learned them with her father's help.

After going over them several times, Miss Franks asked Edwina to repeat them. "Ummm," she hesitated.

Henrietta raised her hand. "Yes, Henrietta?" Miss Franks inquired.

"May I repeat them? I know them."

"Oh, yes, please let Henrietta go first," Edwina agreed with a desperate head bob.

"All right," Miss Franks agreed. "Please recite the first ten numbers in French."

Henrietta stood from her seat and recited them back perfectly. She grinned, her attention focused on Thomas. Now he could see how clever she was, she reasoned.

Henrietta slid back into her seat, pleased with herself.

"Oh," Edwina said, wringing her hands. "I can never come close to being that flawless."

Thomas leapt to his feet. "Do not worry, Edwina. I shall help you. Follow my lead." He flashed her a grin and began with number one then paused for Edwina to follow him. By ten, she grinned at him, blushing and gushing about his help.

Henrietta's smile faded to a frown. She jutted her chin out and narrowed her eyes at Edwina. Her plan had backfired. Instead of being impressed at her cleverness, he'd preferred to play hero to Edwina's ignorance.

Perhaps Mrs. Winston was correct. Perhaps men did not prefer a clever girl. The thought dampened Henrietta's spirits. She sulked for the rest of the lesson and most of the walk home. Clifton babbled in her ear about pirates and French until they reached the house. She slogged through the front door and stamped up the stairs, ignoring her mother's question about how the lesson went.

Clifton was more than happy to fill her in on his escapade and their first day of French. Meanwhile, Henrietta preferred to brood in her room.

CHAPTER 4

1785

French lessons continued for several weeks. While Henrietta excelled at the language, she found her mastery of it did little to catch Thomas Cranston's eye. As they sat through another lesson, Henrietta found herself daydreaming rather than paying attention to Miss Franks.

In her mind's eye, she was several years older. Her dark curls framed her pale skin. Her rose lips formed a smile as her mother placed a bouquet in her hands. She wore a rose-colored dress with lace accents. Rose always brought out her best coloring, her mother said.

She climbed into the waiting carriage as her mother pressed a handkerchief to her eyes and sniffled. When they arrived at the church, her father helped her from the carriage and led her down the aisle. Waiting at the end stood Thomas Cranston. He smiled broadly at her, and she offered him a demure look.

Within the hour, she would be Mrs. Thomas Cranston. They would have a large, prominent home in Savannah. She would be the president of the flower society. And everyone would pay her calls. Everyone would know Henrietta Cranston.

"Henrietta? Henrietta!" Miss Franks voice sounded.

Henrietta pulled her gaze from the window and her daydream. "Yes, Miss Franks?"

"Thomas believes the appropriate phrase for 'Do you speak French?' is 'Parle pas français??' Do you agree?"

Henrietta raised her eyebrow. All eyes turned to her. She glanced among their faces. She knew very well this was incorrect. Miss Franks raised her eyebrows at her as she awaited her answer. Clifton eyed her. Thomas cocked his head at her. Edwina wrung her hands.

"I must admit," Edwina interjected into the silence, "I am not certain, though I trust Thomas is correct. He is knowledgeable in so many things."

Thomas's face broke into a wide grin at her statement. "Thank you for the vote of confidence, Edwina," he said. "Let us determine now if Henrietta agrees."

Henrietta swallowed hard. She did not, however, she would win no points with Thomas Cranston if she proved herself more clever than he. She cleared her throat and with another glance to Thomas, she said, "Yes, I agree Thomas is correct."

"Are you certain?" Miss Franks said, her face showing surprise.

Henrietta nodded and ignored the whispered "Ri!" emanating from Clifton.

She plastered a weak smile on her face and nodded.

"He is, in fact, not correct. Since none of you knew that, you shall all write the correct phrase twenty-five times before tomorrow."

Clifton's hand shot into the air. "Miss Franks!" he whined. "I DO know the correct phrase."

"Oh?"

He stood from his chair and said, "Parlez-vous français."

"Correct, Clifton! Well done!"

Clifton beamed as he slid into his chair. Edwina smiled sweetly at him. "Boys are always so smart."

Henrietta's stomach turned at the sickening statement. She should have stated the correct response. Instead, she had played dumb for the attention of one specific male. She bit her lower lip. It would work to her advantage though, she was sure of it. It stung but, in the end, she would be triumphant.

Following the lesson, Henrietta and Clifton ambled home past the neatly kept houses near the Winstons. Clifton skipped and bobbed, leaping over divots in the path and racing ahead of Henrietta.

As she caught up after one of his sprints, he spun and stalked beside her. "Why did you do that earlier, Ri?"

"Do what?" she inquired.

"Why did you tell Miss Franks Thomas was correct? You knew he wasn't."

"I'd forgotten."

"I do not believe you," Clifton answered.

"Believe what you like."

"You know very well how to ask if someone speaks French. You have repeated that phrase at home several times."

"I was not paying attention and did not hear the question," she lied.

"That isn't true either."

Henrietta clamped her jaw closed as annoyance surged through her.

"So, why did you lie and agree with Thomas?"

"You would not understand if I explained it to you. And besides, Edwina believed him. Why should I not have?"

"Edwina is a nincompoop."

"Clifton!"

"Well, she is, Ri. She is quite stupid." They strolled a few steps further. "So, why did you do it?"

Henrietta's shoulders sagged. "Because had I disagreed, Thomas would not like me."

"Why?"

"I told you you wouldn't understand," Henrietta lamented. "Boys do not like girls who are more clever than they are. If I corrected Thomas, he would have preferred Edwina to me."

Clifton narrowed his eyes. His jaw flexed as he parsed through his sister's words. "So?"

"So, I rather like Thomas and I want him to like me."

Clifton wrinkled his nose. "I still do not understand. You are more clever than I in many things and I like you."

"You are my brother, you are forced to like me."

"That's not true! William Johns has a sister and he detests her."

"I doubt that is true."

"It is! Only last week he pushed her into a mud puddle and ruined her dress just because he does not like her."

"Boys like Thomas prefer girls who are less clever, trust me."

"But why do you care, Riri? Leave the less clever girls to boys like Thomas."

"But I like Thomas."

"Why would you like someone who wishes you to be stupid?"

Henrietta grew weary of the conversation. "Just leave it be, Clifton."

He spun into her path, blocking her from moving

forward. "Do not pretend to be stupid to gain someone's attention, Ri. It can only make you unhappy."

Henrietta's brow furrowed at the boy's statement. "Race you home!" he shouted a moment later, a mischievous grin crossing his face. He spiraled away from her and darted down the street.

Henrietta stood motionless, still processing the young boy's statement. It sounded profound, yet it could not have been. He could not know this. He could not understand the intricacies of life yet. No, she ruminated, he was wrong.

1788

"Ouch!" Henrietta cried. She stuck her index finger in her mouth. The metallic taste of blood stung her tongue.

"Pricked yourself again?" Clifton inquired.

"Tend to your book," Henrietta admonished.

He pulled a handkerchief from his pocket and waved it at her. She grimaced at him.

"If you get blood on your needlepoint again, Mother will scold you. Again."

Henrietta snatched the handkerchief from his hand and wrapped it around her finger. She returned to her work. After a moment, she let the hoop flop into her lap. "It is impossible to work with my finger wrapped," she huffed.

"You'd better finish it, Ri."

"I cannot."

"You are going to be scolded!" the boy sang.

"Then I shall be scolded."

"Who shall be scolded?" Miriam asked as she entered the room. Trailing behind her was four-year-old Carolina. Miriam glanced at the embroidery hoop in Henrietta's lap. "You still have not finished your sampler!"

"No, Mother, I have not. Instead, I have injured myself. And now I shall likely have a purple bruise on my finger."

Miriam sighed. "You must take more care in your work, Henrietta," she said as she stalked to her eldest daughter's side and examined her finger.

"Take more care," Carolina repeated, waving a finger at Henrietta.

"Why must I learn needlework? It is most useless."

"It has several household uses. I have explained it to you before."

"Several mousey uses. I explained before!" Caroline mimicked.

"Household, dear, HOUSEHOLD," Miriam said slowly and loudly.

Henrietta rolled her eyes. "Henrietta, do not do that. It is most unattractive! Now finish your sampler."

"No," Henrietta said. She crossed her arms obstinately and grimaced.

"Yes," Miriam argued.

"No," she answered defiantly.

Miriam's eyes went wide and she set her jaw. "Finish the sampler at once or you shall not go to the parade!"

"But Mother!" Henrietta objected.

"No, but Mothers, dear. Finish or you shall stay home and finish whilst we go to the parade."

"You wouldn't dare!" Henrietta said.

"I am certain your father will agree. Now finish the sampler," her mother said. She gave a curt nod and spun on her heel to depart from the room. "Come, Carolina," she called as she exited.

"Finish or you shall stay at home!" Carolina said.

"Oh, shut up," Henrietta shouted at her as she left the room.

Henrietta sighed and stared at the embroidery hoop in her lap. Clifton gave her a sideways glance.

"You'd better finish, Ri. You do not wish to miss the parade, do you?"

"Of course not, but I refuse to finish this menial work! There is no need for me to learn this stupid task."

"I shouldn't like you to miss the parade. There are to be fireworks after!"

Henrietta shoved the hoop from her lap. It clattered to the floor. "Ri…" Clifton began.

Henrietta ignored him, storming past him and up the stairs to her room. She fumed as she entered and slammed the door behind her. Squeezing her eyes shut, she leaned against the door. After a few moments, she opened her eyes and breathed out a deep breath. Her vision focused on the desk across the room.

With a smile crossing her features, she wandered to the desk and pulled several blank pages from it. After dipping her quill in ink, she began to scratch words across the page. Writing calmed her. This work was worthwhile and meaningful.

Two hours passed as she lost herself in the work. Her door burst open, pulling her attention away from her story.

"There you are!" Miriam said, exasperation filling her voice. Henrietta's unfinished needlepoint hung in her hands.

Henrietta stacked her papers neatly and slid them into the desk. "Is it time for the parade?"

"Yes, but not for you."

Henrietta's jaw gaped open.

"You did not finish your sampler. As I explained earlier, you shall not go to the parade unless you finished the sampler. You did not even make an effort!"

"There is no reason for me to finish it."

"Henrietta, every woman should know how to form a proper stitch!"

"I will not need to know this. I shall have servants."

"Well, aren't we miss high and mighty," Miriam said as she placed her hands on her hips. "Even women with servants know how to stitch."

"I have far better uses of my time, Mother," Henrietta countered. "I have finished another chapter in my book."

Miriam squeezed her eyes shut. "That book. That book! I grow weary of listening to you prattle on about these childish things."

"Writing books is not childish!"

"It is when you avoid the tasks you have been instructed to complete!" Miriam shouted.

Henrietta crossed her arms. She arched an eyebrow at her mother. "Are you *really* going to make me stay home?"

"Yes, Henrietta. You disobeyed me and you must be reprimanded."

"How will you explain my absence to everyone?"

"I shall say you are under the weather."

"Then you shall lie? Is this not something to be avoided?"

"Would you prefer I tell them the truth? That you are a naughty child?"

"You wouldn't dare."

"Wouldn't I?"

"No, because it may ruin any chance I have at making a good match."

"Your marriage is not that imminent that it will matter. All children are naughty some times. At least they will know I've striven to raise a well-behaved child."

"Yet you have failed to this point since your child is at home being punished for naughty behavior."

Miriam rolled her eyes. "Then I shall say you are ill and resting in bed."

Henrietta shook her head and stomped to her desk. She collapsed into the chair. "You are not to write while we are away. You are to finish your sampler!" Her mother threw the embroidery hoop onto her bed.

Henrietta twisted to eye it. With an indifferent expression, she turned away from it. "Did you hear me?"

"Yes," she answered.

"I expect it to be completed when I arrive home." Henrietta gave no response. "Do you understand?"

"Yes, I understand."

"Good." Her mother scurried from the room.

"Though I have no intention of completing it," Henrietta added after her mother was safely away.

She pulled several sheets of paper from her desk and began to write. She gazed out the window as movement caught her attention. Miriam, John, Clifton, and Carolina ambled down the path toward the street. Clifton glanced back to the house as though searching for her. He said something to both their mother and father. John shook his head and tugged on the boy's arm. Reluctantly, he spun away from the house and followed his parents.

As the skies darkened, Henrietta slid from her desk chair. The unfinished sampler stared at her from her bed. She narrowed her eyes at it. "If you want a finished sampler, Mother, fine. I shall finish it." She snatched the hoop from the bed and plopped onto her chair.

After forty-five minutes of careful work, Henrietta held out the hoop. A smile crossed her face. Perfection, she mused. She'd place her completed sampler on her mother's reading chair. She skipped down the stairs and dumped the hoop on the wing-backed chair. With a grin, she spun on her heel and scrambled back up to her bedroom.

Miriam, John, and Carolina had returned home before the fireworks. Clifton had been permitted to stay with friends to watch them, but Carolina had grown too weary and wished to go to sleep.

Miriam checked on Henrietta after settling Carolina. "Did you finish the sampler?"

"Yes," Henrietta assured her. "I placed it on your reading chair."

The woman offered Henrietta a sweet smile and stroked her hair. "There's my good girl. I shall review it tomorrow morning."

Henrietta returned the expression. Her mother kissed the top of her head before leaving the room.

Henrietta curled in her bed as the stars began to poke through the dark sky's canvas. With a book in hand, she studied the words on the page with great interest.

A noise sounded at her window. She gasped and a tremor shook through her. With wide eyes, she peered at the darkened sky outside. The pounding sounded again. A small face peered into her window.

Henrietta puffed out a sigh and shook her head. She climbed off the bed and scurried to the window and unlatched it. "What are you doing, Clif?" Clifton crouched on the roof outside her room.

"Come on, Ri! You can still make the fireworks!"

"Are you suggesting I climb from my window and flee into the night like a thief?"

"Well, you cannot waltz through the front door. Mother and Father may catch us."

Henrietta considered it.

"Hurry, Ri!" Clifton whined. "We'll miss them!" He grabbed her hand and tugged.

A mischievous grin crossed her face and she offered him a nod. He pulled her through the window and onto the porch roof. They scrambled across the small, low-pitched roof to the side of the house. Clifton dropped to his belly and swung his legs over the edge. He climbed down the rose trellis and hopped to the ground below.

Henrietta peered over the side. "Clif!"

"Put your foot over onto the trellis, Ri!"

Henrietta groaned and glanced at the ground. "Hurry, come on!"

She moaned again. "I'm a bit afraid. I'll go back."

"No!" Clifton scurried up the trellis again. "Lay on your belly and dangle your foot."

Henrietta winced but did as he instructed. She felt his hand grasp her leg and place it on the trellis. Her other leg swung freely. He steadied it and placed it into another groove.

"Now, reach one foot down to find another rung."

Henrietta wiggled a foot free and lowered it until she struck a rung. "That's it," he encouraged. "Keep going."

He clamored down the trellis and leapt to the ground below. Henrietta proceeded slowly but neared the ground within minutes.

"Jump, Ri. I shall break your fall!"

Henrietta hopped from the trellis and toppled onto her brother. The two rolled on the lawn before coming to a stop. Clifton was the first on his feet. He hurried to her side and pulled her to standing. "Come on!"

Together, the two children raced into the night. They hurried to the park where Clifton found his friends waiting near an oak tree.

"I didn't think you'd make it, Nichols," one said.

Clifton puffed with exertion. "I told you I was fast."

"Yeah, but dragging a girl with you slows you down," another chimed in.

"Not Ri!" Clifton said. "She's fast."

Further conversation was stunted by the start of the fireworks. Henrietta bit her lower lip as the large bursts colored the black sky. She smiled at them, pleased Clifton had retrieved her. She felt free watching them. Free of parents, free of control, free. She spread her arms wide and giggled as she basked in the fireworks' glow.

When the display ended, Clifton spent a few more moments speaking to his friends while Henrietta enjoyed the warm night air. "Clif," she said after a few moments, "we'd better get back before we are missed."

Clifton nodded at her and grasped her hand. They ducked through the crowd, heading toward home. As the throngs of revelers began to depart, the crowd grew thick. The two children were jostled around among the adults as they tried to press through the crowd.

"We must get home soon. Mother and Father will expect you."

"Come on," Clifton urged, tugging her as he darted between people.

A few fair-goers issued complaints as the children bumped into them. As Clifton bounced off one grisly-looking man, he shouted, "Hey!" As he swung to face them, he broke the contact between Henrietta and Clifton. Henrietta stumbled back a few steps and tripped, landing hard on her rear. Her ankle twisted as she fell. "Ouch!" she cried out.

"What do you two brats think you're doing?" he hollered.

He hovered over Henrietta as she rubbed her sore ankle. "Need a good whipping if you ask me," he growled at her.

CHAPTER 5

1788

"Hey! That's my sister! And I won't let you hurt her!" Clifton shouted, leaping between them. He cocked his fist and landed a blow on the man's potbelly.

"Oof!" the man groaned as air blew from his lips. He doubled over, and Clifton used the time as the man recovered to pull Henrietta to her feet and urge her past the man and down a side street.

She slowed to a stop as the crowd disappeared behind them.

"Wait, stop," she cried.

"What is it?" Clifton asked.

"My ankle," she whined.

"Can you bear weight?"

"Give me a moment," she said, testing it. She sucked in air as a dull pain shot through it. After a moment it eased. She hobbled a few steps and nodded. "It has eased."

"Are you certain? I can help you."

She shook her head. "I can make it."

"Okay," he said. "But I will still help you." He put his arm around her waist and helped her along.

She stopped after a few steps. "What is it, Ri? Does it hurt?"

She shook her head. "Thanks, Clif," she said.

He squeezed her middle and offered a wide grin. "You're welcome. I shall always take care of you, Ri."

They toddled home. Henrietta eyed the rose trellis as they approached the house.

"I shall go in the front door and speak to Father. He is waiting in his study." Clifton pointed to the light streaming from the room. "I'll pretend to march up the stairs then I shall sneak you in the back door."

"I can try to climb…" Henrietta began.

Clifton shook his head. "No. I do not wish to test your ankle. This plan will work. Trust me, Ri." He winked at her and left her near the back door while he darted around the side of the house.

Henrietta waited under the dark sky, hidden in the shadows. Ten minutes passed before the door she eyed popped open. A small face appeared and a white hand waved her into the house.

She hurried to the door. Clifton waved her to a stop. He pointed to her shoes. She pulled them off, clutching them to her chest. He raised a finger to his lips. Henrietta nodded and tiptoed inside.

Clifton pointed a finger toward their father's study then toward the back stairs. Henrietta nodded and they snuck up the narrow staircase. She tiptoed to her room and eased the door shut. A smile crossed her face. They'd successfully snuck out and returned. The feeling was exhilarating. Even the pain in her ankle had subsided from the rush of adrenaline she felt at the achievement.

Henrietta rose early the next day, still buzzing from her previous night's experience. She leapt from her bed and raced to her writing desk. The experience had given her fuel for several story angles, and she wanted to document them all.

Before she finished scrawling the last idea on her paper, a scream ripped through the house. She stiffened in her chair, recognizing her name being shouted. She swallowed hard as she slid from her chair. Still in her nightgown, she inched her door open and peered outside.

Her mother's voice filled the air again. "Henrietta Nichols, come downstairs this instant!"

Henrietta bit her lower lip and stalked from her room and down the stairs. Her mother met her at the bottom. Henrietta pursed her lips as she spied the item in her hand. Her sampler. Miriam waved it at her. "Is this some sort of joke?"

"No," Henrietta offered.

"I am not amused, Henrietta."

Henrietta's eyes found her mother's and she shrugged. "I have practiced every stitch given to me."

Her mother narrowed her eyes and stared at the sampler. She spun it to face Henrietta. "'This is stupid' is NOT what I instructed you to stitch."

Henrietta cocked her head. "I thought it best to make a statement more worthwhile for my practice."

Miriam's face reddened. John entered the hall from his study. "Here, here, ladies, what is all the shouting?"

"It is this," Miriam said, handing the sampler to John. "I instructed Henrietta to finish her sampler whilst she stayed home last night and THIS is what I received."

John accepted the embroidery hoop from Miriam. His jaw popped open before he clamped it shut. An amused expression crossed his face but he held any chuckles inside.

He swallowed and attempted to force a severe expression on his face.

"Henrietta," he said, "this is most unladylike."

Henrietta stared up at her father as Clifton plodded down the stairs. "Was someone shouting?" he inquired.

"I'm sorry if I woke you, dear," Miriam said as she rubbed the boy's cheek.

"Is something wrong?" he questioned.

"No, merely Henrietta has done something… naughty."

He raised his eyebrows, his eyes sliding sideways to Henrietta to determine if they'd been caught. She gave a slight shake to her head and yanked the sampler from her father's hands.

"I practiced all my stitches as instructed. Mother did not care for the message." She thrust the hoop toward Clifton. His eyes grew wide and he gave a hearty laugh.

"It is not funny, Clifton," Miriam scolded. "Henrietta, you were told to stitch the Lord's Prayer. And you shall! I expect you to spend the day working on another sampler."

"Fine," Henrietta said with a roll of her eyes as she stomped up the stairs.

"Do not roll your eyes, Henrietta!" She heard her mother mutter, "Oh, John, I do not know what we will do with that girl!"

Henrietta inched across the porch roof after climbing from her bedroom window. On her hands and knees, she climbed up toward the window. With her fingernail, she tapped against it. Clifton's head popped up from his pillow.

With squinted eyes and a scrunched-up nose, he glanced around while laying on his belly. Henrietta knocked at the window again. He spotted her and flipped onto his back. He sprung to sitting, a surprised expression on his face.

She waved him toward the window. Clifton tossed off the covers and scurried around his room. He pulled on his trousers and doffed his nightclothes in favor of a shirt. After sticking his feet in his shoes, he tiptoed toward the window and pulled it open.

"Ri!" he whispered. "What are you doing?"

"Sneaking out," she breathed. "I thought you might like to come."

He climbed out the window and onto the roof.

"Where are you going?" he asked as they crawled across the roof to the rose trellis.

"Summer is nearly over," Henrietta said. "And it's been months since we snuck out last. I thought we could sneak into town."

"Why?"

"Do we need a reason?"

"You want to sneak out because you've had another row with Mum," Clifton deduced.

"I just want to feel free," Henrietta answered as she swung her leg over the roof's edge and began her descent down the trellis.

"Careful of the thorns!" Clifton warned.

Henrietta leapt to the ground below and waved at him. Clifton scrambled down the trellis and landed next to his sister.

"Where to?" he inquired.

She grabbed his hand and they raced into the night. Henrietta and Clifton hurried down the darkened streets of the town. An occasional drunk roamed the alleys that shot off from the main roads.

"Let's go to the park," she said. "And lay in the grass and count the stars."

"We could have counted stars from our own yard, Ri."

"And what fun is that?"

"Let's do something better," he said with a grin.

As they discussed their plans, the doors to one of the town's taverns opened. The din of the interior floated outside. Two men spilled onto the street. Gripping each other, they sang loudly, chuckling and swaying as they wove down the street.

Henrietta and Clifton pressed into the shadows against the building. As they watched the men depart, another man approached them from the opposite side.

He poked at their chests. "What are you two children doing here?" he questioned. His breath stunk of liquor and spittle covered his mouth as his lips struggled to form words.

"None of your business, old-timer!" Clifton shouted.

"What did you say?" He grasped the boy's shoulders. Henrietta stamped on his instep. He released his grip on Clifton and grabbed at his hurt foot as he hopped on the other. Clifton landed a blow to the man's gut before he grasped Henrietta's hand and pulled her down the street.

"Where are we going?" she asked as they dashed off.

"You'll see!"

Within moments, Clifton wound through the streets and approached his destination. Docked ships bobbed in the water. Clifton pulled Henrietta toward a stack of shipping crates. He crouched low behind them, pulling her down too.

"What are you doing?" she whispered. Her eyes darted around. A few less-than-reputable types milled around the docks.

"I am going to sneak aboard that ship and pilfer something."

"What?!" Henrietta exclaimed. "Clif! Are you mad?"

Clifton held a finger to his lips before he dashed off toward the waiting ship.

Henrietta huffed at him but sank behind the crate. She risked a glance over them. The eleven-year-old boy stood near the ramp leading aboard. He whistled and waved before scrambling up the ramp.

Henrietta waited for fifteen tension-filled moments. She chewed on her lower lip until it pained her. She kept her eyes trained on the ship's gang-plank. Every muscle in her body was stiff. Her muscles began to ache and tremble as she crouched, unmoving.

After what seemed an eternity, movement caught her eye. A shadow moved down the plank. Her breath caught in her throat and her heart pounded in her ears. As the figure leapt to the dock, she exhaled a breath she didn't realize she was holding. Clifton hurried across the docks to her location.

He ducked behind the crates with her. A grin crossed his face. "I did it, Ri!" he exclaimed.

"You're daft!" she said.

"Daft and better off than I was before." He flashed a gold coin at her. "I snatched it from inside the captain's chambers."

"Clif! Put it back!"

"No way! I took it and it's mine! He won't miss it. Besides, I'm not sneaking back on board to put it back. I may get caught."

"You weren't worried about getting caught when you stole it."

"Such is the life of a pirate," he said with a smirk. With that, he flipped the coin and caught it mid-air. He grabbed her hand and pressed the gold piece into her palm, closing her fingers around it.

"I don't want the filthy stolen thing!" she protested.

"Yes, you do. Besides, it comes with a promise."

"A promise?"

"Yes. I shall always take care of you, Ri. That is my promise."

1793

Henrietta strolled through the park on the bright summer day. One week ago, she had celebrated her seventeenth birthday. She had grown into a beautiful woman, her father said. And soon she would catch some man's eye and be taken away from him. He said those words with a wistful look in his eye, though Henrietta did not understand why. She couldn't wait to escape from her home. She could strike out on her own. No more rules, no more expectations. She would be free.

And she would be free sooner rather than later if she had her way. Never mind catching some man's eye, she was certain she'd already caught a particular man's eye. And he had caught hers.

Albeit, he had caught hers years ago. She thought back to her French lessons. To Thomas Cranston as a younger boy. He'd outgrown his freckles but his peach complexion remained, framed by his now slightly darker blonde hair. His light blue eyes were the color of the sky on a cloudless day. She could get lost in those eyes. And her heart melted when he offered her that sideways half-grin, half-smirk, flashing his dimple at her.

He liked her. She knew it. And she liked him. And soon, he'd make an offer. She'd make him court her, of course, but she would become Mrs. Thomas Cranston soon enough.

Her mind wandered as she meandered under the trees, laden with leaves in the heat of the summer. Her eyes drifted to the sky and a smile crossed her features as she imagined her father walking her down the aisle.

She halted in her tracks as an object thudded against the back of her head. She reached her hand to her hair, pressing where it hit. Another small item smacked her back. He spun and searched for the source of the whacks.

She heard a giggle and spotted movement behind one of the larger oak trees. Her eyes narrowed and she glowered at the tree. "Come out," she insisted.

She received no response. Setting her jaw, she tapped her foot against the ground in agitation. "I said come out," she said, her hands settling on her hips.

Chocolate brown hair poked from behind the tree along with those mischievous brown eyes. He smirked at her before he strolled over.

"Why are you throwing things at me?"

"I wanted to get your attention, Ri," Clifton said, his voice now low in pitch. He hovered over her, several inches taller than her. Though he had shot higher than she several birthdays ago.

Henrietta glanced up at him, her hands still on her hips.

"Smile, Ri, it is a beautiful day."

"I was smiling until you threw an acorn at me," she answered.

"You should be happy I hit you."

Henrietta furrowed her brow at the statement. He grinned at her. "My aim has improved. Only last year, I would have missed."

"Bravo, a skill I am certain will be useful."

"Indeed," he said as he offered her his arm.

"I am busy, I do not have time to wander about with you."

"Humor me, Ri," he said. "I shall walk you to wherever you are going."

"Why?" she questioned. "Has Mother sent you to check up on me?"

"No," he said with a chuckle. "Should she have?"

"What does that mean?"

"It means is there a reason Mother should be checking on you. Where are you going?"

"My business is my own."

"I harbor no judgment. Though I am curious since you're being quite secretive."

"I am not." Henrietta began when several boys romped through the park.

"Clif! We're going to have a game," one shouted, tossing a ball back and forth. "Coming?"

"Go ahead, I must take my sister to her appointment," he shouted back.

"That is not necessary," Henrietta insisted. "Go have your game."

"Awww," another boy yelled. "Come on, Clif! Leave her to her tea and flower shows!"

"Perhaps later," Clifton hollered back.

The boy with the ball pointed at Clifton in a silent challenge before he spun away, galloping across the park with his rowdy bunch.

"Go, Clif," Henrietta encouraged. "I am perfectly capable of taking care of myself."

"I know you are, but that doesn't mean you should."

"I can get to my tea on my own."

"Hmm, it is for this very reason I shall escort you there." Henrietta cocked her head at the statement. "You are not going to a tea unless I take you to one."

"Are you saying I am lying?"

His lips formed a closed-mouth smile. "I haven't hurled any accusations. And if I accompany you, you will not be a liar. I will make sure to see you inside Mrs. Winston's door for the Junior Ladies Flower League." He offered his arm again, his smile faltering. "That is where you're going, isn't it?"

The sparkle in his eyes suggested he knew her intentions

were not to attend the league meeting. She threaded her arm through his. "Of course it is," she said.

"As I suspected," he said. "What else would a young lady such as yourself be doing on a beautiful summer's day but talking about all things flowers?"

Henrietta's stomach sank as her mind whirled through her former plans. They wandered from the park through the residential streets. Henrietta bit her lower lip and glanced toward an alley as they passed.

CHAPTER 6

1793

"You know," Clifton said, "I've heard rumors that some young ladies are meeting young men alone in alleyways. Can you imagine?"

"How scandalous," Henrietta feigned.

"Most untoward, I agree."

"Untoward? And this coming from a man who idolizes pirates," Henrietta retorted.

"What have pirates to do with clandestine meetings between lusting young men and the ladies who have captured their attention?"

"I imagine pirates do much worse in addition to meeting ladies after which they lust."

"A debate for another day," Clifton announced as they reached the Winston home. "Here we are. And just in time, it seems."

Edwina stood at the door, greeting several other girls.

"Oh, Henrietta!" she called. "I did not think we would see you today."

Henrietta offered an unimpressed smile and called, "Yes, I've had a change in plans." Her eyes remained on Clifton as he raised his eyebrows and offered an amused glance.

"Hello, Clif," Edwina called.

"Good day, Edwina," he replied with a wave.

"Well, go on, Clif," Henrietta said with a nudge. "Here I am, safely delivered to my tea with the ladies."

"I said I'd see you safely inside. Now off with you." He shooed her toward the house. With a roll of her eyes, she plodded to the house and entered.

Henrietta's eyes glazed over as she sipped at her tea. The ladies chattered about their contribution to the upcoming flower show. Her interest was not piqued until her ears detected the mention of Thomas Cranston.

"Mother says Thomas Cranston shall be the one who pins the ribbon on the person with the winning bloom," Edwina said.

"I would like to have him pin a ribbon on me," Abigail said with a giggle.

Expressions of faux shock and giggles went up through the ladies.

"Such talk from ladies!" Mrs. Winston said as she entered with a poised smile and a plate of tea sandwiches. "Abigail, what would your mother say?"

Abigail's face turned several shades of red. "Oh, I meant nothing lascivious. Only that Thomas is likely *the* most eligible bachelor in Savannah."

Mrs. Winston offered a practiced smile at the girl. "Yes, I imagine whoever catches his eye will be a lucky lady." She thrust her chin in the air as she strode from the room. "Carry on, girls!"

"A lucky lady, indeed," Abigail whispered amidst a cloud of giggles.

Henrietta scowled at Abigail. She set her teacup down with a loud clang and stood. "I am sorry, ladies, I really must be going."

"Oh?" Edwina said. "Are you quite all right, Henrietta?"

"Yes," Abigail said, her nondescript brown ringlets swinging as she whipped her head to stare at Henrietta, "you look a bit… red."

"No more than you!" Henrietta said. "Good day, ladies."

Henrietta hurried from the room and to the front door. Whispers erupted behind her. She rolled her eyes as she pushed into the warm summer air. She pulled the door closed behind her and collapsed into it. Why had Clif shown up when he did? It had ruined her plans. And she'd been forced to go to that ridiculous tea and ladies meeting. She hated them. Perhaps she'd enjoy them better when she ran them.

Mrs. Winston would not reign as queen of Savannah society forever. She would. After she became Mrs. Thomas Cranston. Though she could not secure her throne if she continued to miss meetings with Thomas.

After he'd expressed his obvious interest in her, he'd pressed for them to meet privately. She'd asked him to call at the house as with a proper courtship. Thomas insisted he would, but he'd also confided in her that he was unsure he could stand a proper courtship. Her beauty drove him wild and he was sure he'd overstep his boundaries, angering her father. He'd prodded at her to meet with him alone. And she'd agreed.

Perhaps if she hurried, he'd be waiting for her. She raced away from the house toward the alley where they'd agreed to meet. Ducking between the homes, her eyes scanned the area. Her heart sank she as found herself alone.

She bit the inside of her cheek as tears stung her eyes. He hadn't waited. What if he'd gotten the wrong impression, believed she'd avoided him. Why had she run into Clif in the park? She sighed and pressed her hand against her forehead as she paced the small area.

With slumped shoulders, she trudged from the alley, slogging through the streets toward her home. Perhaps she could comfort herself with her writing.

* * *

Noise startled Clifton awake. He rubbed at his eyes and glanced around the darkened room. What was that noise, his tired brain questioned? Movement caught his eye and he twisted to face his window. A figure crawled past on the porch roof.

Realization dawned on him. With a shake of his head, he climbed from his bed and thrust the window open.

"And just where do you think you're going?" he whispered into the night air.

The figure froze. Falling back to her haunches, Henrietta twisted to face him. "Out," she said simply.

"Sneaking out? Really, Ri, what are you thinking?" he chided.

"You taught me how to do it!" she said, her voice incredulous.

"Yes, but I did not mean for you to use it for nefarious purposes."

"As you do, to pilfer items from local merchant ships?"

"I misspoke. I did not mean for you to use it for nefarious purposes that did not involve me." He grinned, his teeth gleaming in the moonlight.

"Go back to bed, Clif," Henrietta said as she inched toward the trellis.

With a roll of his eyes, Clifton pulled on his clothes and shoes and followed her. She'd already shimmied down the trellis by the time he peered over the corner of the roof. "Wait!" he whispered.

He caught up to her as she strode toward town. "Mind if I join you?" he joked.

"Actually, I do," Henrietta answered, her arms wrapped tightly across her chest.

"And what are we doing that we must do alone?"

"WE are doing nothing. I have an appointment."

"An appointment? In the middle of the night?"

Henrietta stopped and faced him. Her dark eyes focused on his in the moonlight. "It is private." With that, she strode away from him.

"Henrietta," he called after her, "do not meet with him."

She wavered, her brow furrowing as she hesitated in her steps. After a moment, she raised her chin and thrust her shoulders back taking a determined step.

"I am serious, Henrietta," he called again.

She spun to face him. "And what will you do to stop me? Tell Mother and Father? Will you really ruin any chance that I have at marrying Thomas Cranston?"

Clifton shook his head at her. "He will not marry you, Ri."

Her eyes widened and she turned several shades of crimson. "How dare you!" she shouted at him.

"If he wishes to marry you, he will court you. Tell him that."

"He will court me. He only wishes to steal a few moments alone with me. It is his love that drives him to seek this."

Clifton approached her. "It is his lust, not his love, sister. I do not wish to see you hurt."

"Thomas would not hurt me. I can tell by the way he speaks, the way he looks at me."

"He looks at you as a wolf eying a farm animal."

A crisp slap landed against his face after the comment. He rubbed at his cheek. Henrietta twirled on her heel and started away from him. He grabbed her arm, pulling her back. "Let me go with you."

"That's hardly romantic."

"I care not for his romantic desires, I care for you."

"Clif…"

"Ri, if he truly feels this way for you, he should be delighted to see you no matter who is with you."

"He cannot express his true feelings with my brother hanging over me."

"No, I imagine not." Clifton grasped her wrist. "Not again," he said, preventing her slap. "You got the first one for free."

She huffed at him. "I shall not interfere with your liaison, but I insist you do not go alone."

With no other options, Henrietta acquiesced. Clifton ambled next to her as they wove through the streets. Henrietta remained silent, annoyed by his presence.

She turned down a darkened alley. A figure paced near the end, limned in moonlight. Her heart skipped a beat at the sight of him. Even in the dim moonlight, she recognized Thomas.

"Thomas," she said, her voice breathy with excitement. He spun to face her. The smile on his lips faded as he spotted her escort.

"You brought Clif?" he inquired.

Henrietta wrung her hands as she explained. "Yes. Oh, he will be no bother, but…"

"Do not mind me," Clifton interrupted. "But I insisted she not walk the streets alone. Quite surprised you asked her to, really."

Henrietta elbowed him in the gut before Thomas dragged

her a few feet away from him. "Henrietta, this is most unexpected!" he hissed at her.

"I know and I am sorry, though there was not much to be done."

"Who else is aware of our meeting?"

"No one!" Henrietta insisted. "Clif caught me sneaking from the house. It was all I could do to keep him quiet."

Thomas's jaw flexed as he pinched his lips together, his aggravation apparent. Henrietta laid a hand on his forearm. "Thomas?" she asked, a question in her voice. "It does not matter, does it? It is enough just to see me, isn't it?"

"Yes, of course, but…" His voice betrayed his annoyance.

Henrietta awaited the completion of his statement.

He lowered his voice, attempting to steady his temper. "I expected to have you to myself under the moonlight, is all. I feel… crowded. Watched."

They glanced to Clifton who paced several feet from them. He smiled brightly, his eyes constantly on them despite his aimless ambling.

"Might we have a few moments?" Henrietta called to him.

Clifton waved his hands in the air. "Please, take all the time you need."

"Alone," she clarified.

He narrowed his eyes at the pair of them before he turned his back.

Henrietta sighed. She wouldn't get much more from her stubborn brother. She hoped it was enough. Henrietta placed her hand on Thomas's chest and gazed into his eyes.

Thomas stood stiff, avoiding her stare. "Thomas, please. Let us not waste the time we have."

After a moment, he grabbed her hand in his. He forced a smile onto his face. "You look so very beautiful in the moonlight."

She smiled broadly at him. "Perhaps you should pay a call to the house," she suggested.

"Henrietta, please do not rush this," he said, annoyance creeping into his voice again.

"But…"

"I have already explained."

"Surely you can…"

"Henrietta, please!" he said sharply. Clifton glanced over his shoulders at the harsh words. Thomas tempered his voice. "I cannot ask for your hand before I am capable of preparing a home for you. And if I should overstep during our courtship, your father may not permit us to marry. Please, Henrietta, understand. My feelings for you are so deep, I must tread carefully."

Disappointment filled her, but she offered an accepting nod. She must learn to be an understanding companion. She would support him through thick and thin as his wife. She should start now. "I understand. My feelings for you also run deep." She gazed longingly into his eyes.

His eyes slid sideways toward Clifton before offering her a brief smile. His thumb rubbed her hand before he squeezed it. "Well, I suppose you should be getting back. Perhaps we can find another time when we can be truly alone."

"I have a few more moments." She eyed his lips, hoping he might press them against hers.

Instead, he stepped back, dropping her hand from his. "You should go."

She bit her lower lip and blinked back the tears that stung her eyes. She could offer no verbal response. She gave him a clipped nod and turned toward Clifton. He spun away from her as she stepped away. She glanced over her shoulder, hoping for a loving gaze or amorous smile. He kept his back to her.

Her heart ached and anger burned inside her toward Clifton for ruining their moment.

"Finished?" Clifton asked with a grin as she approached his side.

"Thanks to you, yes," she barked.

He smiled as though his job was complete. "And will he call at the house and ask to court you?" Clifton inquired as they meandered through the streets on their return trip.

"Yes."

Clifton's eyebrows lifted high. "Tomorrow?"

"No."

"The day after?"

"No."

"When?"

"I do not know the day or date," Henrietta confessed, "but he will come."

Clifton remained silent at the statement.

"He will, Clif," she insisted.

"We shall see."

Henrietta stopped walking. "Must you be so cruel?"

"Ri, I do not mean to be cruel but practical."

"He loves me."

"And if he does, he shall prove it. He shall ask for your hand, not encourage you to clandestine meetings where he can take advantage of you."

"He could never!"

"Couldn't he? He has a reputation, Ri. You are not the only girl who has caught his eye."

"You are wrong!" Henrietta shouted. "You are cruel, Clifton Nichols." A sob escaped her. "And I hate you for it!"

"Ri!" he called as she dashed past him. Tears streamed down her cheeks. "Ri, wait!" With a sigh, his shoulders sagged. She could not see the truth if he held her eyes open and made her watch. His sister was hopelessly in love with

Thomas Cranston and insistent on planning a life with the dreadful man.

He had not lied to her, he ruminated as his feet carried him toward his home. Thomas Cranston did have a reputation. And not just with marriageable girls. With the staff in his home, with women who frequented the docks with painted faces and questionable clothing, with even a married woman whose husband spent too much time at sea.

Thomas Cranston was an incorrigible cad. A man who would ruin his sister. He could not allow her to throw herself away for such a man. He had to be stopped.

CHAPTER 7

1793

Clifton waited in the alley outside one of Savannah's busiest taverns. Earlier, he'd witnessed Thomas Cranston enter with several friends. Through the window, he spied them tossing back multiple ales. He'd also spotted Thomas's hand wandering inappropriately along the barmaid's body on several occasions.

His disdain for the man grew with each passing second. Becoming Mrs. Thomas Cranston may have been high on Henrietta's list, and certainly, the woman who achieved that dubious goal would be in a position to reign over Savannah society, but she'd pay a terrible price for it. He was determined to ensure Henrietta did not pay that price.

After two hours of imbibing, Thomas stood amidst groans from his companions. He waved his hands at them, a devilish grin on his face as he spoke a few words before departing. He emerged from the noisy tavern and filled his lungs with the warm evening air.

He strode down the street away from the bar. Clifton hurried to catch up to him.

"Thomas," he said, clapping him around the shoulders.

"Clifton," Thomas answered, his brow furrowed with surprise.

"Drinking night?" Clifton questioned.

"A man's allowed to blow off some steam now and again, isn't he?"

"From what I hear, you blow off quite a bit of steam on a regular basis."

Thomas offered him a smarmy smile. "And what's that supposed to mean, Nichols?"

"You've got your sights set on my sister."

"She's a beautiful girl."

"Leave her alone."

Thomas chuckled. "You may want to ask your sister about that. I think she'd be highly upset to lose my attention."

"What are your intentions with Henrietta?" Clifton asked.

"None of your business."

"Do you intend to marry her?"

Thomas ceased walking and burst into laughter. His amusement at the question incensed Clifton. "If you do not intend to marry her, then leave her alone."

"I do not believe she'd prefer that."

"What she prefers is to be treated like the lady she is. What she prefers is an offer of marriage. She gives in to you to secure this. Have you any intention of asking for her hand?"

Thomas shook his head at Clifton. "What do you think?"

"I think you don't deserve her."

He snorted at the statement. "That's where you're wrong, Nichols." Thomas flexed his jaw and broadened his chest, taking a step closer to Clifton. When they stood nose to nose he said, "I'm a bit too good for her. She'd be taking quite the step up marrying me. Though my mother would be dead in her grave before she saw me marry a social climber like Henrietta."

"You bastard!" Clifton shouted, slamming Thomas against the nearby building. He thrust his forearm against his throat, pinning him. "You leave my sister alone or so help me, Thomas, I'll put you six feet under."

Clifton offered a final shove before he pulled himself away from him. Thomas adjusted his collar as he straightened. "Your sister can't seem to stay away from me. I make no promises." He strutted down the street.

"I mean it, Cranston! I'll kill you if you hurt her!"

* * *

Henrietta stared out at fluffy clouds obscuring the sun. Ready for the flower show, she awaited the rest of her party impatiently. What took them so long?

Her mind wandered as she tapped her foot in the air. Thomas would be at the show today. She had not seen him in several weeks. Not since their clandestine meeting that Clifton had insisted on attending.

Since then, he'd avoided her. She sought him out on several occasions. She could not blame him. He'd been angry that their romantic encounter had been ruined. Perhaps he assumed her feelings were not genuine toward him because of it.

She would rectify that today. She must assure him of her feelings, encourage him. If she must, she would make plans for another secret meeting.

Carolina clomped down the stairs behind Miriam. "Are you looking forward to the show, dear?" Miriam asked her.

"Quite," she said with a wide grin. "I shall be delighted to see all the flowers."

Henrietta sauntered over to them. "And your friends, no doubt."

"Oh no," Carolina answered, "I much prefer my books to the silly talk of the girls."

Henrietta's brow furrowed. "Are you not going to scold her, Mother?"

"Over what, dear?" Miriam asked as she fingered a lock of her hair into place in the foyer's mirror.

"Her attachment to her books. At this age, she should be learning to run a household."

"She is, dear."

"When I was her age you scolded me to no end about my writing."

"Yes, though reading is a very appropriate behavior for a wife."

Henrietta's mouth gaped open in indignation.

"Let us not argue about it, dear," Miriam said, closing Henrietta's jaw. "Ready?"

John and Clifton appeared at the bottom of the stairs. "Yes, dear," John answered.

"Oh, I do hope today comes off well." Miriam fretted, wringing her hands.

"I have no doubt it will given all the work you've done."

Henrietta raised her eyebrows. Her mother had fussed over details for weeks, agonizing over arrangement placement and order, afraid of snubbing the wrong person. Henrietta considered it nonsense, though it seemed a grave matter to her mother.

Either way, Henrietta happily went to the flower show. She'd see Thomas and hopefully be able to secure a meeting with him.

Clifton stepped onto the polished wood floor next to her. He offered his arm with that irresistible grin. Henrietta accepted it and they exited the house to the street in silence.

"You're quiet today, Ri," Clifton said as they rounded the corner out of their property.

"There is nothing to discuss."

"Isn't there?"

"Besides, I should still be angry with you."

"Angry with me? Whatever for?"

"For ruining my tete-a-tete with Thomas. I have not heard from him since you insisted on tagging along to my private meeting with him."

"Hmm, what a terrible shame."

"Why are you so insistent on ruining my chances for a good match?"

Clifton rolled his eyes. "He is not a good match, Ri."

"He is an excellent match. Arguably the most eligible bachelor in Savannah. Explain to me how he is not a good match."

"He will make you miserable, sister."

"I do not see how. I would want for nothing. I would reign over the city as social queen."

"And you shall spend your nights alone as he burns his way through every woman in Savannah."

Clifton slid his gaze sideways. Henrietta rolled her eyes.

"Do not roll your eyes at me," Clifton said. "One day you shall thank me."

"I would not hold your breath, Clif."

They arrived at the social hall where the flower show was being held. The thick smell of floral arrangements overpowered the senses as one entered. Henrietta scanned the crowd, searching for Thomas. She found him across the room, engaged in conversation with the Winstons.

A smile curled the edges of her lips as she spotted him. It quickly faded as she witnessed Edwina laughing heartily at something Thomas said. She narrowed her eyes, shooting daggers at the girl. What a fool she is, Henrietta thought.

Clifton noticed her gaze and steered her away toward a large display of roses. "Isn't this arrangement lovely?" he said.

"Oh, I would so agree," another voice answered before Henrietta could. From behind the table, Abigail Spencer popped her carrot-colored mop; her freckled face grinned at them. Well, particularly at Clifton.

"My sister was just admiring it," Clifton said.

"As was I. There are so many things to admire today." She offered him a sweet smile, her face turning a shade of bright pink.

An amused expression crossed Henrietta's face and she wiggled her eyebrows at her brother. "Yes, so very many things," she murmured.

"Do you enjoy flowers very much?" Abigail asked. Henrietta was unsure who the question was meant for. Men didn't tend to take any interest in flowers, yet Abigail's eyes remained fixed on Clifton.

"Clif simply adores them, don't you, brother dear?"

"Oh, quite," he answered. "And there are so many to see. I dare say we had better move along or we shall miss some."

"Oh, but..." Abigail began.

"Good day, Abigail," Clifton said as he dragged Henrietta away.

"Hurry, Clif, we wouldn't want to miss any flowers," Henrietta teased.

Clifton rolled his eyes at her. "Do not roll your eyes at me," she added.

"I suppose I shall not hear the end of this."

Henrietta held in a chuckle as she glanced back at Abigail, who stared after them.

"I dare say she is quite in love."

"She does not know me well enough to be in love."

"She loves what she already knows which appears to be enough for her."

"Too bad for her I plan to be a man of the world, with little time for what she would expect from me."

"I expect she expects a gaggle of children and a lovely home from you."

"Things I am not willing to provide."

"Oh, but, Clif, you are being short-sighted. Think of all those lovely carrot-topped children running around your home. And Abigail standing star-struck each time you arrive there after your long day of house calls."

Clifton answered with a shake of his head.

"Oh, really, Clif, you can't keep putting it off. You're nearly a grown man. You must marry someday."

"Must I? I do not agree. I told you, I plan to be a man of the world."

"I'm quite sure Father still believes you will follow in his footsteps."

"Then Father will be sorely disappointed."

Henrietta shrugged as she stopped to admire a bouquet filled with pink flowers of various kinds. "I suppose Mother and Father have only themselves to blame. They encouraged your outlandish desires from a young age."

"It is hardly outlandish to desire wealth. You do."

"But the means by which I shall achieve it are quite different from yours."

"Not really."

"How do you possibly fathom them similar?"

Clifton shrugged, the corners of his mouth turning downward. "You believe I will compromise my principles to gain wealth. I contend you will do the same with your marriage."

"And round we come to Thomas again. I do not understand why you detest him so."

"He is a louse. A bigger scoundrel than any pirate you've accused me of idolizing."

"We shall agree to disagree. And you shall have to accept him as brother-in-law soon enough."

"We shall see."

They rounded the corner and Henrietta rose to her toes. She'd lost sight of Thomas during their debate about the direction of their lives. She squeezed her lips together as she set her heels on the ground. Thomas was nowhere to be found.

With a huff, she continued to parade around the room with Clifton in the hopes of finding him. As they rounded toward another set of displays, she caught sight of him. He and his father spoke with several gentlemen. His father clapped him on the back and gave him a shake as the men burst into laughter.

Thomas glanced in her direction. Her heart skipped a beat. She offered a furtive smile and a discreet wave. He shifted his gaze without even acknowledging her. Perhaps he did not wish to betray his feelings in front of the crowd. She would cling to that as she shrugged off the encounter.

Henrietta tried several more times to gain Thomas's attention, though she had no luck. Finally, after awarding the blue ribbon to Mrs. Edgar for her rose display, she saw him duck from the room. Clifton engaged in a conversation with a school chum, and she took the opportunity to slink away into the outer hall.

She scanned it, finding herself alone. The door leading outside eased shut. She smiled and hurried toward it. At last, a moment alone with Thomas. As she stepped into the warm late summer air, she searched for her beau. He stood near the corner of the building and seemed to be engaged in a conversation with someone.

"Thomas!" she called as she hurried down the steps and toward him.

His eyes went wide, betraying surprise on his part. As

Henrietta approached him, she noticed a woman hurrying away. "Who was that?" she questioned.

"Oh, just one of my sister's friends. Asking after her. I told her she was inside."

Henrietta smiled and nodded. "I am glad to have caught you. I tried several times though it seems you were ignoring me."

"Did it?"

"Yes. And have been for weeks. Thomas, I am sorry about our encounter with Clifton, but my feelings for you have not changed."

His lips twitched before forming into a smile. "I must admit neither have mine. Though there is a reason I have avoided you."

"Oh?" Henrietta felt her stomach churn. Had she lost her opportunity?

"I am loath to admit it to you as it may change how you feel about me."

"Oh, my darling, that could never happen," she said, grasping his hand and squeezing it.

His eyes flitted around at their surroundings before he sighed. "After our meeting, though my heart was enflamed so by seeing you…"

"Yes?"

He licked his lips and shrugged his shoulders. "Clifton made a nasty threat against me. The truth is he was rather violent. I am ashamed I was not more of a man to stand up to him, but I feared upsetting you."

Henrietta's jaw unhinged. "He threatened you?"

"Mmm, yes, he did. He was quite insistent I stay away from you. He threatened to kill me."

Henrietta clamped her jaw, anger coursing through her. "I feel like such a coward, Henrietta. But the truth was I wondered if maybe you preferred me to stay away, too. And so I did."

"Nothing could be further from the truth!" Henrietta insisted. "I shall speak to Clif."

"Oh, please, do not cause any trouble."

"No," Henrietta said firmly. "Clifton has no right to interfere in my life this way. In our love."

Thomas opened his mouth to reply but before words left it his eyes widened. He dropped Henrietta's hands.

Henrietta's brow furrowed and she glanced behind her. Clifton marched to them, his jaw tight and his hands formed into fists.

CHAPTER 8

1793

"What did I tell you about staying away from my sister?"

"Stop this at once!" Henrietta insisted. "It is I who approached him. And you have no right to interfere."

Clifton grabbed him by the collar. "Stop this!" Henrietta shouted.

"She came to me!" Thomas cried as he tugged on Clifton's arms, trying to wiggle from his grasp.

"And you should have walked away," Clifton maintained.

Henrietta pushed between the two of them. "Stop!" she cried. Clifton let go of Thomas's collar. Thomas stumbled back a few steps, gasping for breath. "You have no right, Clif! No right to interfere in our relationship."

"There is no relationship." He looked over Henrietta's head toward Thomas. "If you love her, come ask for her hand."

Thomas remained silent. "Nothing to say? I am not surprised," Clifton added.

Henrietta slapped him across the face. He offered her a stunned glance. "Why slap me? He's the one who deserves your anger!"

Thomas backed away from the scene. "No, Thomas, please," Henrietta begged.

He waved his hands in defeat with a grimace. "It is best that I go. Your brother is quite out of sorts." He spun on his heel and stalked away.

Tears streamed down Henrietta's cheeks as she watched him depart. Clifton wrapped an arm around her shoulders. She shoved him away. "Don't you dare!" she shouted.

"Ri–" he began.

"No! You have ruined everything for me! If Thomas does not come round to court me, it is your fault!" She poked her finger at him in frustration. "I hate you!"

"Ri, wait!" he called as she fled from him.

Henrietta raced away from the building. The tears in her eyes made it difficult to see in front of her. She slowed her pace, stopping when the building disappeared behind her to catch her breath and choke out more sobs. She glanced behind her, glad to find the path empty. She could not bear another encounter with Clifton. His arrogance knew no bounds. How dare he threaten Thomas?

Her stomach somersaulted as she pondered her future. Had he ruined her chances with Thomas? Could she repair the damage? The crinkle between her brow deepened as she held back more tears.

She wiped at her face as she continued along the path toward her home. When she arrived, she pushed through the front door and stormed up the stairs, throwing herself across her bed. Sobs overtook her again. She cried until she had no more tears left.

She heard the front door open. Voices floated up to her. Everyone was home.

"Shall I check on Henrietta?" Miriam said.

A murmured response answered her. Footsteps climbed the staircase. Henrietta buried her head in her pillow. A warm hand grasped her shoulder.

"Ri?" Clifton's voice soothed.

"Get out," Henrietta croaked.

"Ri, please."

"I said get out!"

His shoulders sagged. "I only mean to prevent you from any harm."

She turned her red-rimmed eyes toward him. "Then remove yourself. For you are the cause of it."

His eyes dropped and he swallowed hard. He remained silent for a moment before he replied, "I shall apologize to Thomas."

Henrietta glanced at him as she sniffled. "Then nothing shall stand in his way if he wishes to court you."

"He does!" Henrietta cried.

"Then I shall not stand in the way," Clifton relinquished. "I shall make my apologies to him. I do not wish to see you upset, Ri. Please do not cry." He wiped at a tear rolling down her cheek with his thumb.

Henrietta grabbed his hand and squeezed it. She forced a smile onto her face. "Thank you, Clif. And you will see, he means to do right by me."

He offered her a weak, fleeting smile and a nod. "I shall apologize tomorrow at the fair."

* * *

1793

Clifton adjusted his collar before pulling on his overcoat.

He'd promised Henrietta he would apologize to the contemptible Thomas Cranston. He'd even try to appear as though he meant it. But he did not trust the man. And he preferred him to keep his distance from his sister.

Her heart would end up broken, he knew it. But she would not see reason. She would not realize she was far better off without him. With Henrietta's sharp mind and strong will, she was likely far better off without any man, but she'd insisted she must follow convention.

Still, following convention with any man outside of the dastardly Thomas Cranston seemed preferable in Clifton's mind. As he pictured the man in his mind, he hoped he could get the words out without bile creeping up his throat.

At least, though, with the apology made, Henrietta could see that he had no intention to court her. She would come to the realization on her own. And, painful as it may be, she would be better for it and she would not blame him.

He caught sight of Henrietta as he descended the stairs. She waited impatiently, tapping her foot against the polished wood floor. Her eyes, still a bit puffy, sparkled with excitement. She would be crushed when Thomas rebuffed her. Hopefully, he would do no lasting damage to her. Clifton would have to keep a careful eye to ensure he did not.

Miriam appeared at the top of the stairs, tugging Carolina behind her. "Come along, Carolina, there will be plenty of time to read before bed."

"But will there not be fireworks?"

"Yes," Miriam answered.

"And will I not be made to stay to watch them?"

"No, not if you prefer not to."

"Why would you not wish to see fireworks?" Henrietta questioned her younger sister.

"I find them a bore."

"If you do not get your nose out of a book, Carolina, you shall never make friends nor find an appropriate husband."

Carolina shrugged. "Do you not prefer to spend time with your writing?"

"That was a childish impulse that I have grown out of."

"I am still a child. I have not yet grown out of it," Carolina responded.

"I do wish you hadn't given up on your writing, Ri," Clifton said.

"Perhaps in another time in my life," Henrietta said.

"I dare say you may find the time after you've raised your family," Miriam said. "Shall we go?"

The family paraded from the house and to the park. Bright sunshine filtered through the many trees as town members talked and laughed under the cloudless sky. Clifton slid his eyes sideways as they entered the crowd. Henrietta's eyes darted around. He knew whom she searched for.

His stomach revolted as he considered the task ahead of him. Henrietta grasped his elbow, her chin raised high in the sky as she stood on tiptoes. "I see him," Clifton answered, following the direction of her gaze.

She turned her eyes toward him, a silent plea in her eyes. "Come along," he said, intending to make good on his promise. They closed the distance to Thomas, who chatted with a few of his friends.

"Thomas," Clifton said after clearing his throat. "A word?"

Thomas set his lips in a thin line and arched his eyebrows. "Gentlemen, if you will excuse me for just a moment," he said to the other men.

They stepped a few paces away and Thomas eyed Clifton. Clifton cleared his throat. "I would like to apologize for my behavior on the last two occasions we've spoken. I was out of line and had no business inserting myself into your affairs with my sister."

Henrietta flitted her eyes between the two of them, trying to gauge Thomas's reaction.

"How honorable of you to take the initiative to offer your apologies," Thomas said.

Clifton forced a smile on his face. "I have seen the error of my ways. It is wrong of me to stand between you and your desires."

Thomas offered him a smile that bordered on a smirk. He thrust his hand out. "I suppose we shall consider the matter closed then."

"I appreciate it," Clifton said as he accepted the man's hand.

He glanced to Henrietta. She offered him a nod. Thomas began to retreat toward his friends, but Henrietta stopped him. "Oh, Thomas, wait."

Clifton left her, retreating several steps and disappearing around a large oak. He circled it, remaining hidden as he glared at the pair of them. Henrietta placed her hand on Thomas's forearm. She leaned in toward him, her eyes pleading. With a smile forced upon her face, she uttered a few words. Thomas narrowed his eyes and glanced around then a smile spread across his face. He set his predatory gaze upon her and spoke a few words. She bit her lower lip and nodded.

What was that bastard up to, Clifton wondered? He'd keep a close eye on the situation.

* * *

Henrietta waited for a few breaths as Clifton retreated. She fixed her gaze on Thomas. "There, darling, you see? It's quite all right now. Everything is smoothed over."

Thomas stared after the man as he disappeared around the tree. Henrietta clutched at his forearm. "Thomas?"

"Did he mean what he said, that is the question," Thomas answered.

"Oh, he did! He did. He realizes he should not have interfered. I'm certain he recognizes the deep feelings between us."

"Yes," Thomas murmured. "I'm sure he does realize."

"Then it is settled? You will come around to court me?"

His eyes settled on Henrietta. He studied her perfectly formed lips, her dark hair framing her porcelain skin, her sparkling, dark brown eyes. "I cannot wait that long to see you again. Will you meet me tonight? Just before the fireworks?"

"But we could spend time together now, and tomorrow you could call…"

"No, we cannot call attention to our relationship before I've spoken with your father. As much as it pains me, we must separate for now. But please, come to me before the fireworks."

"Where?"

"The alley behind the pub."

Henrietta bit her lower lip and nodded. He brushed her arm, giving it a quick squeeze before he returned to his friends.

* * *

As dusk settled over the park, Clifton kept a careful eye on his sister. He'd spent most of the day watching the movements of Thomas Cranston. The man had spoken with a variety of people. He was being groomed by his father, one of the richest men in Savannah, to be a titan among men.

Clifton noticed they spent a large amount of time with the Winstons. As night began to fall, Thomas had left his family and the Winstons and gathered with several friends to share an ale.

Something tugged at his jacket as he glowered at the man. He turned to find Carolina. "Are you coming, brother?"

"No, Carolina," he answered. "Tell Mother and Father that Henrietta and I plan to watch the fireworks with several friends. We shall meet them at home."

She nodded at him. "All right," the nine-year-old girl said. "I shall tell them."

"Thank you."

Clifton followed the departing form of his baby sister as she ran back to find their parents. After she met them, he waved at his mother who returned the gesture, then returned his gaze toward Thomas.

The man had disappeared. Clifton cursed under his breath as he scanned the area. He spotted the man heading away from the park and hurried to follow him. He pushed through the crowd, his eyes fixed on Thomas's back.

Thomas cleared the crowd and wandered around the street toward the pub. He passed it and ducked down an alley. Clifton continued to shuffle through the crowd awaiting the fireworks.

* * *

Henrietta stared up at the starry sky. She waited in the dark alley behind the pub. She'd been early, afraid to miss Thomas. With things settled between Thomas and her brother, nothing stood in their way.

Tonight, they would declare their love for one another and tomorrow Thomas would ask her father to court her. She'd ensure the courtship did not last too long, long enough to seem appropriate before an engagement. Then they would marry. Henrietta already planned what she might wear. She'd ask for a new dress. Nothing she had would really do. It would be a wedding gift from her parents.

She bit her lower lip as she imagined Thomas standing at the end of the church aisle awaiting her. She visualized his blue eyes staring into hers as they said their vows. Her heart melted as he slid the ring onto her finger.

A noise sounded behind her. A figure approached. She recognized Thomas in the dim light. He hurried toward her. A grin spread across her face.

He marched toward her, nearly running into her. He pulled her close. "Thomas!" she giggled.

"Yes?" he asked, his voice husky.

She giggled again. "Control yourself!"

He tightened his grip. "I cannot," he answered. He pressed his lips against hers. She wrapped her arms around his neck, enjoying the moment. Her body stiffened as his hands began to travel up and down her body.

"Thomas," she whispered as he pressed his lips into her neck. "Thomas!"

She felt his breath hot against her neck as he began to lift her skirt.

"Thomas, stop!" she insisted, pushing away from him.

"I thought you loved me?" he questioned.

"I do, but I…" Her voice trailed off as her brow furrowed.

He pulled her toward him again. "Then do not deny me. I cannot control myself around you." He pressed against her. A cloud of doubt formed in her mind as he again attempted to lift her skirt. This was not what she imagined, but perhaps it was expected from her. She'd assumed he'd prefer her to maintain the proper customs. To remain chaste until their wedding day. Apparently not. Though she hadn't imagined an encounter as coarse as this in a dim alley like some lady of the night. Misgivings crowded her mind and her heart. She did not want this, but did she have a choice?

His arms tightened around her. He squeezed her close. His grip began to hurt.

"Ouch, Thomas! That hurts!" Her pleas fell on deaf ears.

Could she break away if she tried? She wasn't sure she could overpower him. Perhaps the best thing to do was give in.

As she considered giving in to him, a voice broke the silence. She gasped as she recognized her name. Thomas's body stiffened. Henrietta leapt back a step, running a hand over her dress to smooth it.

The voice called again. "Henrietta? Are you there? Hurry, you'll miss the fireworks."

Clifton's voice echoed in the narrow alley. "Henrietta, don't go," Thomas whispered. The heat of his breath wafted across her cheek.

"Henrietta!" Clifton called again.

"I'm sorry," she breathed. "I must. But I shall see you soon, my love. Until then." She squeezed his hand and hurried past him down the alley.

* * *

Clifton jogged to the alley after breaking free of the crowd. He peered into the darkness. Hushed whispers reached his ears. Dark figures danced near the end. He contemplated storming toward them, but a better idea sprang to mind.

"Henrietta!" he shouted down the alley. "Henrietta? Are you there? Hurry, you'll miss the fireworks."

He squinted into the darkness as he waited for a response. Hushed voices spoke.

"Henrietta!" he called again.

He waited another moment, shifting his weight from foot to foot as he counted the seconds before he approached them. He shook his head and took a step down the alley when Henrietta appeared in front of him.

He studied her in the light filtering from the pub. She seemed upset. Her face was flushed, her hair mussed, and her breath seemed to stick in her throat.

"There you are," he said, testing the waters. Was she upset with his interruption or for some other reason?

She forced a smile on her face. A fake smile. He'd know that from a mile away. "Here I am!" she said in a voice that exuded a bit too much enthusiasm.

"I did not wish you to miss the fireworks," Clifton said.

Her smile widened and she pushed a lock of hair from her face.

"Are you all right, Ri?" Clifton inquired.

"Yes," she gasped out. "Perfectly fine. What would be the matter?"

He narrowed his eyes at her. "Hurry, let's find a spot to watch the fireworks," she added, slipping her arm into his.

Clifton slid his eyes sideways as they strolled back to the park. The firework display began before they made it. Henrietta stopped and admired them from the street. She seemed lost in them as if allowing the scene to absorb her so her mind did not wander to something else.

What happened in that alley? Clifton's mind could hazard a guess and the implication made his blood boil. In any case, the display seemed to calm her nerves. She gazed up at the large bursts of color against the night sky. They reflected in her dark brown eyes.

"Are you certain there is nothing amiss?" Clifton ventured.

Henrietta offered a fleeting glance before she wrapped her fingers around his hand and squeezed. "Yes, I am certain. Thank you for retrieving me so I did not miss the display."

Henrietta remained quiet for the remainder of the night.

Quieter than normal. On the walk home, she barely said two words. She went straight to her room when they arrived at home, claiming exhaustion.

Clifton climbed into bed curious but realizing he may never know what happened in the alley.

* * *

Henrietta slipped between the sheets of her bed. She drew the covers up to her chin despite there being no chill in the night air. She chewed her lower lip as her mind wandered over the encounter with Thomas.

It was not at all what she expected. When she hurried to the alley to meet him, she anticipated a romantic encounter. Her mind foresaw Thomas gushing over her beauty, whispering in her ear about its effect on him. She thought he may steal a sweet kiss. And she would feign shock over it, though she would secretly enjoy it.

The actual events that occurred contrasted sharply to the vision she'd built in her mind. Thomas was not gentle and loving, he was rough and demanding. His expectations of her were also not in line with what she supposed would happen.

Tears stung her eyes as she clung to her sheet, her knuckles white. Her mind sought to make sense of the situation. She convinced herself the behavior was normal. Thomas loved her. Of course he hoped to share her body.

All would be resolved tomorrow, she decided. Thomas would call and he would ask to court her. Soon they would be married. A shiver shook her body and she pulled her knees to her chest as she settled on her side. Once they were married, everything would be settled. She soothed herself to sleep with that thought.

CHAPTER 9

1793

Bright sunshine streamed through her window the next morning. Henrietta rose and stretched. She hopped from her bed, excitement filling her. Today would be the day her relationship with Thomas became official. It did not matter the events of the previous evening.

Henrietta glanced at her writing desk and bit her lower lip. With a shake of her head, she dismissed the idea of penning any words. Soon, she would have a household to run. She had no time for childish things like writing.

Henrietta presented herself early for breakfast, finding herself the first one at the table. Her father joined her a few moments later, offering her a kiss on her forehead.

"You are up early, dear. I should have thought you would sleep late given the full evening."

A smile beamed from Henrietta's face. "Though I was quite tired last night, the rest did me well. I feel wonderful this morning."

"Wonderful?" Clifton inquired as he entered the dining room.

"Yes, quite wonderful," Henrietta said with a nod.

Clifton's brow furrowed, but he did not pursue it further since Miriam and Carolina joined them just as she finished her statement.

"Good morning, everyone," Miriam said as she took her seat across from John.

They chatted as their breakfast was served before Miriam made an announcement. "We have been invited to a party this coming Saturday. Isn't it lovely?"

"Oh?" Henrietta questioned.

"Where, Mummy?" Carolina asked.

"Well, not you, dear. You are a bit too young. But Father, Clifton, Henrietta, and I were invited to the Winstons."

"What is the occasion?" John inquired.

"She did not say, but she seemed quite enthusiastic about it. I gather it is to be quite a large party. I hope you do not mind, John. I accepted. She seemed so desperate over it."

"Not at all," John answered. "I think we shall all be looking forward to it."

Miriam smiled at him. Henrietta's mind churned. "I suppose the Cranstons will attend," she said. "Along with several other families?"

"Oh, I am certain. They spent a good amount of time together at the fair yesterday. I can imagine they will attend, yes. And she mentioned the Williams family, the Hughes, and the Butlers. Though I am certain there will be several more. I imagine all the ladies from the flower league have been invited."

"And business associates of Reginald, to be certain."

Miriam smiled and nodded. Henrietta smiled, too. By Saturday, she and Thomas would officially be courting. She would so enjoy spending time at the party as an almost engaged woman. She would try to be careful not to lord it over the other girls. She hoped she could contain her excitement.

After breakfast, Henrietta settled with a book on the window seat overlooking the front lawn. The book lay in her lap while her gaze flitted out the window almost constantly.

"Looking for someone?" Clifton asked her as he passed through the room.

"No," Henrietta fibbed.

"Hmm," he offered as he exited to the foyer.

The morning hours dwindled and the afternoon approached. The sun rose high overhead, and Henrietta found her stomach filled with butterflies. Surely Thomas would arrive in the afternoon.

Clifton passed through again in the early afternoon. "Still staring out that window?"

Henrietta had begun to grow perturbed. "So?" she spat.

"It is a beautiful day, Ri. Take a walk! Enjoy the sunshine."

Henrietta set her gaze on the front walk, her arms wrapped across her chest tightly. Clifton rolled his eyes at her. "Come, let us play a duet," he said motioning toward the piano.

"No," she answered, her lips puckered in a pout.

"You will not miss any visitors if you step away from the window," he insisted, tugging on her arm.

She flicked her gaze up to his face. "I am not…"

"Not waiting for anyone. Yes, I know," he said with a coy grin. "Then it should not disturb you to leave the window."

Henrietta acquiesced, allowing herself to be dragged to the piano and plopping onto the bench next to Clifton.

"Move over," he complained. "I cannot play the low end."

"You must learn sometime."

"No, I mustn't. Not really. Now shift down and allow me to play the high end."

"You are such a child, Clif," Henrietta said as she scooted down the seat, allowing him the upper end of the piano.

"And I shall continue to be since you give in to me," he said with a grin as they selected a song.

Music filled the room as their fingers flew across the ivory keys.

"You are playing too slow, keep up," Henrietta scolded.

"You are playing too fast, slow down," Clifton retorted.

Henrietta raised her eyebrows as her fingers darted up and down on the keys. "I shall play faster."

"And I shall play slower."

"You're ruining the song," she cried.

"As are you."

The pair continued their antics, creating a comical display of a too-fast undertone with an exceptionally slow melody.

A giggle escaped Henrietta's lips as she hurried to rush her playing.

"You'd better slow down, I am handicapped as a player and you know it," Clifton said with a laugh.

"Oh, fine," Henrietta said, still chuckling. "I shall slow my playing to match your substandard skill at the piano."

"We cannot all be as brilliant as you, Ri."

She smiled at the compliment, offering a coy sideways glance at him. "Terrible shame," she answered.

"Truly," he said. "You are quite a brilliant woman, Ri. Do not waste it."

Henrietta's hands faltered on the keys and she ceased playing. She spun to face him. "What does that mean?"

"Nothing. Keep playing." He continued with the melody.

"No, you said it and you meant something by it. Tell me what!"

Clifton's hands slowed to a stop and he twisted to face

her. "Oh, Ri, only that you are so talented, and I've noticed you've stopped writing of late. Please do not give it up."

Henrietta turned away from him, shaking her head. "Childish things must be left behind when one is no longer a child."

"It's not childish. And it gives you such delight. Please do not give it up. Not for Mother, not for Father, not for anyone."

Henrietta focused on him. She studied the earnestness in his face and offered him a slight smile. "I shall not… if you can keep up with the next duet." She offered him a broad grin and a giggle before she placed her hands on the keys.

He chuckled and faced the piano. "I am ready for the challenge."

They frittered away the afternoon hours with their piano playing followed by a card game. "That's the fourth round I've won," Henrietta said as she spread her cards on the table.

"Do not remind me," Clifton said.

She raised her eyebrows. "Are you letting me win?"

"Who, me? You know I'd never do anything like that!"

She narrowed her eyes at him. "You're acting strange. All day."

He shrugged. "I am not."

"You are. Why?"

He shrugged. "You seemed upset last night. I thought perhaps you'd enjoy the company."

She lifted her chin. "I was not upset."

"No?"

"No, not at all. Only tired."

"I see. Well, I am glad to hear it. And now I shall show no mercy in the next round."

Henrietta's brow furrowed as Clifton shuffled and dealt the cards. She'd been so caught up in their afternoon antics, she'd lost track of the time. She glanced at the clock. It read nearly 5 p.m. She chewed on her lower lip. No one had arrived at the house all day. Perhaps Thomas planned an evening call. Though that seemed odd.

"Well, come on, then, your go," Clifton said.

She swept up the cards and tried to focus on them. One question continued to bounce around her mind for the duration of the evening: where was Thomas?

* * *

Thomas Cranston did not pay a call to the Nichols house the day after the fair or any day following that week. As each day passed, Henrietta grew concerned over his lack of appearance. Perhaps business kept him tied up. Yes, that must be it, she decided. Or perhaps he was ill. That could be, she mused.

She smoothed her dress as she readied herself for the Winstons' party. Thomas would attend unless he was ill. She'd sort it out then. She smiled as her heart fluttered in her chest. She gazed at her reflection. The rose-colored dress worked well with her coloring. Thomas would surely notice.

She hurried down the stairs, finding her father and Clifton already waiting. Miriam appeared a moment after her, trailed by Carolina. She kissed the girl on the cheek.

"Now, do not give Sarah any trouble," she warned.

"I promise, Mummy," Carolina replied.

"Good. Good night, dear." She kissed the girl again. Henrietta tapped her foot on the floor as she waited.

"Patience, sister," Clifton whispered to her.

Miriam fussed over Carolina for a few more moments before she announced herself ready to depart. With the weather still warm, they walked the distance to the Winston home.

Several people already filled the home's interior. The din of chatter floated on the night air as guests talked and laughed. Henrietta spotted Thomas chatting with several gentlemen, all holding brandies.

She could not approach him now, but soon enough the guests would mix and she'd have the opportunity to speak with him. After an hour, the Cranstons and Nichols found themselves together. Thomas approached the group. Henrietta's face lit with a smile.

"Hello, everyone," he greeted cordially.

"Hello, Thomas," Henrietta answered with a demure glance.

They made polite chatter for a few minutes as a group. Henrietta was about to suggest she, Thomas, and Clifton step away to admire a painting when Mrs. Cranston waved and nodded. Henrietta followed the direction of her gaze. She spotted Mrs. Winston smile and nod.

"If you'll excuse us," Mrs. Cranston said.

"Certainly," Miriam replied. "Lovely chatting with you."

Henrietta bit her lower lip over the missed opportunity. Later, she promised herself.

Servants filtered throughout the room, carrying trays laden with champagne flutes. Henrietta's brow furrowed at the development. Was this a celebration of some kind?

Mr. Winston flicked his finger against the side of his glass as he stood on the main staircase. People gathered around. Edwina and her mother stood next to him on one side, the Cranstons on the other. Edwina fidgeted as though she was about to burst. She bit her lower lip, glancing out at the crowd, her face flushed.

"Ladies, gentlemen," Mr. Winston called. A hush fell over the crowd. "We would so like to thank you for joining us this evening. And what an evening it will be! For tonight, I have the good fortune to announce the engagement of my daughter Edwina to Thomas Cranston."

Murmurs escaped from the crowd and applause rang out.

Thomas stepped forward and grasped Edwina's hand. She giggled and stepped toward him as party-goers rushed to congratulate her.

For Henrietta, the moment was surreal. Her stomach somersaulted, her knees felt weak, her face lost its color as the blood drained from it. Her lower lip trembled as she eyed the scene on the stairs.

She felt tears sting her eyes. An audible groan, mostly covered by the crowd's excited chattering, escaped her lips. She spun away from her family, seeking the cooler air of the August evening.

* * *

As the engagement was announced, Clifton slid his eyes sideways to Henrietta. Her reaction was as he expected. He spotted the shock on her face, noticed her trembling lip and the tears welling in her eyes. A moment later, she spun and hurried from the house. Miriam stared after her, a concerned expression on her face.

Clifton smiled at his mother and waved a hand to suggest he'd determine the source of Henrietta's quick exit. Unfortunately, he knew the source all too well. She'd assumed Thomas Cranston would court her and marry her. The fact that this would not occur was not all too plain. Even Henrietta could no longer deny the man had used her and lied to her.

Still, he was certain her heart was broken at the moment. He hoped that was all that was.

* * *

Henrietta flung herself through the door and stumbled forward on the porch. The railing caught her. She clung to it as she fought back sobs. Thomas… engaged? To Edwina Winston, nonetheless. What had happened? How had this come to pass?

She glanced down at her right hand, still clutching the champagne flute. With a grimace, she tossed it into the grass. Footsteps sounded behind her. She hastily wiped the tear that had fallen from her cheek.

"Ri?" Clifton's voice said softly.

"I… I just needed some air. It was very warm in there," she stammered, keeping her back to him.

A warm hand squeezed her shoulder. "I am fine, really," she choked out.

His hand did not budge. He remained silent, attempting to provide comfort without speaking a word. Henrietta's hand trembled as she fought to control her emotions.

Another tear rolled down her cheek and her brow crinkled with emotion. She pressed her lips together until they hurt. Her shoulders rolled forward and her head fell into her hands.

Clifton spun her to face him. He wrapped his arms around her as she leaned into his chest and sobbed.

"He is not worth your tears, Ri. You are better off."

"I'm not," she sobbed.

"You are. If he kept his engagement secret all the while encouraging you he is not deserving of you."

"I thought he loved me."

"He loves no one but himself."

"And her," she spat out.

Clifton shook his head. "No. He does not love her either. The man cares for no one but himself."

"How could he do this?" she squeaked.

"It is not worth wasting your time considering it."

"How could I be so stupid?"

"You weren't stupid, just too trusting."

"That louse!" Henrietta twisted Clifton's jacket between her fingers.

"Let's go home, hmm?" Clifton suggested.

Henrietta sniffled. "What will people say?" she breathed.

"You care too much what people say. I shall make excuses. Something you ate did not agree with you. The champagne turned your stomach. Sit here," he said as he guided her to a rocker. "I shall tell Mother and Father and then return to take you home."

Henrietta offered a silent nod as she retrieved a handkerchief from her purse. She wiped at her face as Clifton disappeared into the house. She swallowed hard and blew out a long breath as she stared into the night sky beyond the porch roof.

A myriad of thoughts still crowded her brain but she tried to push them aside. She could deal with them later. Feet shuffled on the wooden floorboards.

Henrietta twisted, shifting her gaze to the front door. She expected to find Clifton. Instead, Thomas Cranston faced her. Emotion rushed back to her, and a lump formed in her throat. She bit her lower lip to stop it from quivering as she hopped to her feet.

CHAPTER 10

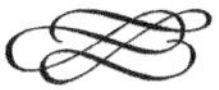

1793

She stared at him for a moment before she took a step toward the stairs leading down to the yard.

"Henrietta, wait, I can explain."

She arched an eyebrow at him. Unsure if she could formulate a response, she remained quiet for a moment.

He took a step toward her. Henrietta retreated one step back. Clifton stepped onto the porch behind Thomas. His expression soured in an instant.

"Shouldn't you be celebrating your engagement, Cranston?"

Thomas kept his eyes on Henrietta. She flitted her gaze to Clifton. "Give us a moment, Clif."

A grimace passed over his features and he gave his head a shake but acquiesced. "I will wait by the street for you."

Thomas waited until he disappeared from their sight. Once Clifton's form was no longer visible, he took another step toward Henrietta. She backed away again. "Please," he said, motioning for her to duck around the corner to the side porch.

"You said you could explain," she said as they rounded to the private location.

He shook his head and closed his eyes. "This is not how I hoped things would happen."

"You knew and you said nothing," Henrietta said, her voice raising.

He held out his hands in an attempt to quiet her. "Henrietta, please," he said in a low tone, "lower your voice."

"Lower my voice?" she shrieked.

He rushed toward her and grasped her arm before she could retreat. "Please, Henrietta, this is an impossible situation. And it has nothing to do with what I feel for you."

Her eyes widened. "Thomas, you are engaged. At the fair you…" Her voice stopped. "You are engaged. This did not happen overnight."

"No. My parents insisted. I hoped Edwina would change her mind, but she did not."

"You knew. You knew at the fair and still, you lured me to the alley."

"I did not lure you, Henrietta. You came willingly because you feel toward me the way I feel toward you."

"And what way is that? If you loved me you would not be marrying another."

"I have little choice in the matter. My parents pressured me. The Winstons are in a good position to further our business."

"You are marrying her to further your fortune?"

"I haven't a choice, Henrietta."

Henrietta turned from him, her mind clouded with questions. "Still, you knew. And you said nothing. And you expected me to… Why, Thomas? Why would you do that?"

"I told you, I have no control around you."

Henrietta swallowed hard. He inched closer to her. His arms wrapped around her waist. His face hovered close to hers.

"Thomas," she breathed.

"Oh, Henrietta," he said, pressing his lips into her neck.

"Thomas!" she hissed as she pushed him away. "We are outside the party announcing your engagement!"

"My engagement to a woman I do not want as much as I want you."

"Yet you will become her husband!"

"Not by my choice."

He stepped toward her and slipped an arm around her waist. "It is you I want."

She shook her head in protest. "It does not matter, now. You are engaged."

"Yes, but we can still be together. There is a way."

Henrietta shifted her gaze sharply to him. "What way?"

He shrugged and offered her a sly smile. "No one must know. It will be our secret." He pressed his lips against her cheek.

A groan escaped her lips. "I will not be your mistress," she spat. "I expected a courtship and a proposal, not a summons to warm your bed outside of your marriage to another woman."

He rolled his eyes. "Oh, come, Henrietta, you can't be serious."

Her jaw gaped open at his remark. He released his grasp on her waist. He continued, "You must have realized we'd never marry."

"No," she said with a shake of her head. "No, I did not realize. Why would I? You led me to believe we would!"

He scoffed. "No, you led yourself to believe we would. I led you to believe I wanted exactly what a girl like you should provide."

She stood in shock at his words. "A doctor's daughter?" He gave another harsh laugh. "You are not exactly high society, Henrietta."

The comments ripped through her heart like barbed wire through flesh. "I would have taken care of you. I would have offered you allowances you'd not have received otherwise. Your life would step up."

William, one of Thomas's friends, rounded the corner. "Ah, there you are. A few people are asking after you."

He nodded, his gaze remaining on Henrietta.

"Go," she said, firming her jaw.

"In a moment," he said, his eyes narrowing at her. He tilted his head, his eyes remaining on Henrietta. "Tell them I'll be along in just a moment. There is something I must take care of first."

William chuckled and licked his lips. He clapped Thomas on the back before disappearing around the corner.

Henrietta raised her chin. "There is nothing more to be said, Thomas. You are released of any obligation on my part."

He snickered. "You are a fool, Henrietta, to turn me down. Not that it matters. I shall simply take what I want from you and treat you like the lowly whore that you are." He grasped her arms and yanked her toward him. She struggled as he pressed his lips against hers roughly, unable to break free of his grasp.

She wiggled as he pushed her against the house's side and clamped his hand over her mouth. He reached down to hike her skirt. "After all, what kind of a girl meets a man in a dark alley alone?"

Tears streamed down her cheeks as she pushed against him. He smirked at her futile attempts.

Suddenly, his eyes went wide. The pressure against her body released and Thomas stumbled backward. He lost his footing and flew back several yards, landing on his backside.

Henrietta heaved a sigh of relief as she spotted the source of his fall. Clifton placed himself between Henrietta and Thomas. "I told you once before to keep your hands off my sister."

Henrietta clung to Clifton's shoulder. "Please take me home," she cried.

Clifton clasped her hand and squeezed. He wrapped his arm around her. "Touch her again and I will make good on my promise to kill you." He guided Henrietta past the man still sprawled on the floor.

"The whore was asking for it," Thomas retorted as he climbed to his feet.

Clifton dropped his grip on Henrietta and spun on his heel. He swung his fist, striking Thomas on the chin. Thomas stumbled back a few steps before he raised his clenched fists. He swung but Clifton leaned away, avoiding the blow. They danced around each other.

"Clif, no!" Henrietta shouted.

Clifton lunged toward Thomas, pinning him against the house where Henrietta had been immobilized moments ago. He pressed his forearm into Thomas's throat. With a grunt, he mashed his arm tighter against the man's windpipe.

"Gentlemen! Is there some sort of problem?" Mrs. Winston squawked.

Clifton sneered at Thomas as he stepped back. Thomas adjusted his collar. "Just a friendly congratulatory sparring match," he said as he rubbed at his chin.

Mrs. Winston eyed the scene, her eyes passing over Henrietta, Clifton, and then settling on Thomas. "Thomas, you're needed inside."

"Of course," he said, pushing past Clifton.

Mrs. Winston gave Henrietta and Clifton another once over before she followed Thomas into the house. Left alone, Clifton hurried toward Henrietta. "Are you all right?"

She nodded, her eyes fixed on the porch floor, unable to push words from her lips. Clifton tilted his head and tipped her chin up. "Ri, are you certain? Did he harm you?"

She shook her head. "No," she pushed out. "No, I am fine. You arrived at an opportune moment."

He pressed his lips together in a firm line. She grabbed his hands and squeezed them. "Thank you," she choked out as tears threatened again.

"Come on," he said, "let's get you home."

Henrietta's lower lip trembled as she nodded at him. He wrapped his arm around her waist and guided her from the porch. They rounded the corner and proceeded toward their home. Henrietta remained silent for much of the walk.

As they passed under a willow, Henrietta slowed. Clifton reached an arm out to steady her. She licked her lips as she stared at the ground below her feet.

Her face scrunched with emotion and she clapped her hands over her face. "How could I have been so stupid?" she cried.

"The blame does not fall on you, Ri," Clifton said as he pulled her into an embrace.

"You warned me and I did not listen." She continued to sob against his chest.

"I hope you have learned that I am always correct," he said, pushing her away and offering a playful grin.

"Ugh," she groaned as she sunk her head against his shoulder again.

"I thought that was rather humorous," Clifton said as he patted her shoulder.

"It was not."

"No? What a terrible shame it has done nothing to cheer you. Perhaps this approach will help. I consider you quite lucky."

"Lucky?" Henrietta questioned. "How do you equate what I've just experienced with luck?"

"Because, Ri, you have narrowly escaped a miserable life with a horrible man. Poor Edwina, though. I fear those rosy cheeks and her happy grin shall soon fade when she realizes he cares nothing for her. You really should focus your energy on pitying her."

"It does not feel like escape." She sniffled.

"I know it hurts, Ri. What he did to you was horrid. But do not focus on that. Focus on the fact that this will not be your life going forward."

"He treated me like a…"

"Shhh," Clifton interrupted. "He is a fool who does not know your worth. You are too good for him."

"Not according to him."

"And we have already established he is a fool."

Henrietta sniffled again and pushed away from Clifton. She wiped the tears from her cheeks. He offered her a tentative grin as she glanced at him. "Better?"

She blew out a long breath and offered a nod. "A bit."

"He is not worth your tears."

Henrietta forced a faltering smile onto her face and nodded. With her emotions in check for the moment, they continued down the street. "Thomas Cranston will not stay on top of the world forever," Clifton said. "He'll have his fall. You'll see."

Henrietta ceased walking again and spun to face Clifton. "Do not harm him."

"Ri, you cannot possibly defend him still."

"It is not him I defend. It is you. I do not wish to see any further harm come to either of us because of Thomas Cranston."

"Do not worry, sister, I will do nothing to harm him unless he provokes it."

. . .

1794

"Henrietta! Henrietta!" Miriam called up the stairs.

Henrietta's shoulders sagged in aggravation. The woman called again. "Yes, Mother, just a moment," she answered as she set her quill down. She pushed back, leaving her latest novel-in-progress spread across her writing desk.

"What is it?" she inquired as she hovered at the top of the stairs.

"Come down here, please," Miriam said.

Henrietta clomped down the stairs. "What is it, Mother? I am writing."

Her mother appeared as though she'd seen a ghost. Her skin was a shade paler than normal and she twisted her handkerchief in her hands. Her purse still hung from her forearm and she still wore her hat.

"Please, come inside the sitting room."

"It must be important, you haven't even removed your hat," Henrietta said.

"It is cheek like that that has gotten us into this trouble," her mother said as she collapsed in a chair.

"What trouble?" Henrietta inquired.

Her mother shook her head and bit her lower lip as she stared out the front window. "Today at the ladies' flower league, Mrs. Winston whispered to me a most shocking rumor."

Henrietta raised her eyebrows. Miriam's face fell and she scrunched her lips as though the words tasted bitter in her mouth. "She told me a rumor is circulating that you..." Her voice broke and she took a moment to steady herself. She lifted her chin and continued. "That you have been inviting advances from men. Even meeting them in secret like a... "

She paused again before she spat out the final words. "Like a lady of the night."

"What?!" Henrietta said as she sprung from her chair. "Who has hurled this accusation?"

Miriam averted her gaze. "I should not need to remind you that if this rumor reaches Mr. Barriweather's ears your engagement may be called off!"

Henrietta sank to the chair in a heap as she considered it. After the debacle with Thomas, she'd struggled to move on, to trust someone. However, her mother continued to encourage her to seek a suitable match. Without knowledge of the fiasco the previous summer, she did not understand the reluctance on Henrietta's part.

Over the winter holidays, Henrietta met Steven Barriweather, a lawyer in the Savannah area. After meeting on several occasions while visiting during the holiday season, he had formally begun to court Henrietta and offered marriage as the seasons turned from spring to summer. Their engagement was to last nearly one year, ending in a springtime wedding.

"Say something!" Miriam said.

"Hello, Mother, back from the ladies' guild already?" Clifton asked as he entered the room.

He took in the scene, his brow furrowing. "What is it? Is something wrong?"

Miriam pursed her lips. Henrietta leapt from her seat and paced. She rubbed the back of her neck as she explained. "Someone has spread a nasty rumor about me."

"What? What rumor?"

"A rather vulgar one about your sister's activities with men."

"What?!" Clifton barked.

"If this reaches Mr. Barriweather, I fear he may call off the engagement."

"That bastard!" Clifton said, slamming his hand onto the drink cart.

"Clif!" Miriam exclaimed. "Mr. Barriweather would be most within his rights to do so. We cannot blame him for…"

"Not him, Mother," Clifton corrected, "Thomas Cranston."

"Thomas Cranston? What has he to do with this?"

"I am certain the rumor has come from him."

Miriam's jaw gaped open. "Why would you imagine so?"

Henrietta stood with one arm wrapped around her waist as she stared out the window. "Clif, don't."

"Why, Ri? She should know!"

"Know? Know what?"

Henrietta squeezed her lips together before she turned to face her mother. She swallowed hard and her lips parted. A pained expression crossed her face as she attempted to explain.

Clifton took the initiative as her voice faltered.

"A year ago, Thomas Cranston made several advances toward Henrietta. They ended in him nearly forcing himself upon her even while he attended his own engagement party. I am certain given her recent engagement, he is attempting to punish her for her rebuff."

"What?" Miriam queried, her face a mask of confusion.

"It is true, Mother. Before his engagement, he pretended to be unattached. He asked me on several occasions to meet him. I thought him sweet on me, though, as I learned at Edwina's engagement party, it had all been a ruse."

Miriam's lips moved but no words emerged. After a stunned moment, she murmured, "I simply cannot believe it. Thomas Cranston? And all this happening to my own daughter, and I never knew."

"Thomas Cranston has quite a reputation, Mother," Clifton said.

"He has?"

"Yes, he has. He has already been unfaithful to Edwina on several occasions. Both before and after their marriage. No doubt you've heard this rumor from Mrs. Winston, who likely fuels the fires of it to reduce the embarrassment there surely is on her daughter's part."

"Before she imparted the news, I heard a whisper about Edwina returning to their home in the middle of the night. I thought perhaps there had been some emergency, but now…"

"Likely the emergency was she could stomach no more of Thomas," Clifton said.

"Still," Henrietta said, "what is to be done about my reputation? Thomas is a cad, yes, but an influential one. And with Mrs. Winston spreading his gossip around, what shall we do?"

"I suppose we must deny them," Miriam answered. "Perhaps, though, Henrietta, it would do best for you to stay away from the public."

"That's unfair!" Henrietta shouted.

"Unfair or not, that is hardly the issue. Containing the damage is the issue."

"I feel that would make matters worse," Clifton contended. "Henrietta has done nothing wrong. To hide herself away implies guilt."

"Then what do you propose?" Miriam asked.

"Simply deny the rumors. Fretting about them and avoiding everyone only fuels the fires. Henrietta did nothing more than trust the wrong man's interests in her. And when she realized her mistake, he attempted to take what he wanted. He is still bitter over it, I am certain."

"Perhaps you are correct, Clif," Miriam said. "All right, we shall deny the rumors and hope they do not sway Mr. Barriweather should they reach his ears."

CHAPTER 11

1793

A week passed with little to no mention of the salacious rumor Miriam Nichols heard from Mrs. Winston. Henrietta prepared to attend the town's fair with her fiancé. Memories of the prior year's fair flooded her mind as she dressed for the occasion. She shook them off, focusing on the positive aspects of her life. This year she would attend the fair as an engaged woman. And soon, she would be married. Her life could settle.

She met Steven at the park. Together, they strolled arm-in-arm around. She side-eyed him as they paused to study a local farmer's wares. Twelve years her senior, he was a bit older than she envisioned in a husband. His eyes already had begun to crinkle at the corners and he'd developed a bit of a belly. Already a portly fellow, it added to his jolly countenance. Unfortunately, he had little interest in Henrietta's writing, but he was keen on the idea that she could entertain their children with bedtime stories.

He faced her, and she offered him a smile. He returned the gesture. He would provide a stable life for her, she couldn't deny that. And he was kind and considerate. Her mother told her he was a good match and that she would grow to love him.

They rejoined the rest of her family. She glanced around the fairgrounds. "Where's Clif?" she inquired.

* * *

Clifton chuckled as he meandered through the fair with several friends. "At any rate, we'll be sorry to see you go," Peter said to Adam.

"I will not be," Adam retorted. "I shall be glad to escape this accursed heat."

"It is not always hot," Clifton countered.

"It is always hot enough. I shall find Williamsburg quite a welcome change."

"I doubt you will find the studying a welcome change," Peter said as they took cover from the bright sunshine under the shade of a large oak.

The trio continued to exchange barbs when Clifton's ears pricked, hearing a familiar voice. He allowed the conversation between Peter and Adam to flow as he inched toward the tree trunk. Voices floated from around it.

"… quite surprised that is still happening," Thomas Cranston said.

"He's getting the better end of the bargain, I'd say," a male voice answered him.

"If you like that sort of girl… you know, the, ah, experienced type," Thomas said with a harsh cackle.

"Well, you certainly did," another answered.

"Yes, I did. What a wild ride…"

Clifton swung around the tree before Thomas could finish his statement.

"Nichols, fancy seeing you here," Thomas said with a smirk on his face.

"I told you once before if you troubled my sister again–"

"You would… oh, what was it? Kill me?" Thomas laughed at him. "I'd like to see you try." He swung his arms out as an invitation. "Well, come on." Clifton glared at him but didn't budge. "No?" He laughed again. "That's what I thought."

Clifton lunged at him, swinging his fist. Thomas danced back a few steps. Clifton swung again, this time connecting with his target. He struck him square on the chin, knocking Thomas onto his backside.

Thomas wiggled and rubbed his jaw as he attempted to sit up. Clifton straddled him, landing another blow. He grasped Thomas by the collar and pulled him upward before he struck him again.

Shouts broke out, and several of Thomas's friends attempted to pull Clifton away. He continued to pummel him with several more blows before he was yanked away. A crowd had gathered as the fight ensued.

Thomas scrambled to his feet with the help of two friends. He wiped at his bloodied nose, his hands shaking.

"You are insane!" he shouted.

Clifton stumbled back a step, panting with effort. "I told you once before to leave my sister alone. Do not speak of her ever again, or I swear I will kill you."

Clifton stared at him for another moment before he stalked away. As he passed the oak tree, he found Henrietta's eyes on him. Her brow crinkled as she stared at his bloodied knuckles. Her eyes met his, full of concern.

Steven caught sight of him as he approached Clifton. "Gracious me," he said as Henrietta closed the gap between them. "What in the world happened?"

Henrietta frowned. "Thomas?" she asked.

Clifton nodded. "I hope he has learned to keep his mouth shut. And if not, he has enough bruises to make it painful when he does open it."

"Thomas Cranston?" Steven inquired. "Whatever has he done to prompt such behavior?"

Henrietta's eyes went wide as they slid toward Steven. "He has the tendency to open his mouth and allow lies to spill out. Someone needed to correct the impulse."

Steven's mouth flopped open. Violence was not something familiar to him.

"Clifton Nichols!" Miriam shouted as she gaped at his bloodied knuckles. "What have you done?"

"I am fine, Mother."

"And what of the man on the other end?"

Clifton's jaw tensed. "He deserved every blow and more."

"Son," John said. "You should not let violence rule your actions."

He nodded. "You are correct, Father."

"It's all right," John said, clapping him on the back. "We all lose our tempers at times. The important thing is we learn to control them."

They wandered away as John provided his fatherly advice. As evening descended, they found a spot to wait for the fireworks. Steven hurried toward them from across the park. His face was flushed and his mouth opened and closed like a fish seeking water.

"Steven, what is it?" Henrietta asked.

"Simply terrible!"

"What is?"

He scanned the faces of the family. "I've just heard the victim of Clif's earlier outburst is tossing about the idea of pressing formal charges."

"Oh, no!" Miriam said, her fingers flying to cover her mouth that hung agape.

Clifton shook his head and slammed the leaf he'd been twirling in his fingers to the ground. "Thomas Cranston is no victim."

"I do not understand," Steven said. "What did you say prompted the attack?"

"I told you, I overheard him spouting off his usual lies."

"Which are?"

"It doesn't matter."

Steven's brow crinkled. "I cannot imagine a lie that would prompt such a reaction, is all. And it may very well matter if charges are brought against you."

Henrietta swallowed hard. She would not allow Clifton's actions to be construed as that of a madman's in order to protect her reputation. "The truth is…"

"Ri, don't. There is no need to repeat it."

Henrietta shook her head. "I…"

"NO!" Clifton shouted. "We shall deal with the reason if necessary. For now, there is no reason to dwell on it. We should enjoy the fireworks."

"But…" Steven said as the first firework burst in a colorful display, painting the night sky and silencing him.

After the display ended, Steven said his goodnights to the family. With a sideways glance at Clifton, he offered Henrietta a final smile and a kiss on the cheek before he hurried away.

Carolina yawned and tugged on Miriam's hand. "Please, Mummy, may we go home now?"

"Yes, dear."

"Go on ahead, we'll catch up," Clifton said.

Miriam smiled and nodded, looping her arm through John's. "Be safe, dear. Henrietta?"

"I shall return with Clif," Henrietta said.

Miriam eyed them both for a moment before she nodded. "Take care of your sister, dear."

"I always do."

The pair waited until the rest of their family were away before Henrietta set her gaze on Clifton. She raised her eyebrows at him. "What are you up to?" she inquired.

"What do you mean, Ri?"

"You clearly did not wish to return with Mother and Father."

"I am a young man. The world is my oyster."

"Don't you think you've gotten yourself in enough trouble today?"

Clifton stared at her, his chocolate brown eyes melting through her. "Thank you, by the way, for not saying anything about what prompted your… outburst."

"I would never, Ri."

She bit her lower lip. "You should not have to suffer for my sake."

"And you do not need to fall on your sword for me. I am a grown man. I can make my own choices."

"And what choices might those be?"

He raised his eyebrows at her.

She cocked her head at him. "You're acting strangely." He avoided her gaze. She craned her neck to catch his eye.

He shook his head but raised his hand. He clutched a scrap of paper between his thumb and forefinger. Henrietta snatched it from his hand. "What is this?" She unraveled the note and read it. Her head shook as her eyes scanned the words.

Henrietta read the note aloud. "Meet me outside the Colonial Tavern at midnight unless you want charges brought. Thomas. What is this?"

"It appears to be a note from Thomas."

"You mustn't go!" Henrietta said.

"Mustn't I?"

"No! Of course not! Clif, this could be a chance to make matters worse and ruin you."

"If I do not go, I could be ruined, anyway. You heard Steven."

"You cannot go alone, take someone."

"I will not subject anyone else to this. The actions were my own. I must face the consequences."

Henrietta bit her lower lip. "Then, I shall go with you."

"Absolutely not," Clifton argued.

"Try and stop me."

"Ri," he warned, "you have been harmed enough. I do not want you involved."

"And you are about to be harmed for defending my honor. You cannot ask me to leave you."

"Fine, then I will not go."

"Really?" Henrietta said, her eyebrows raised and her hand on her hip.

"Yes, really. Come, I shall escort you home."

She cocked her head and crossed her arms. "I will not go, Ri."

"Give me your word."

He hesitated. "Ah-ha, I knew it!"

"Ri, this is far too dangerous."

"I shall stay out of sight."

"Then why go at all?"

"I can summon help if need be."

"I am not going to win, am I?"

"Likely not," Henrietta answered.

"Fine. Stay out of sight. Do not involve yourself."

Henrietta nodded. "I mean it, Ri. Let me handle this."

"I agreed!"

They snaked through the crowd and Clifton led Henrietta toward the Colonial Tavern. After hiding her in the shadows with a view of the alley, he proceeded forward toward the shadowy figure looming at the end.

"Well, Thomas," Clifton said as he approached. "Here I am. Why the summons?"

Thomas smirked in the dim light, the shadows cast across his face distorting his expression into something ugly. Two men rushed from the shadows on either side of Clifton, grasping hold of him.

Clifton struggled against them to free himself. "What is this?" he growled.

"What indeed," Thomas said as he paced in front of the captive Clifton.

"Payback," Clifton concluded. "Well, go ahead, land your blows while I am held captive. Though if you were a real man, you'd have your companions release me and we'd fight this out."

The comment earned a punch to his gut. He doubled over for a moment as the wind left him.

"Oh, come, Thomas, is that all you've got?" he taunted with a chuckle. "No wonder you require the added help."

Another blow landed, this one against his jaw. "You embarrassed me earlier, Nichols."

"That's not hard to do. You embarrass yourself."

Thomas wheeled around and struck him again. Blood dripped from his split lip. He spat more red liquid onto the ground.

"You need to be taught a lesson," Thomas lectured. "You should not speak ill of others." He punched him in the gut again.

"You could stand to learn that as well. You are determined to ruin my sister's reputation. And all because she refused your indecent advances."

"She was all too willing to offer herself to me," he said.

"Quite the little tramp, your sister. Already engaged to another man only months after our little indiscretion."

Clifton roared as he struggled against the two men's grips.

"But I digress," Thomas said. "Regardless of the truthfulness of my statements, you stepped out of line by confronting me. You had no right."

"I had every right."

"No, you did not. I OWN this town, Nichols. I can do what I want. And now you will pay the price for stepping out of line."

Thomas landed another blow against his cheek. He held his chest as he drew his knee sharply upward into his rib cage. Clifton groaned as the air was forced from his lungs.

"Oh, please, do not allow me to have all the fun, gentlemen," Thomas said to his companions. "Feel free to join in."

With a harsh chuckle, one of them pounded his elbow into Clifton's back. He struggled to remain on his feet as Thomas issued an uppercut. Clifton steadied himself, pressing his palms to his thighs as Thomas wound up for another punch.

CHAPTER 12

1794

Henrietta hid in the shadows as Clifton wandered down the alley toward the waiting figure of Thomas Cranston. She held her breath, wondering what the outcome may be. Why had Thomas summoned Clifton? What did he hope to gain by it? Why did he suggest he would not press charges if they could meet?

Voices drifted in her direction but she couldn't make out every word. She squinted into the dim light, trying to read their postures for a hint at what transpired yards from her. Suddenly, two men emerged from the shadows, hidden by the buildings on either side of the alley. They grasped hold of Clifton.

Thomas approached and paced in front of Clifton. After a few utterances between the two of them, Thomas thrust his fist into Clifton's gut, doubling him over.

Henrietta gasped, her hand flying to her open mouth. She stumbled back a step as the assault continued.

It soon became clear that there was no end in sight. The other two joined in. Clifton would be overpowered easily in this game of three-against-one.

The assault continued. Henrietta searched the deserted street for help. She glanced toward the tavern window. Could she elicit help there? Likely not.

Her panicked gaze flitted back to the alley. Clifton would not last much longer. Her pulse raced as she stepped from the shadows.

She only heard her pounding heart in her ears as she raced toward the men. "Stop!" she shouted, her voice high in pitch, betraying her panic.

The men stopped, surprised by her sudden appearance. Then Thomas began to laugh. "Oh, this is just too perfect," he said. He gestured to one of the men who approached her.

"Stay away from me," she said, backing down the alley.

"Ri, get out of here," Clifton warned as he struggled to regain his posture.

"Leave my brother alone."

The man caught up to Henrietta and grasped her by the arm. He yanked her further down the alley toward Thomas.

"Let her go, Thomas," Clifton shouted as one man held on to him. He struggled against him as the other tossed Henrietta toward Thomas. She stumbled several steps before falling against him. He caught her in his arms.

"And here we are again. You cannot seem to stay away from men in dark alleys, can you?"

"Let go of me," Henrietta said as she tried to wiggle from his grip.

"Oh, I will, as soon as I am finished with you. Let's make those rumors true."

The second man had grasped hold of Clifton, further preventing him from moving. Thomas twirled, pushing Henrietta against the building's side. "Don't worry, gentlemen, there's enough for everyone to have a turn after I've finished." He let out a harsh laugh and hiked Henrietta's skirt.

"Stop, Thomas," Clifton shouted.

Thomas's only response was a chilling laugh. Henrietta fought against him but found herself unable to overpower him. A scuffle sounded behind Thomas. She peered over his shoulder with tear-clouded eyes. Clifton had smacked one of his captors in the nose by slamming his head into it, sending the man stumbling back several steps as blood poured from his nostrils. He spun and gave the other man a strong blow against his cheek.

Freed from any restraint, he reached into his boot, withdrawing an object. He cocked it and pointed it at Thomas.

"Stop or I will kill you, Thomas," he warned.

Thomas's head swiveled and he caught sight of the pistol. He spun to face Clifton. He breathed out a shocked breath. "Now, Clif, let's not be hasty."

"Oh, I am not being hasty. This is the last time you will harass my sister."

"Let's talk this out like men," Thomas implored, holding his hands out in front of him.

"Ri, come to me."

Henrietta nodded. With wobbly legs, Henrietta slid away from the wall and stepped toward Clifton. She spotted movement behind him. "Clif, watch out!" she shouted.

He twisted to face his attacker, shifting his weight to avoid a punch. The man grasped hold of the gun and the two struggled for a moment. Henrietta rushed forward, snaking her arm around the man's neck and tugging. It did little good. The other attacker pulled her away. As she struggled to free herself a deafening blast filled the alley. Her ears rang as she tried to orient herself, stumbling forward when her attacker suddenly let go.

She lurched toward Clifton, grabbing hold of his arm to

steady herself. Her eyes raised to his face. His jaw hung agape and his eyes were wide. Henrietta followed the direction of his stare. Her lower lip trembled as she discovered the source of his shock.

The other two men eyed the scene before backing a few steps away and fleeing into the night. Thomas collapsed to his knees. He touched his stomach with a trembling hand, a grimace forming on his face as he withdrew it and stared at his blood-stained fingers.

Clifton swiveled toward Henrietta. "The pistol went off. I didn't mean to..." he gasped out.

Henrietta rushed toward Thomas as he fell forward. With Clifton's help, they turned him onto his back. His blood-soaked shirt clung to him.

"Oh," Henrietta choked out, "there's so much blood."

Thomas gasped for air. "Help," he cried. Tears fell from the corners of his eyes.

"What do we do?" Henrietta asked Clifton.

"I do not know. I am not certain if we can do anything."

"We must take him to a doctor!"

Clifton swallowed hard and nodded. As he lifted Thomas's shoulders, the man gurgled. Blood spilled from his lips before his head fell sideways. His unseeing eyes stared forward.

Henrietta's jaw unhinged and her eyes widened further. Her lower lip trembled as she glanced up to Clifton. "He is... he is dead."

Clifton remained silent for a moment before locking eyes with Henrietta. "I didn't mean to..." he repeated.

She squeezed his hand. "I believe you. But... what do we do now?"

"You must go home. Immediately. Forget what you saw here."

"No!" Henrietta insisted. "I will not leave you."

"You must," he insisted. "You cannot be party to this."

"But I can testify that you did not mean to kill him."

"Testimony that will be considered tainted since we are siblings. Ri, you must go."

She shook her head. "No, we need advice. Options."

"From whom?" Clifton questioned.

Henrietta pondered for a moment before grabbing his hand and pulling him along with her. "Come with me."

"Ri, where are we going?" Henrietta ignored him, winding through the streets.

He pulled her a stop after several moments. "I really must insist you return home and allow me to handle this."

"No. It is I who got us into this situation with Thomas. Now come along."

They continued for several more blocks before Henrietta slowed. She came to a stop outside a townhome. Clifton groaned. "Ri, no."

"We have no other options," she said. She marched up the three steps and rapped against the door. A few moments passed with no answer.

"Ri, let's go," Clifton said from the sidewalk.

"No," she said, pounding against the door again.

A flickering light appeared inside. The flame grew larger before the door popped open. Steven Merriweather, in his dressing-gown, peered out.

"Henrietta?" he questioned, squinting into the night.

"We need your help," she said simply.

With shock apparent on his features, he stood back and allowed them entrance.

"What has happened?" he asked as Henrietta gripped the fireplace in his sitting room. Dying embers still warmed the room and she stared at the red glow emanating from them.

"I require a bit of legal advice. Thank you, Ri, for making

the appeal on my behalf, but you should return home now," Clifton explained.

"No," Henrietta said, spinning to face them.

"Legal advice? Does this concern Thomas Cranston?"

"Yes," Clifton answered.

"Has he filed charges already?"

"No," Henrietta answered. "And he will not be filing charges."

"Oh, what a relief!" Steven said as he plopped into an armchair. He stared between the siblings and his brow furrowed. "Then what legal advice do you seek?"

Henrietta bit her lower lip and glanced at Clifton. He shook his head. Steven's gaze flitted between the two of them. "Something prompted you to seek my advice in the wee hours. I would very much like to be apprised of what that was."

"Thomas Cranston is dead," Henrietta said.

"What?" Steven exclaimed. "How?"

"There was an incident…" Clifton began.

"Clif received this note from Thomas," Henrietta interrupted, pulling the note from her purse and handing it to Steven.

As he accepted it he stared at her hand before grasping it. "Is this blood?"

She swallowed hard. "Yes."

He stared at her and she pointed to the note. "Clif felt it best to meet him but I did not wish him to go alone. So I followed, remaining hidden in the shadows."

"Go on," Steven prompted after perusing the note.

"Thomas lured him to the alley then, with the help of two friends, attacked Clif."

Steven's eyebrows raised and he glanced to Clifton, eyeing the bruises on his face.

"I presented myself to attempt to stop the attack and…"

"And?" Steven questioned, leaping from his chair and pacing the floor.

"Thomas grabbed me. And he…" Her voice trailed off again. Her face, ashen in color, fell.

"I had a pistol. I drew it and told him to stop," Clifton continued. "A struggle ensued and the gun went off. The bullet pierced Thomas's gut. He died moments later."

Steven's jaw flapped open. He searched for words but none came.

"He did not mean to kill him, Steven. What can be done?"

He arched his eyebrows and tilted his head as though considering the question. "Were there witnesses?"

"Two of Thomas's friends. They fled the scene when the gun went off."

He nodded. "Did either of them sustain any injuries?"

"Perhaps a few. There was a brawl."

"Clif's injuries are much worse! They attacked him, three on one!" Henrietta cried.

"It does not matter," Steven contended. "Clifton argued with him earlier. A very public argument. He attacked him, unprovoked. This will all be brought into evidence, you see. Trying to prove self-defense or even lack of forethought could prove impossible. What was the nature of the argument?"

Clifton and Henrietta shared a glance. "Does it matter?" Clifton inquired.

"You have come to seek my help. I must know the details in order to advise you."

"It's fine, Clif," Henrietta said.

"No, it is inconsequential. The fact of the matter is, we argued in public and now he's dead."

"By your weapon. Where did you acquire it?"

"From a man on the docks."

Steven's shoulders sagged as he shook his head, his eyes

pinched closed. "I am afraid it does not look good. One word from the others present, and you shall be arrested and tried. He is… or rather was a prominent man. Unless we can work to discredit him somehow, which would be tricky given his status, or to provide some reason for the violence, you would likely be sentenced to hang."

"And if we could provide a reason?" Henrietta asked.

"The odds are significantly improved that a death sentence would not be sought, but prison would remain the most likely outcome."

Henrietta collapsed onto the sofa. "And it would depend on the reason," he added.

Henrietta's head sank into her hands and she sobbed. "I am the reason," she choked out.

"Ri, no. There is no need to say anything further. We have our advice. We should go."

She shook her head as she sniffled. Tears stained her cheeks. "Thomas has been spreading rumors about me. Saying I am a woman of questionable morals who has met with several men."

Steven stared at her for a long moment. "It is not true," Clifton said.

"Is there more to this story?" Steven questioned. "What would prompt such a tale from him?"

Henrietta licked her lips. Clifton shook his head at her but she continued despite his disapproval. "A year ago, Thomas led me to believe he was interested in courting me. Though it was a farce, I believed him genuine. I… met with him privately. Despite his actions, nothing came of the meeting as Clif showed up and I left. Days later, his engagement to Edwina was announced. It was then that he confessed his interest in me to be only… carnal. I refused him, and he took exception. He nearly forced himself upon me, but Clif intervened. After that night I'd have nothing more to do with Thomas. Following our engagement, though, it appears he became enraged and began to spread rumors about me."

"And your reaction was to beat the man senseless?" Steven posed to Clifton.

"The man is a pig. He deserved far worse than that fate."

"Far worse than being left bleeding in an alley? Pig or not, he is a man!"

"A man who twice attempted to force himself upon my sister. A man who despised her so he hoped to ruin any chance she had at happiness by spreading gossip."

"Violence does not solve the issue."

"I'd argue it has," Clifton retorted.

"I think you'd better leave," Steven answered.

"Steven, please," Henrietta said, leaping to her feet.

He shook his head. "Both of you."

Henrietta's brow furrowed and she drew in a sharp breath. "Do you mean…"

"I am sorry, Henrietta," Steven said, "but I believe it is best that we part ways."

"But…"

He shook his head at her. "If my involvement in this ever came to light… never mind. I am very sorry for the distress this will cause you, and if asked I will give away no details to paint you in a poor light, but I cannot enter into a marriage with you."

Henrietta's face displayed the shock that burrowed inside her.

"Please do not punish my sister for my actions," Clifton attempted.

Steven stood firm and shook his head. "It is not a punishment, merely the realization that we are not well-suited."

"Steven," Clifton tried again.

"Please, leave. Both of you."

Clifton offered a nod and a muttered thank you as he grasped Henrietta's arm and tugged her toward the door. They exited into the summer night's warm air. The distinctive sound of a lock turning behind them sealed their fate.

"Ri," Clifton said as she stood staring at the ground below them.

"Even from the grave, he ruins my life," she murmured.

"Ri," he repeated, guiding her away from the house. They found a nearby bench and sat down. "We must discuss what to do."

"What can we do?"

"I must leave."

"No!" Henrietta argued.

"Ri, I must go. You heard Steven. I could be tried and sent to prison or worse."

"But you did nothing wrong!" Tears shone in her eyes. The law will not see it that way."

"Please, you cannot go."

"I must, Ri. I will sign onto a ship. But I will return. Once this dies down. The stories will end and I will come back to town. I'll be a famous pirate by then." He grinned at her but his joke did little to lighten the tension.

"No," she argued. "No, we'll go somewhere else. Both of us. We'll leave tonight."

"No," he said. "I shall leave tonight, but you will not."

"No, Clif. I cannot bear to stay here alone. Not after this." Her voice filled with emotion and she choked back a sob.

"Ri…"

"You cannot leave!" she shouted, leaping from her seat. "You cannot leave me here!" She covered her face with her hands and sobbed.

Clifton wrapped her in his arms. "You will survive, Ri. And I will return. I will always return to take care of you."

"You are abandoning me," she cried.

"Only for a little while."

"I cannot bear it. Not after the last year. Not after tonight."

"You must. Keep up your writing. I shall expect two… no, three novels finished by the time I return."

"No," she said and pushed away from him. "No, you do not get to decide for me."

"All right, Ri," he said. "We shall both go."

"Really?"

"It appears you will not allow me to leave on my own."

She smiled and raised her chin. "No, I will not."

"Then I suppose I have no choice. We will return home, pack a few items, then depart."

She nodded, wiping at her tears.

When they arrived at the house, Clifton whispered, "Pack a few things and meet me in my room when you are ready."

"All right," she said with a nod. She dashed up the stairs with Clifton following her. She offered him a smile and a nod as she disappeared into her room. Pulling a small travel bag from under her bed, she hurried to the wardrobe and stuffed in several items. She pondered between two dresses, wondering if she had room for them both. She had to hurry, she warned herself, as she tossed one aside. There was no time for indecision.

She raced to her desk, gathering her writing and adding it to her packed items. Perhaps wherever she and Clif started over, she could use her writing to help. She'd have better prospects outside Savannah. They would support each other and eventually, they'd both find happiness.

She smiled to herself as she closed the bag. She lugged the bag from her room. Careful not to make too much noise, she tiptoed toward Clifton's bedroom.

"Clif, I…" she began as she entered. She scanned the darkened space. Her heart skipped a beat. Her gaze fell on a paper tented and sitting on top of his desk. "Ri" was scrawled on it.

She shook her head as though it would change the outcome. "No," she murmured as she crossed to it. With trembling hands, she snatched the paper with her name. Another sat next to it, addressed to her mother and father. She flipped open the paper.

Ri -

I know it will pain you greatly when you realize I have left without you. And for that I am sorry. I have cost you much. But I cannot take you with me. I must make my fortune. Then I shall return. And I will take care of you, dear sister. I will not renege on my word.

Until then, think well of me and take care.

Ever your loving brother,

Clif

Tears welled in her eyes, and she slumped to the floor. She pulled the note to her chest as she collapsed in a heap crying.

CHAPTER 13

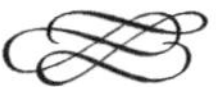

1794

Clifton glanced back once at the darkened form of his childhood home. He'd taken a few possessions with him. He'd had to have been quick to escape his room before Henrietta came for him.

He'd lied to her. He'd told her they would leave together. He had no intention of taking her with him. He couldn't.

He realized she'd be disappointed, hurt, and knowing Ri, likely angry, but he had to do this alone. He'd return for her one day. And he'd take care of her as he promised.

With the silent affirmation, he tore his eyes from the home and strode into the darkness. His feet carried him to the docks. Ships, their sails tied up or missing, bobbed in the waters. He'd heard days ago that the ship, *Cotton Mary*, was preparing to set sail at sunrise. He found the vessel and stared up at its masts. Activity flourished as sailors prepared to shove off.

Clifton stopped one of the men on his way up the gangplank. "Excuse me. Who would I speak to about working aboard?"

"Captain. He's aboard in his quarters."

Clifton nodded to the grisled man before preceding him onto the ship's deck. The man motioned again toward the captain's quarters. Clifton approached the door, giving it a solid knock.

A man grunted an acknowledgment and an invitation to enter. Clifton pushed the door open and glanced inside. The captain hovered over a set of maps, two men joining him on either side. He narrowed his eyes at Clifton. "Yes?"

"Captain, I have come to seek employment aboard this vessel."

"We have a full crew," the captain said, returning his attention to his map.

Undeterred Clifton said, "Possibly so, but you have no one of my caliber."

The statement intrigued the captain. "Oh?" he questioned. "What ships have you sailed on before."

"None."

The captain laughed. "None? Yet you claim some expertise in being a sailor? Enough that I should take you on over and above my full crew?"

"Yes," Clifton said with a savvy grin.

"Explain yourself, boy," the man said.

"I am hard-working, amiable, and I will never abandon my crew or my ship."

"Admirable traits, boy, but it is what I expect from all my crewmen."

"Is it what you receive from them without fail?"

"More or less."

Clifton arched an eyebrow. "Is it more or less? I'd suspect the latter. Seamen are rarely known for their overwhelming loyalty, but rather more for their loyalty to beverages of the alcoholic nature."

The captain narrowed his eye at him, an amused but befuddled expression turning up the corners of his mouth. "And what do you propose?"

"Hire me. I shall keep the crew in line."

A laugh escaped one of the other men's lips. "Be gone, boy," he said, waving his hand at Clifton. "Captain Hardinger already has his second-in-commands."

"And they seem to be doing a rather poor job or he would not have entertained my request," Clifton said, his eyes not leaving the captain's face.

Captain Hardinger mulled the statements for a moment before he spoke again. "Can you read a map?"

"Most definitely."

"Captain, you cannot be serious?" one of the men uttered.

The captain ignored the statement. "Can you use the stars to navigate?"

"Yes," Clifton said. "All things I am familiar with."

"I thought you said you never worked a ship," one of the other men said.

"I said I never worked a ship, yes. I did not say I'd never been on one."

"I shall hire you as an assistant to me. You will learn how a merchant vessel operates. If you cannot hack it, I shall leave you at the first port. Do you understand, boy?"

"I do. It is an agreeable arrangement."

"Fine. Find a space below decks to stow your gear and report back here at first light."

Clifton offered a nod and a tight-lipped smile as he backed from the captain's quarters.

* * *

Cotton Mary rocked violently as the waves crashed over her sides and onto her deck. Several men scrambled to keep upright as the slick wood and the perilous pitching of the ship made it difficult to walk.

Lightning lit the blackened sky, illuminating another huge swell. It smashed into the ship, bowling over two men who fought to hold the wheel steady.

Clifton stood on the helm and grasped the spinning wheel to steady the ship.

The drenched sailors climbed to their feet. "Keep her steady," Clifton said.

"Sir, the ship will not make it. We shall be doomed."

Clifton shook his head as one of the men retched over the boat's side before returning to his post. "We shall be doomed if you do not keep her steady. We are too close to the Isle of Danvia. If we do not pull away, we shall be sucked to the island and smashed against the rocks."

"But she will not withstand the waves, sir."

"She will," Clifton assured them. "Keep her aimed there." He pointed toward the horizon. "See the break in the clouds?"

With a worried glance around, the men nodded. Clifton clapped them on the back before descending to the deck below. He picked his way toward the captain's quarters as the ship swayed under him. After pounding and receiving a shouted invitation, he pushed inside. He removed his tricorn hat. It dripped on the floor as water splashed from it.

"Well?" the captain questioned.

"We will make it on time."

The captain raised his eyebrows. "In this weather?"

Clifton mirrored his expression and nodded in affirmation. "The men follow you well, my boy. They like you. They respect you. You are an asset. Which is why I've chosen to promote you."

Clifton offered a half-smile.

"What of the danger of the Isle of Danvia? The storm pushes us ever nearer."

"We should skirt it without much trouble if they keep to the course."

"Good. Your re-routing has saved us yet again."

"Is there anything else, Captain?"

The captain shook his head and gestured for Clifton to take his leave. Clifton staggered from the quarters and across the ship's deck. After a quick check of their course, he descended downstairs. He grabbed a bowl and helped himself to the stew.

"How can you eat?" Walsh questioned. His pale, clammy skin suggested seasickness.

"Relax, Walsh. We will not capsize."

"But the swaying," he said as his stomach threatened to revolt.

"Like a gently rocking swing," Clifton answered.

The chief mate smirked at him. "So brave in the face of danger," he said with a sneer.

Clifton did not respond, merely shooting him a narrow-eyed glance.

"Careful, Nichols. Your calculated risks may just cost us one of these days."

"Oh, I doubt it. I take great care when calculating."

The man grimaced and shook his head. "I do not understand what the captain sees in you. You are brash and arrogant. And I'd wager you have no experience whatsoever in anything meaningful."

Several crew members gathered around as the conversation continued. "I have taken appropriate actions when necessary," Clifton answered.

"Oh? And what might those be?"

"None of your business."

"As I suspected. He has no experience, gentlemen! Not really. If the circumstances turn dire, I suspect we'd find him hiding under his cot." The man gave a harsh chuckle. A few others joined in. Most of the crew members, though, waited for Clifton's response.

Clifton set his bowl down and drew in a deep breath, puffing his chest. He approached the chief mate, drawing close to him.

The man stood firm and asked, "Have you ever had cause to end a man's life?"

"Yes," Clifton said.

The chief mate flinched, showing the slightest hint of surprise. "So, you are a murderer?"

Clifton did not waver. "No. The man attacked a woman with the intention of harming her. I warned him three times not to proceed. He did not listen. I fired. He died."

The man offered a disgruntled smile. "Appears you are not one to be crossed, Mr. Nichols."

"No," Clifton agreed. "I am not."

* * *

1796

Lightning tore through the sky and thunder rumbled overhead. The wooden ship crashed through the rolling waves. Clifton staggered across the slippery wooden deck. The rain pelted him from above. A few sailors clung to the ship's side, their meals not remaining in their stomachs.

Clifton eyed them, realizing they'd not return after they docked next. Perhaps he shouldn't blame them. They were, after all, new, and this storm was one of the worst he'd sailed through.

In his two years aboard the *Cotton Mary*, he'd already become accustomed to life at sea, including stormy weather.

He'd not even become seasick the first time the boat rocked enough to nearly capsize.

His iron-clad resolve had allowed him to move up quickly and become a trusted associate of Captain Hardinger. His mind turned to the man. He doubted he'd make it through the night. In addition to the rough waters, several crew members suffered from scurvy. The captain was counted among those men.

Clifton slipped out of the rain and into the comfort of the captain's quarters. The captain lay in his hammock, his skin blotchy and bruised. His eyes were closed and for a moment, Clifton wondered if he'd already passed. In the dim candlelight, he noticed the shallow rise and fall of the man's chest. Still alive.

Clifton approached him and stared down at the man who'd taught him so much in his brief time aboard. The man stirred. "Clif, my boy," he said in a hoarse voice.

"I'm here, Captain. I have brought some broth."

The man shook his head, groaning in pain. "Do not waste it on me. I will not survive the night."

"You don't know that," Clif said as he filled a spoon with the light-colored liquid.

The captain offered a congested chuckle as he accepted some of the broth. "I do." After a few sips, he waved his hand to stop. "When I go, I shall like to be buried at sea."

"Buried at sea?" Clifton inquired as he set the bowl aside. "What of your family?"

"I have none. I have spent my life sailing these seas. The sea is my family, and I should like to be reunited with her for eternity. I leave the task to you, my boy."

"I shall see that it is done."

"I have no doubt," the captain said. "You are an excellent worker. You will make an excellent captain one day."

Clifton offered him a half-smile as the man's eyes closed. "Perhaps sooner than you'd think," he murmured.

Clifton stayed with the man until he took his final breaths. After seeing to his watery burial as promised, Clifton returned to the captain's quarters to find his chief mate, a man by the name of William Dickerson, lounging with his feet on the captain's desk.

A puff of smoke floated toward the ceiling from the man's mouth. He clutched a cigar between his fingers. His dark hair was slicked back into a queue, accentuating his sharp features. The candlelight further underscored his devilish look.

"Really, William, you could have waited until the man's body was cold before you commandeered his office," Clifton admonished.

"I am the captain now. This ship will operate under my rule. You may call me Captain Dickerson."

Clifton rolled his eyes at the man.

"And it will operate quite differently to the way it did under Captain Hardinger."

"I have no doubt."

"For starters, that attitude will need to be adjusted. Hardinger may have found you tolerable. I do not."

"We will put into port soon. Perhaps I should seek another ship."

"Hmm, not soon. I have another stop to make first. Tell the helmsman to change course."

"To?" Clifton inquired.

The man stood and clamped the cigar between his teeth. He jabbed his finger at the map. "Here."

Clifton studied it then slid his eyes sideways toward his new captain. "And what is there?"

The man smirked, his facial features almost grotesque in the flickering candlelight. "Something very valuable."

* * *

They weighed anchor off the coast of a small island. Several skiffs were organized to row to the island. Clifton's boots splashed in the water as he leapt out and dragged one ashore. He surveyed the deserted beach. Sand spread in either direction. Behind it, thick palm and deciduous trees closed in the rest of the island.

Captain Dickerson squinted in the bright sun as he studied the darkened canopy.

"Hunter, Mitchell, take a contingent of men around that way and into the area I pointed out earlier," he shouted.

The two men nodded and gathered a group of men, setting off down the beach with them in tow.

"Gentlemen, follow me!" the captain shouted. "And keep your wits about you."

Clifton regarded him for a moment as they set off toward the trees. Coolness enveloped them as they stepped under the canopy. Clifton waited for his eyes to adjust before he proceeded. What was Dickerson's aim here, he wondered?

They proceeded well into the depths of the trees. Movement caught Clifton's eye as they approached a clearing. "Sir," he breathed.

"I see them," the man answered.

Several dark-skinned people hovered, hidden amongst the trees. Clifton noted several of them carried spears.

As they entered the clearing, a contingent of men approached. They wore only cloths around their lower halves. Their faces were decorated with black paint. Necklaces made of fangs hung around their necks and onto their bare chests.

"Hello," Captain Dickerson said.

A rail-thin individual, with his ribcage showing through

his skin, mumbled something to the man in the middle of the group. He muttered unintelligible words back.

"He asks what you seek and what you bring to trade," the man reported.

"Right to the chase, is it?" The captain offered a chuckle. "I seek the gold you have. And I have a great many valuable things to trade."

"Such as?" the man inquired.

Captain Dickerson rattled off a list of items including food, blankets, weapons, and valuable gems. Clifton's brow furrowed. They had none of these things aboard available for trade.

The man passed the information along.

"Show us what you have brought," he replied.

"They are all aboard ship. Show us the gold."

"No items, no gold."

Captain Dickerson offered a snort. "You have no choice, really. Give us the gold."

The man sneered at him and conveyed the latest message to his superior. The older man broke into a wide grin and laughed.

Captain Dickerson joined him. The older man spoke in a foreign language. He followed his statements with another laugh.

"What did he say?" Captain Dickerson inquired.

The skinny man continued to laugh. "He said no. It is you who has no choice. You are surrounded. We give you nothing." The man laughed again heartily.

Captain Dickerson joined in with him. After a moment of laughter, his facial features settled into a sneer. "Tell him so is he. And now we'll take the gold."

The laughing man's face turned serious in an instant as Captain Dickerson snapped his fingers. From the trees, more brown-skinned men emerged. Stripped of their spears and with raised hands, they were marched forward at gunpoint by the other contingent of the captain's men.

They paraded the indigenous people toward a waterfall. A village was situated nearby. "Where is the gold?" Captain Dickerson hissed.

The man directed them to behind the waterfall. The captain directed two men to scout the location. They returned with grins on their faces.

"You have your gold, now go," the man spat.

"Begin hauling the gold to the ship."

"And what of them?" Mitchell asked. He motioned toward the men who had led them there.

Captain Dickerson flicked his eyes toward the captive group then the town. "Kill them all, and burn the village to the ground."

Cries went up among the captives as the translator passed along the message. The leader of the indigenous group raced toward the captain. Though Clifton did not understand the language, he appeared to plead with the man.

The other man spoke hurriedly. "Take the gold, take what you want. But leave us in peace. Please, there are women and children. Surely you would not harm them?"

The captain stepped away, ignoring the men. No one moved. "You have your orders," he said after a few steps. "Execute every living soul and burn the village down."

Clifton took a step backward and drew his sword. He pressed it to the captain's neck. "I think not."

Captain Dickerson eyed the sword pressed to his neck, then slid his eyes up to Clifton's face. "Lower your weapon, Nichols, or I'll have you up on charges."

"Our orders for the trading company do not mention this stop."

"No, they don't, but insubordination is insubordination."

"Not when you are not the captain."

Dickerson's brow crinkled. "Have you gone mad?"

"No. William Dickerson, I am hereby removing you from your position and commandeering your vessel."

"On whose authority?"

"Mine," Clifton said.

Dickerson roared with laughter. "You have no authority."

"Don't I? You have made several enemies as chief mate."

"Possibly so, though no man aboard this ship would turn down the bounty we are about to haul aboard."

"A bounty you had no intention on sharing until you found yourself in this predicament, I am certain. Besides, I am not asking them to."

"Gentlemen!" Dickerson shouted. "If you would like to share in the reward, simply ignore this madman and complete the tasks as I've laid out."

Only four other men attempted to follow his instructions, trying to herd the men of the tribe toward the village.

No one else moved. Clifton raised his eyebrows. "Oops," he taunted. "Gentlemen, lower your weapons. Johnson, Tyler, take a contingent and escort former captain Dickerson and his loyal crewmen to the ship and secure them below decks. We'll deal with them later."

The remaining men followed the orders given by Clifton, lowering the weapons held against the tribe. Two men grabbed Dickerson roughly while the others herded the four men. They began to march him forward. "You're all fools!" he shouted. "When I report this, you'll all be out of jobs!"

"I doubt that," Clifton argued.

"We no longer work for the West India Trading Company!" a man shouted.

"Liars and cheats, the lot of you!" another chimed in.

Clifton chuckled at him as he was led away. A wiry blonde approached him. "Thanks for the heads up, Mitchell," he said.

Clifton approached the tribal leaders. "How can I say hello in your language?" he asked the translator.

After mastering the word, he spoke in English again. "I am sorry for former Captain Dickerson."

"The chief wishes to thank you," the man said. "He would like to repay you for your kindness." He motioned toward the gold. "He says take it. It brings us nothing but bad omens and bad luck."

"Tell him for his offering, he should not be troubled again. If you experience any difficulty with the company, get word to me. I shall handle it."

The man conveyed the message. "He is grateful for your protection, Mister." The man paused. "What shall he call you?"

Clifton offered a slight smile. "Tell him he can call me Black Jack."

The man passed along the message. The chief nodded and grinned at him. "He offers his thanks to you again. And his daughter."

"What?" Clifton inquired.

"His daughter. He offers her to you as a wife."

Clifton shook his head. "Please tell him I will not take his daughter from him."

"He insists she is very beautiful."

"I have no doubt she is. But I will not rob him of his daughter or his daughter of her own choices."

"He says take all the gold, you are a most reasonable man."

"Tell him I find him the same."

After concluding his discussion with the man, he climbed atop a rock near the water's edge.

"Gentlemen," Clifton shouted. "Tonight, we cut our ties with the West India Trading Company! Tonight, we declare war on them and men like Dickerson. Tonight, we fly the black sails for tonight, we are pirates!"

CHAPTER 14

1796

"Keep her steady!" Clifton shouted as they sailed through the choppy waters.

"I see her, sir!" a crewman shouted from the crow's nest.

"Good," Clifton said. "Steady men."

They approached the other ship, bobbling in the waters. Clifton's eyes narrowed as he studied it on the horizon. Something was off.

"Walsh, what do you see?" he called up to the man in the crow's nest.

"*The Fenton,* sir! She appears disabled."

"Ripe for the picking, eh, Captain?" Mitchell asked him.

Clifton narrowed his eyes at the scene. Something was wrong. "Hard to starboard!" Clifton shouted.

"Sir?"

"Put her over, now and retreat."

"But sir! *The Fenton* is defenseless! Her limited weaponry will not outmatch us and she is already disabled."

"She is disabled because someone disabled her. Now put her hard to…"

His words were cut off as a cannonball flew past, smashing into the water near them in a giant plume of water. The men ducked and covered their heads instinctively. Clifton raised his and scanned the horizon. From behind *The Fenton*, another ship sailed.

Clifton screwed up his face as he recognized Redbeard's *Scourge of the Seas*. With its pirate flag sailing high, she hurried to gain on Clifton. Cannon's blazed from within her belly.

"Is she hard over?" Clifton shouted.

"Yes, sir, hard over, sir," the response came.

"Ready the cannons and return fire."

"Shall we make a stand, sir?"

"No, she will outgun us. She has the advantage. We run. This time."

Clifton's vessel, now called *Neptune's Servant*, began to turn. As she slid through the water, her cannons returned fire. One struck a blow, splintering the bow and defacing the mermaid gracing it.

Neptune's Servant continued its turn. Clifton stared over at the other ship, spotting the red mane of Redbeard. He narrowed his eyes and sneered at Clifton. They'd been beaten today. Bested by another pirate. It would be the last time Clifton allowed that to happen.

As the ship completed its arc, Clifton gave the order to cease fire.

"Sir, the *Scourge* follows."

"She cannot overtake us, keep to the current course."

"Sir, we should take our chances and stand and fight."

Clifton shook his head. "No, we were bested. Plain and simple. We shall live to fight another day."

"Sir, she is gaining on us!" the man shouted, alarm

sounding in his voice.

"She will not overtake us. Put her to port a tad. We shall steal her wind."

The man nodded and relayed the order to the helmsman. Shouts came from the other ship. They readied to fire again and board. Clifton smirked. They would not have that pleasure today.

With a nervous glance behind them, the man said, "Sir? Your orders?"

"Keep her steady."

The man licked his lips as he glanced between the horizon and the other ship. Within minutes, she dropped back. *Neptune's Servant* pulled ahead, widening the gap between them.

Clifton smirked as he glanced behind them.

"Set a course for Tortuga. We need to regroup."

* * *

Clifton secured the final prisoners from his raid on *The Penylan*. They'd come away with a nice bounty after the ship had robbed local island residents of riches, leaving many of them dead after an ugly battle.

"Sir!" a shout came from the crow's nest. The man pointed toward the horizon.

"Perfect timing," Clifton said with a smirk. "Are we ready?"

"Ready, sir!" Mitchell said. "On your orders sir."

"Good."

The ship sailed ever closer. *Neptune's Servant* made a slow and clumsy attempt to pull away from alongside *The Penylan*. As he expected, *Scourge of the Seas* attempted to slip behind the other ship, using it as a buffer.

Clifton couldn't hold back a chuckle at the Redbeard's

predictability. The last of his men scrambled from below decks on *The Penylan*.

Cannon fire erupted from the warring ship. "Hold," Clifton instructed his nervous crew.

The two men still aboard the disabled merchant ship swung across to *Neptune's Servant*. As soon as they were aboard, Clifton gave the order to pull away.

A cannonball grazed the ship as she turned to her port side. Another one struck her square, blowing a hole through her main deck's railing. Clifton fought to maintain his footing.

Before another barrage could strike, Redbeard's ship slipped behind *The Penylan*. Several of his men boarded her, scurrying below decks to use her weapons hull to attack *Neptune's Servant*. Clifton eyed the ship, waiting for their retreat. Within seconds, the men reappeared on the deck. They shouted and waved their arms. Before anyone could decipher their meaning, a loud boom sounded. *The Penylan* exploded in a fiery burst that shot skyward. Anything left aboard was flung into the sea. *Scourge of the Seas*, which sought to shelter behind her, sustained extensive damage. Fires burst from several spots on her deck and hull. The eruption blasted a large hole into her side. She sat disabled, unable to pursue her intended victims.

Clifton chuckled. They did not sink her, but they blew a large enough hole that Redbeard would be unable to chase them for quite a while. Clifton offered a hand wave and bow toward Redbeard as he shouted orders to assess and repair the damage.

"Sorry, Redbeard, you'll need to do better than that," he shouted.

* * *

1797

Neptune's Servant floated in the waters next to the *HMS Queen Anne*. The crew of the *Queen Anne* huddled on the deck, their hands bound and on their knees.

A gangplank was stretched across to facilitate the unloading of the *Queen Anne* to the other ship. Boots pounded against the boards before they struck the deck. Clifton, dressed all in black, studied the men on their knees.

"And this is the group responsible for the massacre?" he asked his crewmen who were holding them.

"Aye, sir, this is them."

"What have you to say for yourselves?" he asked as he marched up and down the deck.

No one answered. "Cat got your tongues?" He awaited a response but none came. "No matter. Load them aboard the *Neptune*, we'll drop them on our way."

The men nodded and started to pull them to their feet. "Wait, wait," a man near the end cried.

Clifton strutted to him and squatted down. "Have something to say?"

"Yes. I… I didn't want to do it," he admitted.

"Didn't you, now? And did you object before your fellow crewmen slaughtered almost an entire village full of men?"

"They were preventing us from doing the business of the company," another man grunted.

"I wasn't aware the company's business was to murder innocent people," Clifton shot back. He turned his attention back to the upset man. "My question remains: did you object?"

The man's lip trembled. "Not in so many words."

"Not in so many words," he repeated. "And what does that mean?"

"Means he didn't say nothing," another man blurted.

"Just stood there and shook all over. Might as well have cried for his mummy."

Clifton regarded the man. "Are you aware of who I am?"

The man nodded. Clifton raised his eyebrows at him, prodding him for an answer.

"Bl-Black Jack," he choked out.

"Yes, Black Jack, that's right. And are you aware of what I normally do when I've captured a ship?"

"Kill all aboard but one."

"Interesting. The tale is not entirely true, but I'll take it. Your cowardice on the island has earned you the right to be the one man left behind."

"Please, Black Jack, I'll join your crew. I…"

"No," Clifton said as he rose to stand. "You cannot be trusted. You have no guts. Tie him to the mainmast and move the others to the *Neptune*."

"Aye aye, Captain."

Clifton climbed back to his own ship and settled in his quarters to plan his route. Within the hour, the other ship had been drained of its contents. His crew withdrew from the *Queen Anne,* leaving its sole occupant tied to the mainmast.

With the anchor raised, they set sail. "Course set of Altalba, Captain," his second in command, Charleston, reported.

"Good, we'll leave these criminals there for the Altalbans to deal with and drop the other bounty in the usual spot before we set course for Savannah."

"Savannah?" Charleston questioned.

"Yes, Savannah," Clifton answered. "Drop the black sails and raise the standards. We enter Savannah's port under the usual guise of a merchant ship."

"Yes, sir, but…" He hesitated.

"You have a question. Ask it."

"Why are we returning to Savannah? We can sell the textile load from the *Queen Anne* at any port."

"I must return to Savannah," he said. "My sister is getting married."

* * *

Henrietta regarded her reflection in the mirror. The rose pink dress she wore complimented her skin tone, bringing out the rosiness in her cheeks. She forced a smile onto her face. She must try to look happy. It was, after all, her wedding day.

Her smile faded as she recalled that detail. Despite the new dress, despite the gifts she'd received, the wedding brought her little joy. She hadn't told anyone that. She'd barely admitted it to herself.

But she had few other options. Following the dissolution of her first engagement on the fateful night Thomas Cranston died, she'd had few other offers. She'd spent the time since that night almost three years earlier depressed. Her writing had ceased. She'd thrown herself into other so-called interests. She'd become difficult to manage.

It had taken her days to even emerge from her room after that night. Her mother had found her the following morning curled in a ball on Clifton's floor, still clutching the note.

"He is gone," she'd whispered. "They are all gone now."

Her mother hadn't understood. She'd called for her father who scooped her from the floor and carried her to her bedroom. She'd heard the exclamations of surprise as her parents read Clifton's note, detailing his plans to go to sea. He promised to return as soon as he'd made his way.

After the shock had worn off, Miriam had tended to Henrietta. Her jaw had gaped open as Henrietta informed her of the dashed engagement, leaving out most details beyond the gentleman had simply changed his mind.

In the days that passed after those two revelations came the news of Thomas's death. His death rocked Savannah. Henrietta had not attended the funeral services, but she'd heard the whispers from the ladies her mother socialized with regularly.

"Edwina was devastated," they'd started with. The tale slowly turned to "Edwina is shocked yet relieved." Stories of Thomas's liaisons where whispered behind every closed door. His reputation sullied, his death became a matter of "crossing the wrong sort" in the court of public opinion. By the next season, Thomas Cranston was forgotten.

But not by Henrietta. The man had ruined her life. Clifton had left because of him, leaving her stranded here alone and in misery. She would never forgive him for walking out on her.

She'd used her anger toward her brother to slowly reclaim her life. She'd shoved all her other passions aside and focused on herself. In the midst of her transformation, she'd met Captain William Blanchard. The man, fifteen years her senior, had seemed captivated by her. She found it easy to charm her way into his heart and eventually his life.

He offered her marriage soon after they'd begun courting. She accepted. With prospects slim, she jumped at the chance, regardless of her feelings.

It was William Blanchard who informed her of Clifton's latest ventures, too. As they strolled in the park one evening, Clifton's name had somehow come up. The Captain's brow had furrowed as he heard it.

"Clifton Nichols?" he questioned. "Clifton Nichols is your brother?"

"I should prefer to forget that fact," Henrietta said.

"You would do well to."

Intrigued, Henrietta raised her eyebrow at him. "Oh?"

"Henrietta, he is a thug! A pirate. He roams the seas preying on merchant vessels, robbing them and killing their crews."

"What?"

"You did not know? Dear lady, I am sorry to be the bearer of this terrible news."

Henrietta suspected as much, though she had not confirmed it. In fact, she had not spoken to Clifton since the night Thomas died. He'd visited on three occasions in the past three years. Henrietta had conveniently been away from the house whenever he came to town.

It mattered not. Their relationship was over. He was no brother of hers. She shook her head and adjusted her gaze into the mirror as she smoothed her dress again. She would not spend her wedding day reminded of Clif's betrayal.

Henrietta wandered to her vanity table and sank into the chair. She dabbed jasmine-scented perfume at her wrists. Tears stung her eyes as she considered what lay ahead of her. Was she making a mistake? No, she thought with a shake of her head, no, she must proceed.

A light knock sounded at her door. She glanced up at the doorway. Her father peeked inside. "Ready, darling?" he inquired.

She nodded without speaking, offering a wavering smile.

"Before we go, someone is here to see you." Her father smiled and ducked from the room.

Henrietta's brow furrowed. Who would be here?

She rose as she awaited her visitor. Footsteps sounded and a figure entered the room. His cocoa brown eyes studied her for a moment. He looked older, wiser. "Hello, Ri," he said.

Henrietta's posture stiffened and her chest heaved as anger coursed through her. "What are you doing here?"

He did not speak, only gazed at me with those chocolate eyes and a penitent expression on his face.

"Get out!" she shouted at him.

"I suppose I deserve that," he said.

"You deserve nothing," she said, a grimace stuck on her lips.

His jaw flexed as he considered his response. "Ri, I…"

"Stop. And do not call me that."

He sighed, his frustration apparent. He searched the ceiling for some inspiration.

"I said get out!"

"Ri, I understand you are angry but…"

"Yes, I am angry."

He held out his hands. "And you deserve an explanation. But there is time for that later."

"Later? I am getting married today. I can finally leave this horrid town behind."

Clifton shook his head. "Do not marry him, Ri."

"How dare you!"

"You can be as indignant as you want, but, Ri, I am begging you to reconsider. He will leave you with nothing but more misery."

Henrietta let out a laugh. "More misery? More than you did? More than my life has seen already?"

He opened his mouth to speak. "No," she interrupted. "No, the Captain is my ticket out of this horrid little burg."

"At what cost, Ri?"

"None."

"That isn't true. Do you love him?"

"Of course."

Clifton narrowed his eyes at her. "This is not what you wanted from life."

"None of what has happened is what I wanted from life. I am making the best of the cards I have been dealt."

"You do not need to do this, Ri. In a short time, I should…"

"No more," Henrietta said. "I shall hear no more of this!"

"Ri, please listen, I can help!"

Henrietta burst into laughter. "I wouldn't trust you to help."

"Ri…"

"NO!" she screamed. "No. You abandoned me. You left me. You are a liar and a cheat. A scoundrel and a pirate. You are no brother of mine. Get out. If I never lay eyes on you again, it should be too soon."

His face fell and his fingers tightened on the tricorn hat he held in his hands. He offered a silent nod. "For what it's worth, I am sorry, Ri. And I love you."

Henrietta spun, turning her back to him.

"Goodbye, Ri. I wish you every happiness."

Tears flowed down her cheeks and a lump formed in her throat. She bit her lower lip.

"Clif, wait…" she said as she twirled to face him. A sob escaped her as she found herself alone.

CHAPTER 15

1797

The carriage bounced as the new bride approached her home in Hideaway Bay. Henrietta peered from the carriage window.

"Excited?" William Blanchard asked her.

She smiled at him. "Very."

"I hope you will enjoy the house. It has a walk that over-looks the sea."

"What is the name again?"

"Whispering Manor."

"Why is it named so?" Henrietta inquired.

"The breezes from the ocean cause a whispering sound through the house."

"Oh."

"Some people say it is haunted, but I've never found any ghosts."

The trip from Savannah had been difficult. They'd foregone any honeymoon, opting to travel to William's home so Henrietta could settle in before William departed again for the sea.

He'd chosen to tell her only after they were married. They'd quarreled over it on their first night as a married couple. In the end, Henrietta could not use her temper to change his mind. He'd thrown in her face that he needed to continue his merchant work to provide for her. He'd also made a nasty comment about not being crooked like her brother.

She blamed it on the alcohol, which he'd consumed liberally at their after-wedding reception.

Perhaps his departure would be welcome, she thought to herself as the house came into view. She eyed it, not used to the style of seaside homes. A pang of regret coursed through her as she considered the small town they'd just driven through. She'd grown up in Savannah, which dwarfed Hideaway Bay. What a horrid little town, she thought.

Henrietta stepped from the carriage and stared up at the house. A nip in the nearly-fall air sent a chill up her spine.

She snapped her head in William's direction as he joined her, offering his arm. "What is that chill?"

He laughed. "Fall, Henrietta. This is not Savannah. The chill is already upon us here."

A sinking feeling grew in the pit of her stomach as he led her into the house. Overall, it was not bad. It certainly needed a woman's touch, but with a generous allowance, she could make it a home.

* * *

The week passed quickly as Henrietta attempted to settle into her new home. She would have enjoyed walking the shores but the chillier-than-she-was-accustomed-to weather drove her inside every time.

"Is the weather ever pleasant here?" she inquired of William.

He checked his pocket watch.

"William, are you listening?"

"Hmm?" he inquired after a moment.

She shook her head, her jaw hanging open in astonishment. "I asked if the weather was ever pleasant here."

"I think you'll find the summer's quite temperate," he said with a nod.

"That doesn't give me much hope. Summer seems a long way off. I…"

"Henrietta," he interrupted. "Something has come up. I must leave earlier than I anticipated."

"What?" she asked.

"I am sorry."

"But, William! We are less than a week married!"

"It cannot be avoided, darling. I am sorry."

"Well, when do you sail?"

"Tomorrow."

Her jaw gaped open further. "Tomorrow?! William, you cannot be serious."

"I am sorry, I am. My apologies, dear, but such is the life of a sea captain."

"And when will you return?"

"Perhaps for the Christmas holiday."

"Perhaps?"

"Yes. I hope to return then, but I may not."

"So, I am to spend my first Christmas alone?"

"It is unavoidable, dear. I shall do my best, but I cannot promise." He kissed her cheek before stalking from the room.

* * *

The following morning, William kissed Henrietta on the cheek before departing. She stood on the roof walk, watching his ship sail from the harbor. Left alone in the house, she tried to busy herself with setting up her household.

Days turned to weeks, and the weather continued to worsen. As the leaves changed and abandoned their posts on the trees, Henrietta sent an invitation to her family to join her at Whispering Manor for Christmas. She bundled against the icy wind as she returned to the manor after posting her letter.

"Hello, Mrs. Blanchard," a white-haired gentleman greeted her as she hurried along, her arms wrapped firmly around her.

"Good day," she said with a curt nod.

"Oh, in a hurry?" he inquired.

"I am. Attempting to escape this dreadful weather."

"Dreadful weather? It is quite a lovely fall day!"

"Lovely? With this frigid wind?"

The man chuckled. "The sea breeze is invigorating, but it is quite warm for the season."

Henrietta's eyes widened at the statement. "Oh, I dare say if you find this cold, you are in for a rude surprise when winter sets in."

"Oh," Henrietta murmured, her voice full of disappointment.

"Anyway, I hoped to speak with William."

"William departed several weeks ago."

The man's brow furrowed. "Oh, I did not realize. I suppose I should have since I have not seen him about town."

"He left only days after we returned."

"How odd," the man said, his brow crinkling further. "I would have thought he would stay for several months as you set up your household. Well, no matter."

"Yes, I would have thought so, too, but the sea calls."

"Well, I suppose when the sea calls, a sea captain must answer!" he said, wagging his finger in the air.

"Quite," Henrietta agreed, her teeth threatening to chatter from the cold. She inched away from the man.

"Oh, if you wouldn't mind, Mrs. Blanchard, could you please ask William to see me the moment he returns. It is quite urgent."

She forced a smile on her face. "Of course, Mister..." She left the last word hanging, unsure of who the man was.

"Mr. Churchill," he said. "From the bank."

"Mr. Churchill, yes. Yes, I will let him know."

"Thank you, Mrs. Blanchard."

With another curt nod and smile, she hurried away to Whispering Manor.

The grey skies of November set in soon after, driving Henrietta inside for most of her waking hours. On several occasions, she'd considered resuming her writing. A childish impulse, she thought as she shoved it away. She'd taken no joy in it. Not since that night.

A new leather book filled with blank pages sat on her desk. A wedding present from her sister, Carolina. Perhaps a journal, she thought. Yes, perhaps that would help her. Her depression had returned of late, but perhaps putting words to paper would release her emotions.

She dipped her quill in ink and began to write.

November 12, 1797

My name is Henrietta Blanchard.

I have begun this journal to provide an outlet for my thoughts and entertainment to amuse myself on the cold winter nights to come.

This season will provide my first winter in Hideaway Bay. As cold winds already whip from the nearby sea, I wonder what madness may have overcome my mind some fourteen months ago when I accepted the proposal of Captain William Blanchard.

William, or The Captain, as he is oft referred, proved capable of providing me with a life to be envied. Or so I thought. Fourteen months ago, I had lived further south in Georgia. What I believed to be cold then would practically be considered balmy here. I am already regretting the chill in the air, and my fellow townsfolk have imparted that the weather will further deteriorate.

I cannot imagine it. When William spoke of his home as we courted, I imagined a magical seaside mirage. Instead, I have been brought to a frigid burg where winds howl daily and nightly like a screaming banshee. Gray skies reign from mid-October until late March according to those who have lived here in previous winters.

The cold weather traps me inside for most daylight and nighttime hours and, from what I have gathered, will continue to do so until the spring thaw. What a horrible, ghastly concept! Why had William not informed me of this dreadful, dreary weather before we wed?

Others in the town continue on, paying no mind to the frosty weather. Some of them even enjoy it, it seems!

"You will grow accustomed to it," they tell me. I cannot imagine so.

To worsen matters, William has sailed on his ship The Atlantic Queen *for trading in southern waters. He shall not return until Christmas at best. If delayed, I shall spend my first holiday as a married woman alone.*

While disillusioned, I do not intend to dwell on my complaints. I have written to Mother and invited her, Father, and my sister, Carolina, to spend the holidays at Whispering Manor. In my letter, I accentuated the beauty of the home the Captain provided for me. Though disingenuous, I did not mention the terrible cold surrounding my beautiful home.

I hope they shall accept my invitation. Then, I shall busy myself planning for the holiday.

Henrietta sat back in her chair and stared at her entry. She felt nothing. Journaling did not have the same effect as her writing did. When writing, she could lose herself entirely, becoming part of the scene itself, conversing with her characters as though they were friends. This was not the case when detailing her own life. Still, she would attempt to continue in the hopes that she grew fond of it.

* * *

Neptune's Servant rocked in the rough seas. Clouds hid the stars from view. Rain poured from the night skies, beating the ship's deck. Clifton rode out the storm in his cabin. He stared at the map in front of him.

A knock sounded at his door. "Enter," he shouted.

A slim man ducked through the doorway, removing his rain-soaked hat. "Orders, sir?"

"Keep on them."

"Even through the storm, sir?"

"I said keep on them!" he exclaimed.

"Aye, sir." He removed himself from Clifton's quarters.

Perhaps it was foolish to pursue the merchant ship during this weather, but the weather matched his mood. They'd sailed from Savannah three nights earlier.

He'd visited Henrietta before her wedding ceremony. She'd been angry. She had every right to be, he supposed, but the fury in her eyes still bothered him.

He would make it up to her, he vowed. He'd return again and again until she forgave him. He owed her that much. It had been his folly that cost her.

She'd married The Captain, as he was called. Clifton had few dealings with the man personally, but what he knew of him, he did not like. The man was cruel. And stupid.

But now his sister had married him. He'd do his best to ensure William Blanchard ruined her life no further.

"Sir," the wiry man announced, ducking his head into the cabin again, "we are within gun range."

A smirk crossed Clifton's face as he pulled himself up to standing. He fixed his tricorn hat on his head. "Raise the Jolly Roger and fire on them."

"Yes, sir."

The man hurried from the room. The door swung open as the ship rocked and swayed. Clifton sheathed his sword and stowed his pistol in his belt. "Time to be a pirate," he said to himself.

* * *

Henrietta glanced through the day's correspondence. Her heart leapt as she found a letter addressed to *Mrs. William Blanchard*. She recognized her mother's writing. This must be the response to her invitation. She twirled as she held the letter out. Her mind spun as she considered preparing for their arrival. She had several things to attend to in order to ready Whispering Manor.

Henrietta hurried to the library desk and sliced the envelope open. She pulled the letter from inside and began to read.

Dearest Henrietta,

I hope you are settling into your new life well. What a shame William had to return to sea so early. Though, I hope it will provide you with a relaxed introduction to your home. I dare say, you may find you prefer to set up your home without the demands of your husband nearby.

I do hope William shall return in time for Christmas. I should like you to have some company over the season.

On that note, I fear a trip north may be out of the question for us. The cold, damp weather that must be present in the winter months may trigger an attack of my bronchitis, and I do wish to avoid such an event as it takes a great toll on me.

I thought the trip may be of interest to Carolina, however, your father would not be able to travel with her, unwilling to leave me alone. And Carolina feels she may become the source of gossip should she travel unwed to your home.

It is most unfortunate. Perhaps we could plan for another trip at another time.

Please take care, daughter.

With love,

Mother

A scowl set on Henrietta's face as she read the letter. Color rose into her cheeks as anger coursed through her. She crushed the letter into a tight ball and flung it into the fire.

"Mrs. Blanchard?" one of the maids asked.

"Not now, Mary," Henrietta said as she brushed past the girl. "I must compose a letter right away."

She stormed up the stairs to her bedroom, slamming the door behind her. She paced the floor, her fists curled into balls. After a few moments, she plopped onto her desk chair and scrawled words across a paper. When she finished, she folded the missive and addressed it to her mother.

Wrapping in a shawl, she clutched the letter in her hand and hurried down the stairs and out the front door. The November cold was already bitter by her standards. She hurried through the cold to the post office.

Anger still coursed through her even after she posted the missive. She returned to Whispering Manor and stamped up the stairs and to her room.

As she sat at her desk, the maid poked her head through the door. "Mrs. Blanchard," she tried again.

"I said not now, Mary!" The girl bit her lower lip and stared at Henrietta. "GET OUT!" she shouted. The exclamation sent the girl backing from the room.

Henrietta closed her eyes and breathed slowly through her nose. She dipped her quill into the ink and set to writing in her journal.

November 20, 1797

I write today in frustration. I have received a response to my invitation for the Christmas holiday. Mother feels it may be overwhelming to travel north, particularly to a seaside town, fearing it may trigger her bronchitis. Mother's bronchitis is a convenient excuse, in my opinion. And Mother's bronchitis has prevented Father from accepting, and even Carolina, who feels she may become a source of gossip should she travel alone and unwed to Hideaway Bay.

Even now, I can feel angry blood course through my veins as I pen these words. In a fit of fury, I quickly scrawled an angry response and sent it away in the morning post. Nonsense, I wrote! Utter nonsense! The Captain's house is well-built and can provide enough warmth to keep Mother's bronchitis at bay. I scolded her for abandoning her first-born child to a lonely Christmas. I reminded her of William's departure and possible post-Christmas return. And I commented on Carolina's ridiculous reasoning to stay at home. Traveling to her married sister's home a source of gossip? Doubtful, I wrote. And how can she ever hope to achieve a match if she cannot bring herself to leave her home?

In retrospect, perhaps I was too harsh. William often reminds me I should not act with hasty action, but rather with thoughtful intent. Unfortunately, he was not here to temper my more volatile nature. It is too late to recall the letter. I hope it has the intended effect rather than the opposite.

CHAPTER 16

1797

Two weeks passed before Henrietta received a response. She held the letter, with her mother's handwriting scrawled on the front, in her hands, pondering it before opening it. "Better to know, I suppose," she said with a sigh as she sliced open the envelope.

Her eyes scanned the words on the page. A slow smile spread across her face. She'd won. Her mother wrote they would travel for the Christmas holiday to Hideaway Bay. Henrietta held the letter close to her chest and bit her lower lip. At least she'd have some family with her this Christmas. Her mother wrote that their plans remained indefinite but that they would arrive for the holiday.

She'd received little to no word from The Captain, but she hoped he would arrive in time to spend a family Christmas.

Henrietta spent the next several weeks preparing for her family's arrival. She arranged and rearranged rooms, planned menus and activities. Word arrived through the post that her mother, father, and sister would not arrive until the week of Christmas. Not ideal by Henrietta's standards, but at least they were coming, she figured.

News had come of William. He would not return home to spend Christmas with his new bride. He'd found a profitable venture and could not return until after the new year.

Henrietta's life was not what she'd hoped. Clifton's words rang in her mind. Perhaps she had made a mistake. Though it was too late to rectify it now. And what would she have done otherwise? With no means to support herself, marriage remained her only option.

She threw herself into domestic tasks as she awaited the arrival of her family.

Their carriage pulled up to Whispering Manor on December 23. Henrietta's stomach fluttered as she caught sight of her family. "I thought you would never arrive," Henrietta said as they stepped from the carriage.

"The journey took longer than expected," her father said.

"Apparently."

"Oh, what a lovely home," her mother said as they stepped through the front door. She shivered. "Though cold. Is it always this cold?"

"I shall have Mary add more logs to the fires," Henrietta assured her, holding back a roll of her eyes.

She showed them to their rooms and allowed them to settle in. Over dinner, they discussed plans for Christmas. Henrietta found herself smiling as they planned to decorate the tree tomorrow evening, Christmas Eve. She settled in bed that night feeling peace for the first time since her arrival at Whispering Manor.

* * *

Henrietta rose as the sun crested the waves. Today, she would decorate her first Christmas tree in her own home. She hummed to herself as she went about her business. As the sun set in the western sky, she gathered with her mother, father, and sister to decorate their tree.

Mary delivered hot cocoa to them as they chatted and laughed over the process.

"Oh, this is more lovely than I expected," her mother said. Henrietta beamed as Miriam clapped her hands together and eyed the tree. "If only Clifton were here."

The hot liquid stuck in Henrietta's throat and she nearly choked on it.

"How dare you bring that louse's name up within these walls!" Henrietta spat out.

"Henrietta!" Miriam exclaimed. "Your language!"

"It is true! That is exactly what he is. And if my husband was here, he would agree!"

"Now, now, dear," John said, patting her on the shoulder. "Mother only means to say how nice for the family to spend the holiday together."

"Then Mother should have said that," she answered with a sigh.

"Oh, you shouldn't be so hard on him, Henrietta. He loves you so dearly. He was so glum when you and he had words again."

"Mother!" she began but was interrupted.

"Henrietta, please reconsider. I have never seen a man so crestfallen as Clifton when he went back to his ship. You must forgive him for leaving all those years ago."

Henrietta's blood boiled. She slammed the cup to the floor. It shattered to pieces, brown liquid splattered across the floor.

"STOP!" she screamed. "I will hear no more of this! I will not have my holidays ruined by the mention of that...

scoundrel! He is no brother of mine. So help me, Mother, if you bring him up again I shall lose my mind!"

Henrietta fled from the room. Her feet pounded up the stairs as tears formed in her eyes. She stumbled into her bedroom and flung herself across the bed. Sobs wracked her body. After an hour, with no one coming to check on her, she dragged herself from the bed and penned another journal entry.

* * *

The holidays passed, and Henrietta found herself alone on a cold January day shortly after the new year. Peace over the holiday season had been fleeting. Miriam mentioned Clifton several more times despite Henrietta's insistence against discussing him.

Despite her outrage at the events, she found herself glum as she studied the winter landscape in Hideaway Bay. Within a week, Henrietta longed to escape from Whispering Manor.

As snow flurried past the window, she sat at her writing desk and penned a letter to her mother.

Dear Mother -

How lovely it was to see you, Father, and Carolina over the holidays. Despite our rather frequent disagreements over Clifton, I very much enjoyed having family in the house.

Though I wish you would see Clifton for what he really is. He is a scoundrel. I do not say this to be callous toward your feelings, it is the exact opposite. I do not wish to see your heart broken when you realize the truth about him. It is also most dangerous for Carolina to admire him as she does. It can lead to nothing but trouble.

But I digress and I certainly do not mean to lecture you, only to explain my behavior during your visit.

When you first left, I felt a bit of relief, not realizing how taxing a visit would be on me as hostess, but I have quickly grown homesick. I detest the weather in this dreary town. And I have heard no news from William regarding his return.

As such, I am writing to secure an invitation home. How I long to see Savannah again and escape the balance of the winter months in Hideaway Bay. I hope you will be agreeable. I should very much look forward to visiting!

I will await your response with bated breath!

Yours, Henrietta

Henrietta smiled at the note as she addressed it before venturing into the frigid temperatures to post it. When she returned home, she stalked into the quiet home. Silence surrounded her. Her lips formed a frown. She roamed the rooms, searching for something to strike her fancy. She found nothing. After an hour, she decided she would begin to prepare for her journey south. This could distract her and settle her mind.

1798

"Clifton!" Miriam exclaimed as he stepped into their Savannah home. With outstretched arms, she hurried toward him before wrapping him in a full embrace. "It is so good to see you."

"And very good to see you, Mother."

"I hope you will be staying longer than your last visit! You set sail so quickly after Henrietta's wedding, I barely got to see you."

"Such is the life of a sea captain, Mother," Clifton said as Miriam guided him into the sitting room.

"Clif!" Carolina shouted, tossing her book to the side and running to him. He swept her into a hug.

"How was your trip north?" he inquired. "Did you enjoy it very much?"

Carolina shrugged. "It was all right."

"All right?"

"I saw snow!" she said.

"You did? Was it as glorious as you imagined?"

"No," Carolina answered. "It was quite cold, and I did not care much for it."

"I see. Well, at least now you know."

She smiled and nodded. "And Henrietta and Mother quarreled constantly, so I had little peace."

Clifton shot a glance to Miriam with raised eyebrows. "Why don't you go read in your room, dear?" Miriam suggested to the girl.

"Okay, Mother." With a kiss on Clifton's cheek and her mother's, Carolina disappeared from the room, book in hand.

Clifton settled into an armchair while his mother escorted Carolina upstairs. He stared into the flames of the fireplace. Carolina's words rattled through his mind.

"Clif!" his father's voice called as he stepped into the room.

"Father," he said as he rose to his feet. They exchanged a handshake before settling into chairs with brandies. Miriam returned moments later.

"Carolina all tucked in?" John asked.

"Yes," Miriam answered, shooting a sideways glance to Clifton.

After a few moments of silence, Clifton ventured, "And how is Henrietta?"

"Oh, perfectly fine. Carolina exaggerates so," Miriam said.

"Is she happy?" Clifton inquired.

"Of course, dear. It is so sweet of you to worry over her."

Clifton's jaw worked as he pondered the statement, staring into the fireplace.

"And William has provided such a lovely home for her. I cannot imagine her being unhappy with it. It is quite large and sits right on the sea."

"I fear she does not care for the colder climate," John said.

"She will become used to it," Miriam answered.

"I am surprised William left her so quickly," John added.

Clifton cocked his head at the statement. "Left her?"

"Yes, the man raced off to sea merely days after they arrived home. You'd think a newly married man might stay for an extended time to settle his wife. After all, they did not even honeymoon. He simply dumped her at the house and left!"

"Oh, it's quite all right, dear," Miriam said with a pat on her husband's hand. "I imagine it is much easier to mold the home to your liking without your husband hovering over you. I told Henrietta as much."

John shrugged as he sipped his brandy. "But let's focus on you, dear," Miriam said. "How long will you be able to stay?"

* * *

Henrietta paced the widow's walk in the frigid air. Her breath, visible in frosty puffs, wafted through the winter air. Despite the cold, she wore only a small wrap. Her anger warmed her from the inside out. She seethed over the letter still clutched in her hand. She'd crinkled the parchment into a tight ball after reading it. Tears had stung her eyes, but she'd bitten them back and climbed to the rooftop perch to calm herself.

After several moments, she smoothed the paper and reread the letter.

Dearest Henrietta,

I am so pleased you enjoyed our visit. It is certainly nice to see you settled into your married life. And in such a beautiful home.

I do hope you hear from William soon and that he will soon rejoin you at Whispering Manor. To that end, perhaps it is best to await his return there. Surely he will find it shocking to arrive home and find his new bride gone!

Besides that, given your resentment toward Clifton, it would pain you to realize he is currently spending several weeks with us here. I am certain, given your behavior over the holidays, you would agree it is best to remain at Whispering Manor lest your temper overcome you. Given the animosity you direct toward him, I should certainly think it best.

I hope you do not find the winter months too depressing and spring is soon upon you.

All the best, Mother

Henrietta wrenched the door open and scurried down the steep staircase. She tore into her room and tossed the letter into the fireplace. She sat at her desk, whipping a piece of paper from her stack and began to compose a letter.

Mother,

I have received your reply and suffice it to say, I am outraged and offended. To realize my own home is closed to me and my own mother bars me from it has stung me to my core. I am certain I will weep bitterly over it once the shock has passed.

And to make this realization that you have chosen that louse over me has wounded me greatly. He does not deserve to return to your home. He should be thrown out on the street before being offered a warm bed under your roof!

What a slap in my face to be shut out of my own family home in favor of a criminal.

You, Mother, shall become the laughing stock of Savannah!

Henrietta

Henrietta addressed the letter and flew from Whispering Manor to post it.

* * *

As the months turned to February, Henrietta sat staring at the sea from her bedroom window. Her mood had not improved. She brooded over her circumstances. Her marriage to The Captain was misery. Stuck in a desolate place alone. Perhaps Clifton had been right to warn her.

Her mind turned to her brother. She felt the familiar fire grow inside her. He had been partly to blame for her circumstances. Had he not left her when he did, she may not have chosen to marry this man. And now her mother had chosen him over her.

What kind of life did she have? Perhaps she should ease her ire toward Clifton, apologize to her mother, and reconcile with him. She considered it for a moment. Had he meant to abandon her? Or had he hoped to save her from a terrible life by disappearing?

A cold gust of air swept past her as she pondered it. She glanced toward the open door. The front door banged shut. Her brow furrowed. Who was using the front door? If the maid had used it, she would reprimand the girl swiftly.

Henrietta rose and stalked to the railing. She glanced over, her heart skipping a beat.

"William!" she shouted.

"Hello, dear," he said.

"Oh, William! I am overjoyed to see you," she called as she hurried down the stairs. She threw her arms around his neck, and he kissed her cheek. "How was your voyage?"

"Perfectly fine. I did not run across your brother at least."

Her brow furrowed at the mention of Clifton. "Clif?"

"Black Jack, as he is called in our circle. The man is a menace. He has attacked more ships than I can count."

"He is at home in Savannah," Henrietta murmured.

"At home? Firstly, dear, this is now your home, so he is merely in Savannah. And second, he should not be allowed in your former home. He is a louse. I'm surprised your mother can stomach him. But let us not speak of him. How have you been faring in the winter weather?"

"Oh," Henrietta said, her lips forming a frown. "I detest the cold. Perhaps now that you are home, we might plan a trip to wait out the remaining winter months. Perhaps somewhere warm."

He smiled at her. "I would love to, my darling, but…" He released his grasp on her and stalked away, turning his back toward her.

"But?" she questioned.

He shook his head. "I must leave in two weeks' time."

"What? Another sea voyage?"

"Yes and no," he said. "I do not return to sea for one month, however, there is some business I must attend to in Raleigh first. So, I shall leave in two weeks then travel to port before shoving out to sea."

Henrietta's jaw clenched and she spun away from him.

"Oh, do not be upset, darling. I am as displeased as you are. But it cannot be helped." He grasped her arms and squeezed.

"You are not home five minutes before you inform me you plan to leave," Henrietta spat out.

"As I said, it cannot be helped. Please, dear, let us not quarrel." He spun her to face him. She refused to make eye contact. He tipped her chin up with his finger.

"Fine, we shall not quarrel," she said as her eyes met his. "Perhaps, though, I can also plan a trip. To Savannah. I can travel with you to Raleigh and then on to Savannah when you sail."

He dropped her arms. "No," he said flatly.

"William!" she objected. "You cannot strand me here in this forsaken place and expect me to be happy!"

"I said no. If your louse of a brother is in Savannah, I want you nowhere near him. Do you understand? You are not to travel to Savannah."

She did not respond for a moment. "Henrietta! Do you understand?"

"Yes," she said, her face a mask of annoyance.

"Good. Now, I must go out. I shall return for dinner. Perhaps then we can discuss something lighter."

He spun on his heel and disappeared through the front door. Henrietta stomped up the stairs and plopped onto her window seat. Her fury had reignited. And she directed it all at Clifton. Once again, he had ruined her life. Forgive him? No, she thought, with a shake of her head. No, no matter his reasoning, he had abandoned her. And he had chosen the life of a criminal. And now he prevented her return to her home. She could not forgive him for that.

When William returned in the late afternoon, he brought with him the post. "There is a letter for you, dear," he said, waving the envelope at her.

"Oh? Thank you. I shall read it at once before dinner."

Henrietta recognized her mother's handwriting. She sliced open the envelope and extracted the missive. Even with William's refusal over her planned trip, she still hoped to find an apology and invitation inside. She would take pleasure in refusing it, at least.

She scanned the note inside, her eyes widening.

Dear Henrietta,

I was very sorry to read the things in your last correspondence.

You are always welcome in my home. However, I will not allow you to continue your quarrel with Clifton. He is your brother. If and when you are willing to temper your acrimony, you are welcome. Until then, you are not.

I am sorry if that ruins your plans to escape your home, but you are a married woman now. You must learn to deal with the ups and downs of married life. Perhaps the fault lies with your father and I. Perhaps we spoiled you too much. I do not know, but I must stand firm by my decision. I will not have the household upset with your misbehavior nor will I throw my son out.

Very truly yours,
Mother

Tears pricked her eyes as she read the letter. She crumpled it and tossed it to the floor before she collapsed to her bed. When William retrieved her for dinner, she waved him away, feigning illness. She could not stomach a conversation with him. Her day had been miserable, as had the days before it. She was certain the days that followed would be no different.

Her life was a shambles. And she wondered if she could find some escape.

CHAPTER 17

1798

Clifton's boot splashed in the water as he leapt from the dinghy. His crew dragged the boats ashore, several laden with bounty from their latest haul.

Clifton stared at the palm trees swaying in the wind. Chests filled with gold coins and jewelry lined the beach.

"Ready, sir?" his second in command inquired.

"Yes." He grabbed hold of one side of one chest. The weight strained his muscles as they lugged it to the heart of the island. They ducked into a small cave opening and Clifton dragged the chest behind him.

An underground river cut through the cave. Clifton trudged through it until he hit a stone barrier. The warm water rose to his chest now. With a deep inhale, he submerged himself, swimming forward underwater.

He emerged with a gasp for breath on the opposite side of the stone wall. Another cavern existed. A small gap in the rock face exposed it to the outside high above. Sunlight filtered in through the hole.

The light glinted off gold stacked on the cavern's floor. Gems sparkled and shone from the darker corners. Clifton wiped the water from his face and tugged the chest toward dry land.

With the help of a crewman, he dragged it away from the water. Pushing the top open, he grabbed a handful of coins, allowing them to fall back into the chest. He eyed the cavern. He'd accumulated much wealth in his time as captain of *Neptune's Servant*. But what was it all for?

And how safe was it? Redbeard had made numerous threats. He searched the islands for Clifton's hiding place, intending to rob him of every last piece, he'd threatened. He needed to find a new place to hide it. But where? And how could he ensure its safety?

"Sir?"

"Yes?" Clifton inquired.

"Will we have a stopover at Tortuga? Some of the men are asking."

Clifton considered it. "Yes, they've earned it."

"I shall inform them. We have nearly finished unloading and should be ready to set sail within the hour."

Clifton nodded as he focused his gaze on his bounty again. His mind plagued him with the same question. What was it all for?

* * *

Neptune's Servant floated away from the small island on the calm Caribbean waters. They'd make port tonight after the setting of the sun. Alcohol would flow freely and the men would enjoy their time off the ship.

A knock sounded on the door as they eased into port. "Enter!" Clifton yelled.

"Sir, the ship is docked. May we go ashore?"

Clifton waved his hand to indicate they may. The man hesitated. "Are you going ashore, sir?"

"In a moment," Clifton answered. His mind remained troubled. Perhaps a drink would settle his nerves.

With a sigh, he climbed to his feet, gathered his hat, and left his cabin. The warm Caribbean breeze rustled his hair as he strode down the dock.

The tavern on the main drag brimmed over with people. Laughter and loud chatter floated to the street beyond.

Clifton wandered through the open door. He spotted several of his men enjoying the local company and the tavern's beverages. He ordered an ale at the bar and spun to face the room as he sipped it. With his elbows resting against the bar's top, he scanned the patrons.

His eyes narrowed as he spotted a familiar face in the back of the room. At a crowded round table, Captain William Blanchard sat, holding cards close to his chest.

Clifton sighed and shook his head as he meandered toward the card game to watch it unfold. He sipped his ale as one man stared at his cards.

"Raise," he said, tossing coins into the center.

Blanchard's jaw tightened as the man next to him folded, tossing his cards in a heap on the table with a grunt.

Blanchard chewed his lower lip and rubbed the back of his neck as he eyed the generous pot.

"To you, Blanchard, what will you do? Go home a loser or try for the win?" another asked.

He nodded and eyed his cards again. "I will continue to play, though I need an IOU."

Laughs rose from a few players. "Throw in your cards, Blanchard, you're too far in debt as it is."

"I'm good for it," he argued.

"Sure you are. You lose too much to be good for it."

He lifted his chin. "Not this time."

"Oh, big talk, is it a bluff?"

"I'll front him," Clifton said, tossing a few gold coins into the pot.

He narrowed his eyes at Clifton. "Declined," he said.

"Unless you accept his money you've got nothing to call with and you're out of the game," a grisly man with greasy hair and a gray-streaked beard said.

With a grumble and a grimace, Blanchard offered a nod. "Fine. Call."

"Show your cards."

Blanchard laid his cards out on the table. "Two pair, kings high."

Clifton raised his eyebrows and peered at the cards. He firmed his lower lip. Perhaps he'd reacquire his money. He slid his eyes to the other man left in contention.

The man's lips formed a smirk. In a dramatic display, he spread his cards across the table.

"Three Aces."

A murmur went up around the table. The man reached both arms in a bear hug toward the pot as a chuckle escaped his lips.

"Wait!" Blanchard shouted, blocking the man's arms. "Again. Double or nothing."

All eyes swung toward the winner. He stared at Blanchard for a moment then shook his head. "Nah. I'm taking my winnings."

"Gentlemen?" Blanchard asked. "Another round?"

"You've got no money left, friend."

"A simple fix, you know I'm good for it," Blanchard insisted.

"You still owe me quite a bit," a black-bearded man grumbled.

"But…" Blanchard began.

Clifton rounded the table as another man pulled him from his seat. He slid between them, knocking the man's grip off Blanchard. "Come along, William," he said.

"Get your filthy pirate hands off me," he spat. He leaned away, stumbling back a few steps.

Clifton grasped him by the collar and dragged him outside. He dunked him into a watering trough. Blanchard gasped as he pulled him from the cold water.

"You are drunk," Clifton said as he tossed him onto his rear.

"You're one to judge, pirate," Blanchard spat.

"Being that I am the sober one of us without a hefty gambling debt, it appears I may be the better of us to judge."

The man climbed to his feet, still dripping. "I do not know what you speak of."

"Really? Have you forgotten the thousands of dollars you are in debt in your drunken state?"

"I only needed one more game to right the course."

Clifton snorted a laugh. "Of course. It's always just one more. That's how you got into the trouble you're in."

"I am not in trouble."

"Oh? I beg to differ. You owe several large debts to several people. And I have it on good authority you've decimated your finances to feed your habit."

"You are awfully judgmental given your line of work, Black Jack," he said, spitting out the last words as though they had a bitter taste.

"You are married to my sister. I do not wish to see her troubled by your bad habits."

"Like she is troubled by yours? I find this very rich coming from the man she cannot stomach."

Clifton's muscles tensed and his jaw worked as his mouth formed a grimace. "I do not wish to see her hurt. Regardless of how she feels about me."

"How magnanimous of you," Blanchard said, waving his arms in the air. "I assure you she could care less if you are dead or alive."

Clifton closed his eyes a moment to calm himself. "Go home, Blanchard. Before you make more of a mess of things. Spend time with your new wife."

"That will be the day I take advice from a pirate." He cocked his head, staring beyond Clifton. "If you'll excuse me, I have urgent business."

He pushed past him and ambled away from the bar. Clifton twisted, catching sight of a shadowy figure disappearing between two buildings. He waited a moment before crossing the street and skirting around the building there. He inched behind the buildings, approaching the alley where the figure disappeared.

Voices floated from the alley.

"How sure are you?" Blanchard's voice questioned.

"Very."

"And it's sizable?"

"Very large," the man assured him.

Silence passed between them for a moment. "Large enough to cover your debts and get you back on your feet," the man added.

"And it's located off the coast here?"

Clifton peered around the corner, eyeing the map held between them. His brow furrowed as he studied the spot where Blanchard pointed.

"Aye."

"Why has no one else pursued this?" Blanchard inquired.

The man shrugged. "It's a bit tricky. Got to know what you're doing with the ship."

The Captain scoffed. "I am an experienced sea captain. The task should be easy."

"From your lips, oh, Captain, my captain."

Blanchard paid the man a hefty sum, rolled up the map and stuffed it into his pocket. "Thank you."

"And the rest of my cut?"

"Yes, you'll get your additional finder's fee as soon as I return."

The man nodded. "Good luck, then, Captain. I look forward to your return with great anticipation."

The man spun on his heel, disappearing down the alley. The Captain waited a moment before he turned in the opposite direction and strolled down the alley toward Clifton. As he rounded the corner, Clifton stepped in his path.

He sighed with disgust. "What was that conversation about?" Clifton asked.

"None of your business."

"You're going after something," Clifton retorted.

"And I suppose you hope to beat me to it."

Clifton shook his head. "I saw the location you pointed out. You cannot go there."

Blanchard let out a harsh laugh. "And who will stop me? You? Will you widow your own sister?"

"No, you'll do that on your own pursuing this supposed fortune."

Blanchard took a step forward, trying to walk past him. "Do not pursue this, Blanchard. The coast there is dangerous, it has claimed many a ship."

Blanchard spun to face him again. "I am an experienced captain with many more years on the sea than you, boy. I know how to skipper a ship! Now stay out of my way!"

He spiraled around and stalked away.

"Do not go, Blanchard! It is an impossible bounty!"

The man continued on his way, ignoring Clifton's warning.

* * *

Under the night sky, Clifton watched *The Atlantic Queen* set sail from the Tortuga port. The Captain had wasted no time in gathering his crew and hoisting the anchor. The three-masted ship disappeared in a speck on the horizon.

Clifton's chief mate, Johnson, appeared at his side. "Longing for the sea, sir?"

"Watching a fool pursue an absurd plan, more like it."

Johnson raised his eyebrows at the statement. "Blanchard is going after Denvia's Folly."

"What? Doesn't he know…"

"That it's impossible? And likely a falsehood? One would think an experienced sea captain would know these things, yes. But he doesn't."

"It is a fool's errand, to be sure," Johnson answered as he searched the horizon.

"And one that will end in trouble, mark my words."

"Why does it bother you, sir?"

"The idiot is married to my sister. And I do not wish any misery to befall her."

"May God be with him, then."

"He shall need God to prevent his demise, yes."

* * *

Clifton lounged in a chair, a beer resting on his belly and his feet propped on a nearby table. With the brim of his hat pulled low on his forehead, he hoped not to be disturbed.

They'd spent several days in the port of Tortuga. Clifton

used the time to consider the questions that had bounced through his brain since he'd last visited his stash of booty.

"Sir!" a breathless voice said.

He didn't answer.

"Sir!" Johnson's voice said again.

"Ugh, what is it, Johnson?"

"Have you heard the news?"

Clifton sighed and set his feet on the floor, pushing his hat to its normal spot on his head. "What news?"

"*The Atlantic Queen*, sir. She's been lost."

"What?" Clifton said, suddenly alert.

Johnson nodded. "Captain Smith of the *Silent Lady* just docked. He brought with him the tale. He'd passed the ship as he circled an island. When he returned, there was no sign of it. He claims to have seen debris in the water."

Clifton considered the tale. He took a final sip of his ale before saying, "Gather the men. We sail in two hours."

Johnson's face formed a mask of confusion. "Sir?"

"You heard me. Gather the men. We sail in two hours in search of *The Atlantic Queen*."

"Yes, sir," Johnson answered.

Within two hours, Johnson had managed to drag the crew of *Neptune's Servant* from the rocks under which they hid. They pulled up the anchor and sailed into the setting sun. Clifton stood on deck, his hands clutching the railing. He hoped not to find what he suspected he'd find. He hoped Captain Smith had exaggerated the situation.

He pressed the crew, setting a hard pace toward the Isle of Denvia.

"Sir," Johnson said, shaking him from his slumber at daybreak two days after they had sailed. "The island is within sight."

Clifton sat up and nodded. "Keep a fair distance and weigh anchor. Any sign of *The Atlantic Queen*?"

Johnson shook his head. "No, sir, none."

"Debris in the water?"

"We are not close enough yet."

"Slow us and circle the island. Search for debris."

"Yes, sir."

The man left and Clifton poured himself a rum and sipped it before adjusting his clothes and donning his hat. With his pistol and sword readied, he stepped onto the deck.

He clutched the railing and scanned the water. A shout descended from the crow's nest. He glanced up, noticing the man's outstretched arm culminating in his pointed finger. He followed the direction. Debris floated on the water's surface.

"Weigh anchor and get skiffs in the water!" Clifton ordered. The man scrambled to fulfill his orders. The anchor thudded against the ocean's floor and the ship slowed to a stop.

"Search for survivors. And a positive identification that this is indeed *The Atlantic Queen.*"

Dinghies were lowered. "Sir?" Johnson inquired. "Why are we concerned?"

"Blanchard is my brother-in-law."

"I did not realize you were close."

"We are not." Johnson raised his eyebrows. "If I can avoid having my sister widowed less than six months after her marriage, I should prefer it."

Johnson nodded. Clifton climbed to one of the waiting dinghies and they rowed closer. "Careful not to get too close to the shore," he advised. "We cannot risk running aground as there is no way to reach us for rescue and these waters are shark-infested."

Using his spyglass, he searched the shoreline for signs of survivors. He found nothing. Driftwood floated by. "Give me an oar," he requested. With one in hand, he reached for a piece of the floating wood and dragged it closer.

Bright lettering covered it. UEEN marked the piece. His stomach turned at the sight. It provided nearly positive proof that these were the remains of *The Atlantic Queen*. Likely it had been smashed on the rocks as it attempted to close in on the island. Rumors of a storm at sea in the area likely made the approach trickier than normal. One misjudgment would have sent them spiraling into a current that dragged them closer to the rocky shores regardless of what they tried to escape.

He swallowed hard and flung the oar to the side. He swung the spyglass upward and scanned the island again. A fleck of navy blue drew his attention toward a grouping of sharp rocks jutting from the water.

"I see something," he said. He removed his jacket and dove into the water.

"Sir!" Johnson shouted. "Wait, the sharks!"

Clifton stroked hard toward the floating fabric. He grasped it as he approached. A blue jacket like the one he'd seen Blanchard wearing at Tortuga. He scanned the area as he bobbed in the water. Caught between the rocks, he spotted something. He swam toward it, identifying it as a body as he approached.

The body floated face down in the water. He squeezed between the rocks and grabbed hold of it. Turning it over, he spotted a bloated face. Difficult to identify after having been in the water for several days, the face could have been William Blanchard's though he could not be certain. He groaned at the sight as he dragged the body back toward the skiffs.

"Sir!" Johnson screamed. "Sir!" He waved his arms wildly and pointed toward something. Clifton ceased moving and scanned the water in the direction Johnson indicated. His eyes widened as he spotted two fins cutting through the waves.

"Make for the boat!" Johnson shouted.

Clifton attempted to drag the body with him, but it slowed his progress. The fins moved quickly through the water. He spotted a third approaching from another direction.

"Leave the body!" Johnson directed. Clifton released his hold on the corpse and stroked toward the skiff. As his men pulled him aboard, Blanchard's body disappeared below the waves. The only remaining evidence was the pool of red foam.

CHAPTER 18

1798

Clifton eyed the horizon as *Neptune's Servant* sailed for Savannah. Visions of the shipwreck clouded his mind. Blanchard's bloated corpse circled there, too. He swallowed hard. As if Henrietta did not hate him enough. This news would kill her.

He'd put into port in Savannah and inform his parents. Perhaps they would know the best way to handle it.

Henrietta stood staring out at the sea from her widow's walk. The weather had improved considerably. The wind no longer stung her face. Perhaps life here would now become tolerable, she thought as the rising sun painted the morning sky and reflected in the water below.

She waited until it had risen high overhead before she retreated inside. She settled at her library desk to catch up on correspondence. With any luck, The Captain would return home soon. Perhaps then she could make good on her promises of invitations for dinner parties.

As she finished her letters, she collected them and meandered to town to post them. The walk relaxed her now that she did not shiver against the cold weather.

The postmaster greeted her as she entered the small office. "Good morning, Mrs. Blanchard. Letters to post?"

"Yes," she said with a smile.

"Ah, a smile today! What has you so chipper?"

"The weather!" she admitted. "It has finally ceased to be so cold."

"Indeed, lovely weather of late."

"Is there any mail for me?"

"Yes, I have one letter here in the early post for you."

She accepted it with a smile, pocketing it for her return trip. When she arrived at Whispering Manor, she eagerly sliced open the envelope. She'd not recognized the handwriting, so she was intrigued.

She read the greeting to Mrs. Blanchard. The next words furrowed her brow.

You do not know me, though I am acquainted with your husband. I regret to inform you of some rather terrible news.

The words that followed caused her to collapse onto the desk chair.

The Atlantic Queen has become lost at sea. The ship and its entire crew were last seen off the Isle of Denvia. No souls have spotted them since this sighting. The crew, along with your husband, are presumed dead. While there is no definite proof of death, it seems the most likely case.

I do regret having to send such news. Please accept my most sincere apologies, Mrs. Blanchard.

Yours,

Captain Henry Smith

Henrietta's lower lip trembled as she read the words. Dead? No, she thought, he could not be dead. Not William. There was some mistake. No, God would not do this to her. He would not rob her of yet another happiness. He would not deliver another blow. William must be alive. Surely, there was some mistake.

Tears escaped her eyes and she hurried upstairs, hoping a journal entry may assuage her fears. The pages of the journal were stained with her tears as she finished her entry. She'd promised herself to cling to the hope that William was alive. He could not be dead, she was certain. She would not lose hope.

She wiped at her cheeks. These tears were wasted. When William returned, she would laugh at how foolish she had been in these moments.

* * *

Clifton stared up at his childhood home. He'd shared so many happy moments under the house's roof. This would not be one of those happy moments. He swallowed hard and approached the door, letting himself into the foyer. Quietness surrounded him as his eyes scanned the entryway.

Miriam walked through with an embroidery hoop in her hand. She halted as she caught sight of him.

A smile spread across her face. "Clif!" she exclaimed.

A slight smile crossed Clifton's face. It faltered after a moment and he bit his lower lip.

"I did not expect to see you again this soon. Though I am thrilled, darling." She wrapped him in her arms and gave him a tight hug. As she pulled away, she studied his face. "Clif? What is it?"

"I have some bad news."

The color drained from Miriam's face and she swallowed hard. "Oh?"

"Shall we go into the sitting room?"

She offered a quick nod as she clutched his arm. "Is Father here?"

"Yes," Miriam answered as she sank into an armchair. "John! John!" Miriam shouted.

Carolina stuck her head into the room. "He is outside, Mummy, would you like me to fetch him? Clif!" The child ran to him and threw her arms around his waist.

"Hello, Carolina," he greeted her, wrapping his arms around her and kissing the top of her head.

"Carolina, please fetch Father," Miriam said, "and then finish your essay."

"But, Mother! I'd like to visit with Clif!"

"And you shall after you finish your essay."

With a sigh and slumped shoulders, the child answered, "Fine."

"Good girl."

Clifton wandered to the drink cart as the child darted from the room and poured himself a brandy. He sipped at it as he waited. Within minutes, his father appeared in the room.

"Son?"

"Hello, Father."

"We did not expect you."

"I've already told him that." She reached her hand out to prompt her husband to her. He approached, grasping her hand. "He says he has bad news."

"Oh?" John inquired.

Clifton took another sip of his brandy before he set the glass down. "William Blanchard is dead."

Miriam gasped, her hand flying to her open mouth. "What?"

"How?" his father added.

"His ship wrecked off the coast of the Isle of Denvia. I searched for survivors but found none."

"Are you certain it was *The Atlantic Queen?*" Miriam inquired.

Clifton nodded. "The wreckage pointed to it. We found a piece of the ship with the letters U-E-E-N."

"And no one survived? Perhaps made it to the island?" John asked.

Clifton offered another head shake. "I... I found a body. It may have been him. I'm not certain. There was nothing I could do. There was no evidence of any survivors."

Silence fell over the room for several moments before Miriam's sob broke it. Clifton hurried to her, kneeling in front of her. "I am sorry to be the one to bring this news, Mother."

She sniffled and used her handkerchief to dry her moist eyes. "It is not your fault, Clif," she said, caressing his face. "You tried to help him."

"I tried to warn him about the rocks near the coast. He would not listen."

"You spoke to him before he set sail?" John questioned.

"I did. He sought something most dare not. I warned him not to try for it. He did not heed my warning. When I heard tale of a shipwreck, I pursued his ship immediately. Alas, I was too late to find anyone alive."

"Have you brought his body?" John asked.

Clifton closed his eyes and shook his head. "No, I'm afraid... there was an incident. The waters are shark-infested. I..."

John nodded. "There is no need to go further with the explanation."

Miriam stared into the empty fireplace. "This will kill Henrietta."

"Perhaps the news is best delivered in person," Clifton suggested.

Miriam glanced at him then John. "Yes," he stammered. "Yes, perhaps Mother and I should take a trip north."

"I would like to go," Clifton said.

"It may be best for you to stay away. This will no doubt upset her and given her anger toward you, it may make the situation worse."

Clifton's face fell.

"Oh, darling, I realize you'd like to support her, but it is for the best to leave it to Father and me."

"You are correct, Mother. My presence would only serve to create more tension in a situation already fraught with it."

Miriam offered a sad smile at him and reached for his hand. She wrapped her fingers around his and squeezed. "She will forgive you one day, darling. But perhaps now is not the best time."

He nodded. "There is something else you should know then before you go."

Miriam regarded him with surprise on her face.

"William Blanchard was a drunkard and a gambler. He has left Henrietta destitute."

Miriam's jaw dropped open. "Oh my!" she exclaimed. "Oh, she cannot know this."

"Mother, do you think that's best?"

"Yes. His death will kill her. She mustn't know the rest. Not now."

Clifton raised his eyebrows but did not argue.

Miriam rose to her feet, stuffing the handkerchief up her sleeve. "Well, I have many things to attend to. We should leave as soon as possible. I should like to deliver the news in person before word reaches her."

"With the journey, that may not be possible," John admitted.

"No, but we have definite information and if she catches wind of it, it will be best to be there for her." She turned to Clifton. "I shall ensure your old room is prepared before I leave, dear. You'll stay?"

"Yes, I plan to stay for several days at least."

Miriam nodded and smiled before disappearing from the room.

They set off the following morning as the sun crept over the horizon. Clifton watched them disappear from his bedroom window. Quietness enveloped the house.

Clifton stalked from his bedroom into the empty hall. He wandered downstairs, eyeing the bookshelf. He ran his finger along the many volumes there. Perhaps he would read something.

His eyes found the window and he focused on nothing in particular outside. Restlessness settled into him already. Perhaps he should return to sea.

As he paced the floor, he imagined the journey north. Imagined the destination. Imagined Henrietta's face as they imparted the news.

His parents would tell her that her husband was dead. What they refused to tell her was the string of bad debts he left in his wake. She would be ruined. Destitute. Her marriage, which she hoped would bring her freedom, would be yet another noose tightening around her neck.

Clifton found himself standing in the doorway of Henrietta's former bedroom. He stared at the room. The last time he'd seen her here, she'd been angry. Had she softened at all?

He stalked to her small writing desk and ran his hand across it. Many a tale she'd written here since she was a child. Most had delighted him. She didn't write anymore, his mother told him on his last visit.

He lifted the lid of the desk. Papers lined the inside. He gathered them together. Before he stalked away, a glint of gold caught his eye. He fished a gold coin from the desk's bottom. He recalled the night he'd given it to her. With the gold coin clutched in his palm, he sank onto the bed's edge.

On the top sheet, Henrietta had scrawled *Over Land and Sea.*

He shuffled to the next page. Henrietta's writing filled the page. He smiled down at the paper as he scanned the words. He imagined her reading it to him, acting out the scenes. Her voice echoed off the pages as he read them.

The stack of papers entertained him through the morning hours. As he reached the last page, he realized the story remained unfinished. "She stopped writing," his mother's voice reminded him.

She hadn't even taken her unfinished work with her. Sadness crept over him again. Henrietta had given so much of herself away to create what she expected to be an enviable life. What did she have to show for it? She'd be ruined by her husband's debts and forced to remarry. If she could, that was. She was pretty enough to achieve another match, but she did not seem to be lucky in love.

Clifton stared down at the pages strewn across Henrietta's bed. An idea formed in his mind. A smile crossed his lips and he gathered the pages up. He searched the desk for any others.

With them all collected, he darted from the room and down the stairs. The bright afternoon sunshine greeted him as he stepped onto their porch. This plan could work, he thought as he hurried toward the docks. He realized the news he imparted would not be welcome, but he could offer her something else. Something to ease the pain. He must go. He must face her. Perhaps this time they could put that fateful night behind them and move forward.

After climbing aboard *Neptune's Servant,* he stowed Henrietta's work in his cabin. He found his chief mate lounging below decks.

"Johnson," he greeted him as he hurried down the wooden stairs.

"Sir?" the man asked, leaping from his hammock.

"Gather the men and ready the ship."

"We're leaving?"

"Yes. I have a plan."

"Plan?"

"A place where we can hide the treasure from Redbeard. And someone who can protect it."

"Where, sir?"

"Hideaway Bay."

The man stood for a stunned moment before he nodded. "I shall gather the crew."

* * *

Henrietta stared at the sea from her rooftop perch. She'd received two letters informing her of her husband's disappearance. They hinted at his death. But she could not believe it.

If William was dead, what did that mean for her? No, she couldn't even consider it. He was not dead.

The door to the house popped open and Mary stuck her head in. Henrietta sighed. "What is it, Mary? I am quite busy!"

"Guests, Mrs. Blanchard."

"Guests? At this hour? 'Tis only mid-morning!"

"It is your mother and father, Mrs. Blanchard. And your sister."

"What?" Henrietta inquired, her brow furrowing. "Mother? Father?" She considered the development. "Tell them I shall be down in a moment."

"Yes, Mrs. Blanchard."

The maid ducked back inside the house. Henrietta's grip tightened on the railing in front of her. Why had her family come unannounced? Perhaps her mother had seen the error of her ways and came to apologize. "I suppose we shall see," Henrietta murmured to herself.

With one last glance at the rolling waves, she entered the house and made her way to the sitting room. Her mother leapt from her chair as Henrietta entered. She wrung a handkerchief in her hand.

"This is certainly a surprise," Henrietta said as she eyed them. Silence filled the room. Miriam gave a furtive glance to John. Carolina pursed her lips. John swallowed hard. "Well, is someone going to say something?"

The room remained quiet. "Really?" Henrietta continued. "Not even a hello? You show up on my doorstep unannounced and then proceed to gawk at me without even so much as a greeting?"

"Henrietta," John finally said. His lips bobbed up and down but no other sound emerged.

"Henrietta, please sit down," her mother said.

The crease between Henrietta's eyebrows deepened. "Whatever for?"

John approached her and placed a hand on her forearm. She stared down at it as though it was a bug. "We have some unfortunate news."

Her eyes flitted to her father's face. She stood stock-still. Her heart rose into her throat. She swallowed hard, her gaze fixed.

"It seems there has been a shipwreck."

Henrietta's jaw firmed and her head began to sway into a gentle shake.

"*The Atlantic Queen* has been consumed by the sea. There appear to be no survivors."

Henrietta's legs wobbled underneath her at the news, and she collapsed to the floor beneath her. Her father knelt beside her, still holding her arm.

"I am sorry, Henrietta," he offered.

Carolina raced from the room as her mother whispered for her to fetch tea. Miriam approached Henrietta as Carolina disappeared. She crouched and stroked her daughter's hair.

"No," Henrietta murmured. "No!" she shouted louder. "No, he is not dead. He cannot be dead."

"I am sorry, dear."

"NO!" she shouted again. "There is no proof. I have heard the rumors. His ship is missing. It could have sailed for a port unknown. He is not dead. No."

"The wreckage…"

"Could have been any ship!" Henrietta contended as her father lifted her into a chair.

Miriam shook her head. "Evidence was found to suggest it was, in fact, William's ship, dear."

"What evidence?" Henrietta demanded as she leapt to her feet.

"A piece of the wreckage contained the letters U-E-E-N," John revealed.

Henrietta's lip trembled. "I have heard from two sources *The Atlantic Queen* is missing. Neither mentioned scanning the wreckage and finding anything such as this."

"We have heard from someone who pursued the ship to verify the story and search for survivors."

"Indeed. He found a body in the water which he presumed to be William."

"Then where is his body?"

Miriam glanced to John again. "He attempted to reclaim it but… it was lost to the sea."

"Who was it who found the body?"

Miriam glanced to John. He shrugged in a silent answer. Miriam's lip quivered as she searched for the words.

"Who!" Henrietta demanded.

Miriam stared at the floor. "Your brother, Clifton."

Henrietta's eyebrows shot up as she stumbled back a step, nearly collapsing a second time. She set her jaw, her lips forming a thin line. "Clifton is a liar."

"Henrietta…" her mother began.

"He is a LIAR!" she screamed. "He spreads this tale for his own gain."

"To what end, dear," Father argued.

Mother nodded. "He was most upset to impart the news."

"Oh, was he?" Henrietta inquired, drawing herself upright. "And he imparted it to you and Father rather than face me with the news. Why? Because I would detect his lies."

"He wanted to come. To support you. We felt it best he stay home."

"He is unwelcome in my home!"

Carolina returned with a tray of tea. "Why not sit down, dear?" Miriam prompted.

"No. I have much to attend to. I assume you will stay?"

"We had planned to," Miriam answered. "To help you with the shock. And the arrangements."

"There will be no arrangements! My husband is not dead! Now, I shall see to your rooms. You may stay while we await news of his return."

She stalked from the room before anyone could answer. After stepping from their sight, Henrietta collapsed against the wall. Grief threatened to overcome her. No, she thought as she pushed it away. She would not believe it. Not when Clifton was the source. He was a proven liar. He had lied to her so effortlessly all those years ago. He was doing it again. No, she would cling to the hope that her husband remained alive.

CHAPTER 19

1798

Two days passed before Henrietta received another visitor. In the mid-afternoon, Captain Reginald Adams arrived on the doorstep of Whispering Manor.

"Captain Adams," Henrietta greeted him. "Please come in. May I offer you tea?"

"No, thank you, Mrs. Blanchard," he said as they settled in the sitting room. "I am afraid I have some rather dire news."

The color drained from Henrietta's face. "Have you found my husband's ship?" she choked out.

He licked his lips before continuing his tale. "We have found wreckage."

Henrietta's lips formed a grimace and she struggled to ready her lower lip from trembling.

"The ship's name identified from the wreckage is *The Atlantic Queen*. I am so sorry, Mrs. Blanchard. There appeared to be no survivors."

"No," she sobbed.

"I am so sorry," he repeated.

Miriam hurried into the room. "No," Henrietta sobbed again. "No, he cannot be dead."

Captain Adams glanced at Miriam. She nodded to him. "Thank you, Captain Adams, for delivering the news. We shall take it from here."

The man nodded and stood as Henrietta remained inconsolable. "I shall show myself out. My condolences, Mrs. Blanchard." He nodded his head at Henrietta before disappearing from the room.

Henrietta let out a wail as the front door slammed shut. John rushed into the room, and Miriam explained the latest development. Together, they led Henrietta to her bedroom and laid her across the bed.

She sobbed for over an hour amidst murmuring that the tale could not be true. Miriam stroked her hair as she sat with her. When her sobs died down to whimpers, Carolina brought a tray of tea. Henrietta could not bring herself to touch it.

Miriam moved to the armchair after John inched it closer to the bed. She held Henrietta's hand. "Perhaps we should think about a service, dear."

"No," Henrietta sobbed.

"I realize this is difficult," Miriam said, "but a funeral will give you some closure and allow you to grieve."

"I do not wish to grieve."

"You cannot continue on this way, Henrietta. Surely now you must see Clifton was not lying. You must accept the news. You must face it."

Henrietta did not respond. "Take some tea, dear." Miriam offered her a teacup.

"I do not want tea. I do not want anything. Leave me."

"Perhaps you should get some rest. I shall leave you to sleep. If you need anything, please call." Miriam kissed her forehead before leaving and pulling the door closed.

Henrietta lay on the bed for another hour, unmoving. She dragged herself from it after she'd ceased crying and plopped down at her desk. She scrawled for a few moments in her journal before she collapsed back on her bed.

She could not bring herself to accept his death.

* * *

Heat rose quickly on the first day of July. Henrietta adjusted her black dress and veil as she readied herself for the funeral. Her parents had made the arrangements, then convinced her to attend.

She still could not believe he was dead. After the shock had passed, she'd struggled to accept it. There was no body. The body Clifton found was conveniently lost to the sea, according to her parents. Perhaps William had survived. Perhaps he was trapped on the nearby island.

That was the story she would tell herself for now. That was the story she would tell everyone else, too. She would lose too much if he was dead.

A knock sounded at her door. "Ready, dear?" her mother asked. She offered a consoling smile. The expression annoyed Henrietta.

She shook her head. "I really do not see the point in this. He is not dead."

"Come to the funeral, dear. I realize this is difficult to process, but when you have accepted it, you will regret not mourning him."

Henrietta rolled her eyes at the statement. "And you will all feel ridiculous mourning him when he returns."

Miriam offered her another consoling glance as she held her hand out toward Henrietta. With John's help, they climbed into the waiting carriage and set off for the church. Expressions of sympathy met Henrietta as John led her up the aisle to the front pew.

As the service began, a coffin was carried into the church and set on the bier. Henrietta stared at it, a curious expression on her face. As the pastor began to speak of William's life, a chuckle escaped her.

"Shh," Miriam warned.

But her laughing fit continued. Gasps from several attendees sounded. She doubled over with laughter.

John leaned toward Henrietta and whispered, "Perhaps a spot of fresh air is in order until you have collected yourself."

"No!" she shouted, her voice echoing off the stone walls. Silence consumed the church, and Henrietta leapt to her feet.

No, I will not be quiet!" she shouted. "Here you all sit, crying and praying over an empty casket. William is not here! You don't know he is dead. None of you! But you are all so willing to accept it, and why? You vultures come to my doorstep to offer condolences when what you seek is a death declaration and a doling out of his fortune.

"Shame on you. All of you! You sit here and mourn a man who isn't dead so you can profit from his death! I will no longer be party to this!"

With a shove, she set the casket toppling from the bier and crashing to the floor below. The jarring against the stone floor flung the lid open, revealing the empty interior.

More expressions of shock rang out as Henrietta stormed down the aisle and into the bright sunshine beyond the church's doors.

As the doors swung shut behind her, she spotted a figure stand from a nearby bench. Her jaw flapped open at the sight.

"Hello, Ri," he said.

She regarded him for a moment before narrowing her

eyes at him and frowning. "How dare you show your face here!"

She stormed down the steps and up the path. Clifton sidestepped, cutting off her exit. "Ri, wait," he said. Henrietta struggled to maintain her composure as he gazed at her with a softened expression.

She attempted to hold her resolve. "For?" she questioned. "For you to lie to me? For you to tell me my husband is dead? I will not believe it! I..."

Her voice trailed off as her knees buckled. As emotion overcame her, she swooned forward. In an instant, the truth rushed into her.

Clifton caught her, steadying her before she fell. "Oh, Riri, let me help you, please."

"I... I do not need your help," she choked. She attempted to right herself, but her legs wobbled and stumbled forward, grasping hold of his arm. "No one should see us together. The rumors... "

"To hell with the rumors, Ri," he answered as he steadied her. "You are my sister. I had no desire to tell you of your husband's death. Truly, when I set sail, I hoped to find him alive. Please let me help you get through this."

Henrietta gazed into his cocoa eyes. "There is nothing to get through," she insisted. Her lower lip trembled as she held back the tears brimming in her eyes. "I do not accept it," she whispered.

"Ri..." he began.

"No!" she interrupted with a shout. "No, he cannot be dead!" A whimper escaped her, and her knees buckled a second time as the tears she'd attempted to hold back spilled onto her cheeks.

Clifton swept her into his arms and carried her to Whispering Manor.

Mary opened the door as he climbed onto the porch with

a weeping Henrietta. "Prepare a toddy for her and bring it upstairs to her room," he instructed.

With a nod, the girl disappeared as he mounted the stairs. Within moments, he laid her on her bed and Mary returned with the hot drink as Clifton stepped out of the room. "Do you prefer to sit in your armchair, Mrs. Blanchard?"

Henrietta declined with a shake of her head and a sniffle. As Mary departed, Clifton appeared. He knelt next to her bedside and wiped a tear from her cheek.

"Leave," she groaned.

"No," he answered. He clutched her hand in his. "You can have your tantrum, but I am your brother. I am not leaving you in your time of need."

"He is not dead," she insisted.

"If it helps to hold on to that hope, then do so, Ri."

She adjusted her hand, wrapping her fingers around his and squeezing. Her eyes closed and she drifted to sleep.

Clifton stared at her for a few moments after she'd fallen asleep. She'd been angry, but she'd accepted his help. Perhaps this was a sign of things to come.

When he was certain she wouldn't awaken, he wiggled his fingers from hers and took up a post in the nearby armchair. He'd wait until she woke to continue their discussion.

After an hour, the maid popped her head into the room. "Sir, might I bring anything?" she whispered.

Clifton shook his head and dismissed her with the wave of his hand. A few moments later, Miriam appeared in the doorway. Clifton pressed a finger to his lips and motioned toward Henrietta. She smiled at her sleeping form then at Clifton before she backed from the room. Clifton followed her into the hallway beyond.

"You got her to sleep. I fear she's barely slept since we told her. I have heard her up most nights pacing the floors."

"She is terribly upset."

"She refuses to accept his death. She had quite an outburst at the church, though I imagine many people will understand."

"She is grieving. Denial is the only thing keeping her going. She will accept it in time."

"I am surprised to find you here with her. I thought you were staying in Savannah."

"I could not bring myself to stay away when she needed me."

"Even so, I am surprised she allowed you in the house."

"Henrietta is all bluster and blowhard. She could barely keep to her feet. Her emotions overwhelmed her, and I carried her here. She insisted I leave, but I refused. She needs our support now. No matter what she says."

"You are a good brother to her, Clif."

He smiled at his mother. "She will likely sleep several more hours if she's not rested properly in the past few days. Perhaps you, Father, and Carolina should go to town. There are several Independence Day events occurring. I'm sure Carolina would enjoy it."

Miriam glanced toward Henrietta's bedroom. "I should sit with her until she wakes."

"I will not leave her."

"But..." she began.

Clifton shook his head. "We must come to terms with each other eventually."

"Perhaps now is not the best moment to do that."

"Perhaps it is. She needs her family. All of us."

Miriam pushed a lock of hair behind his ear. "You are a good brother to her, Clifton."

"She is a good sister to me," he answered. "Now, hurry, you don't want Carolina to miss all the fun!"

She kissed his cheek before spinning on her heel and descending the staircase.

Clifton returned to Henrietta's bedroom and eased the door shut. He slid into the armchair as she continued to sleep.

Henrietta woke as evening approached. She stirred with a slight moan before pushing herself up to sit. She rubbed at her red and puffy eyes and sniffled.

"You're awake. How do you feel?"

"Terrible," she murmured.

"Mother, Father, and Carolina returned from the funeral. I sent them to town. There are some Independence Day events taking place."

Henrietta swung her legs over the side of the bed, clutching her head as it pounded. She swayed and squeezed her eyes shut. "You should have gone with them."

Clifton stood and paced the floor. "I had reason to stay back."

"And what, pray tell, is that?" Henrietta asked as she massaged her temples.

Clifton approached Henrietta and knelt in front of her. He gazed up into her dark eyes. "Brace yourself, sister, you have more bad news coming."

CHAPTER 20

1798

Henrietta groaned. "What could be worse than the tale you've already spread of my husband's demise?"

Clifton took her hand in his and squeezed it but Henrietta yanked her hand away from him. "Do not dally with your dreadful announcement, brother. I am certain you are chomping at the bit to share it."

Clifton's mouth formed a thin line as he stared at Henrietta. "It gives me no pleasure to tell you this, Ri, despite what you may think of me."

Henrietta prodded him to continue with a raise of her eyebrows.

"I am afraid your troubles are only just beginning with William's death." Henrietta's shoulders slumped at the mention of her husband's death. The reality was slowly settling in around her. Hearing it from Clifton himself had made it plain that he was not lying. "He's left you in rather a mess," Clifton continued.

"Yes, quite. He has left me alone in the world," she said, her voice cracking as she choked back emotion.

"That is not true," Clifton countered. "Though it is quite a bit worse than only that."

"Quite a bit worse than widowing me at this age?" she shouted, her voice incredulous. "What are you jabbering on about?"

"Simply put, Ri, he has left you destitute."

Henrietta pulled her chin back, her jaw opening. "What?" she questioned.

Clifton nodded to confirm his statement.

"Impossible!" she shouted as she leapt from the bed and paced the floor.

"You may check with your agent at the bank. Though I am certain you will find your accounts quite low and several bad debts against them."

Henrietta ceased pacing for a moment as she struggled to form words. She pondered what she might do, what might become of her.

She collapsed to the bed, grasping at the bedpost to steady herself. "How?" she choked out.

"The Captain was a drunkard. In his inebriated state, he'd often gamble. I'm afraid he wasn't very good at it. He racked up quite a series of debts with some rather dangerous people."

"You lie!" Henrietta shouted.

"I do not, Ri. No one wishes you to know this. Mother and Father expressly requested you be kept in the dark, in fact. Rather salt in the wounds as they viewed it. But you must be made aware of your circumstances."

Her forehead wrinkled. "No," she said with a shake of her

head. "No, William was not a drunk. He did not gamble. He was an upstanding sea captain! Revered!"

Clifton's jaw tensed and he eyed Henrietta. "I am sorry, Ri. We all have our vices."

Henrietta studied his face. She stared into his eyes, searching them. She searched for the lie, but she could not find it. Her brother shared the truth with her.

"But what of his trade business? Surely it can cover…"

Before she finished the statement, Clifton gave a slight shake of his head.

"Oh," Henrietta groaned as her shoulders slumped again.

She focused on the floorboards in front of her as she processed the dire news. Clifton squeezed her shoulder.

"What will become of me?" she whispered as visions of poverty tormented her.

Clifton tipped her chin up to meet his gaze. A devilish half-grin crossed his lips and mischief showed in his eyes. "I have a plan."

"What possible plan could you have to undo all the poor choices I've made?" Her voice broke as tears filled her eyes again.

"Oh, Riri," he chided.

Henrietta stalked to the window, clutching her midriff. "It is the honest truth. You warned me. I did not listen. You should be gloating."

Silence filled the room. Henrietta twisted to glance at him. "Well, go on. Tell me you told me so. Tell me this is my fault. Tell me I should have listened…" Her voice broke and tears streamed down her cheeks. She covered her face with her hands and wept.

Clifton pulled her into his embrace. She collapsed against him and continued to cry. Pulling her hands from her face, she stared into the darkening sky as tears continued to flow.

She cried until she had no tears left. As her tears stopped, she sniffled and wiped at her tear-stained cheeks.

"Are you quite finished now?" Clifton asked her.

Henrietta sniffled again and shook her head.

"I am not certain you could have many tears left, sister," he said.

"Is this the extent of your plan? To badger at me until I no longer grieve? You always excelled at it when we were children."

This earned a chuckle from Clifton.

"Do not laugh at me," she warned. He continued his snickering. It proved infectious, and Henrietta gave into a giggle.

After several light-hearted moments, she pushed away from him and plopped onto the bed. "Oh, what will become of me now?" she questioned.

"You will be better for it. You will rally."

"Are you quite daft? My husband is dead. He has left me no means to provide for myself until I may secure a new marriage. IF I can…"

"If? You're still a beautiful woman, Ri, though…"

"Though I am now damaged goods," she answered. "A widow. Not a beautiful, young, unmarried girl. My prospects have diminished."

"That's not what I meant."

"Isn't it? Well, dear brother, what insights have you to share?"

"You should have no trouble attracting a new husband if that's truly what you want."

"What other choices have I?"

"You have many, Riri. The world is at your feet."

Henrietta burst into laughter at the statement. "Oh, dear brother," she choked out between giggles, "perhaps it is you who is the drunkard. How much liquor have you imbibed before this conversation?"

"You laugh, yet you shall soon see my meaning."

"Well, please, enlighten me."

Clifton settled into the armchair near the fireplace. He shrugged and said, "I have amassed a fairly large fortune from my excursions."

"You mean your pirating," she corrected.

He offered another shrug, his dark eyes sparkling as he glanced at her. "It's not much different than what your so-called beloved husband did, you realize."

"I beg to differ. He did not pillage and rob."

Clifton smirked. "He did, just not to his own people. It's a moot point, and I am not here to debate."

"Continue," Henrietta directed.

"As I said, I have amassed quite a large fortune."

"I fail to see how your future sets the world at my feet."

He raised an eyebrow. "I need help. I need a hiding spot for my riches. With a keeper. Someone I can trust."

"I suppose the bank will not take stolen funds."

"I need you, Ri."

"Me? To guard your stolen money? Surely you jest, brother."

"I do not."

"You have no trusted associates?"

"None I trust more than you."

"What are you proposing? I fail to see how this sets the world at my feet."

"I am proposing you oversee my bounty in return for a slice of the pie. A generous slice, I might add." He cocked his head as he awaited her response.

Henrietta lowered her eyes as she processed the request. Loose ends dangled in her mind but the pieces of the puzzle began to fall into place.

"Would your generous offer be enough to cover William's debts?"

Clifton rose and paced the floor. "I have already paid down his debts, both to the more nefarious characters and at the bank."

Henrietta's eyes widened in surprise. "Call it an advanced payment for services to be rendered," he said as he noticed her expression.

"So, Whispering Manor…"

"Belongs to you. Well, technically to me, but for all intents and purposes, you, Riri."

"So, I have only swapped guardians. From husband to brother."

Clifton faced her, his mouth in a frown. "I have no desire to play guardian to you. You are a capable woman. I do not mean to control you. Not that I could, anyway."

She raised an eyebrow at him as a challenge. "Under the arrangement you propose, I am free to do as I wish then?"

"Absolutely."

"Travel?"

"Wherever you'd like, sister dear."

"Alone?"

He shrugged. "If you so desire. The world is your oyster. Though Neptune's Servant remains at your disposal."

"Purchase lavish items?"

"Your choice."

"Write?"

"I sincerely hope you do. I have missed your stories."

"Marry?"

He narrowed his eyes at her. "Would you, Ri? Would you prefer to, really? Given the choice of your freedom versus a life tied to a husband, would you remarry?"

"I should think it to be expected of me."

"When have you ever preferred to do what is expected?"

"I learned long ago what I prefer does not matter. It is what is expected that matters," she said wistfully.

"This mentality led you into your first marriage. And this disaster."

"Love led me there," she insisted as she spun to face the window.

"Did it, really? You wept before Father paraded you down that aisle. Did you truly love him? Or did you merely love the life you expected him to give you? Or were you merely out of other suitable options?"

She mulled his statements, and a tear fell to her cheek as her lower lip trembled. She had married William when she'd had no other options. Had she loved him, or had she loved the idea of him?

She clutched her handkerchief, twisting it into a taut rope. Clifton laid his hand on her shoulder. "You can be free now, Ri," he whispered to her.

She spun and flung her arms around his neck. Tears flowed freely down her face, though they were now from relief rather than sadness. She pulled back and gazed up at him. A tiny smile crept across her lips.

Clifton matched her expression. "Are we agreed then?"

She nodded. "Bring the treasure!" Clifton grinned at her and she raised a finger. "Though I have several questions."

"I expect nothing less. This is why I've hired you."

"Well, out with them. What questions have you?"

"First, how do you propose to bring this so-called treasure here?"

"We must be careful. I propose docking in the dead of night."

Henrietta cocked her head at him. "And smuggling it ashore?"

He nodded to confirm her guess.

"Where shall we place it? How large is it?" she fired, her finger pressed to her chin. "And who is guarding it now?"

"A trusted associate."

"Then why move it? Why insist I guard it?"

"It is unsafe where it is. And because even trusted associates can be bribed."

"And I cannot?"

He narrowed his eyes at me. "We are blood. Family. I trust you. Our history proves it."

"Despite our estrangement?"

"A blip. A spat between siblings, nothing more."

Henrietta smiled and squeezed his shoulder in silent thanks. She resumed her pacing. "All right, so you sail under the cover of night. We smuggle the treasure ashore. How large is it? You never answered."

"I fear it may sink the ship."

She ceased her ambling and raised her eyebrows. "You jest."

"I do not. I told you I have been very successful in my endeavors."

"I suppose," Henrietta said, collapsing onto the bed, "I should be more reluctant in aiding you given the way you came into your fortune."

He shrugged and wiggled his eyebrows. "I have never wronged anyone who did not deserve it."

"What does that mean? You robbed from trade ships, did you not? And let us not speak of what you did to the sailors aboard."

"Those trade ships were captained by crooked men already on the take. Men who mistreated their own sailors and those they traded with. I relieved them of their command and offered their men a new life. I'm rather a hero if you really consider it, Ri."

"Crooked men?" He nodded, an amused expression on his face. "So you have robbed the robbers?"

"Rather a Robin Hood, I'd say." He smirked, his charming grin as disarming as it always was in assisting him out of trouble.

Shaking her head, she teased, "You have a high opinion of yourself."

"Someone must, why not me?"

"All right, so it is large enough to sink your ship. And what of the contents?"

"Gold, silver, jewels, and the like."

"I thought you robbed trade ships?" He nodded. "Trade ships carrying jewels and gold?"

He rolled his eyes. "No, Ri, you rob the ship and then sell the contents for gold and jewels. And there was the occasional raid of a ship carrying some valuable contents of the European nobles."

"Stop," she said, holding up her hand, "I should hear no more of this."

"Why? They may prove interesting when you take up writing again."

"If I find myself in need of inspiration, I shall ask."

A bemused smile crossed his face. "Fine. What other questions have you then?"

"I am curious about something else you mentioned rather unrelated to our current discussion."

"Which is?"

"You mentioned a plan when I said I would be expected to remarry."

A naughty grin crossed his face. "If you continue your current course of action, no one will suggest it."

Her brow furrowed. "My current course of action?" she inquired.

"Yes," he said nonchalantly, waving his hand in the air.

"The grieving widow who refuses to believe her husband will not return. Pining away for him. You could even parade about on the widow's walk. Make a real show of it, Ri. You've always enjoyed acting."

Henrietta offered him a wry glance.

"What?" he questioned. "I have vivid memories of sword fights, murders, and more in my childhood bedroom every evening. I'm sure reluctant widow is something you can pull off."

"So, you propose I pretend to await my husband's return from sea in order to remain a widow?"

"It is the perfect plan!"

"Mother and Father will disagree."

"They usually do. You've never seemed to mind."

"I do not," she assured him. "Though that will not stop them from badgering at me."

"Nor you from pitching one of your famous fits. Father always gives in to you then. And Mother only wrings her hands because she does not know what to say or do."

"In an effort to win me to her way of thinking, she did rather spoil me. I am not certain she expected this result."

"In any case, it works to your advantage. Use it."

Henrietta offered a coy smile. "Then it sounds like we have a plan."

"Not quite," Clifton answered.

Her brow furrowed, her grin vanishing. She cocked her head at him, questioning his meaning.

"We still need a hiding spot."

CHAPTER 21

1798

"**H**ow able-bodied are your men?" Henrietta inquired as she strode along the beach with Clifton the next morning.

He glanced sideways at her. "What kind of question is that?"

She rolled her eyes at him. "A perfectly acceptable one when we are discussing hiding treasure large enough to sink your ship. Which one is it, by the way?"

He pointed to the ships in the distance. "There. With the three masts."

"Where is your pirate flag?"

"Well, I don't sail it into port with the Jolly Roger flying, Ri," he said, his voice incredulous.

"Why not? You are quite proud of your endeavors, Robin Hood."

He offered her a wry glance. "I have no regrets, but I still maintain some level of decorum in polite society."

"I see," she answered. "Well, anyway, you have not answered. How able-bodied are you men?"

"What did you have in mind?"

Henrietta ceased walking and motioned in front of her.

He raised his eyebrows. "A cave?"

"A sea cave," she said. "Quite a large and deep one."

"And you propose to put the treasure there."

"More or less."

"I would argue it is too obvious."

"I have a solution for that and a reason for using this particular cave."

"Enlighten me."

"First, let us explore the cave and determine if it provides sufficient refuge for your large treasure."

They disappeared into the opening. Clifton stared at the chamber as they entered. After scanning it, his eyes rested on Henrietta. "Ri..." he began as she eyed the space.

"Yes?"

He rubbed the back of his neck. "At the risk of angering you again, this is rather a poor hiding spot."

She cocked her head at him. "Anyone could meander in. In fact, it's likely one may spot the treasure from the beach."

Henrietta threw her head back and laughed. Clifton raised his eyebrows at her. "I fail to see the humor in the situation."

"Surely you cannot think me that stupid, Clif."

He offered her a confused grin. "You said..." he began.

She grasped his arm and tugged. "I said this cave, more or less. I certainly did not mean this cavern in particular."

"Oh!" he said.

"Oh, Clif. If you truly believed me this stupid, you should not have hired me."

"I shall refrain from comment lest I earn your ire again."

"Wise choice, brother," she said as she led him to the rear

of the chamber. A lantern sat near the back of the cavern. She lit it and held it high.

"Now," she said as she placed her hand against the cool rock. "It is quite hard to see but…" She dragged her hand across the dark surface until it disappeared. "Ah, here it is." She offered a broad smile before she slipped into a crack in the surface.

Clifton stared at the space where she'd disappeared. Light shone through the crack, and Henrietta's features appeared on the other side. "Well, come on," she said, motioning for him to follow.

He found the journey a tight squeeze but successfully made it to the other side. A large cavern yawned beyond the tiny passage. Henrietta held the lantern high overhead, its feeble light struggling to reach the far end of the chamber.

"Well, what do you think?"

Clifton stalked around the area. "It certainly is large enough."

"And hidden. We could block the small passage to cut it off entirely."

Clifton rubbed his chin in thought. "The tricky part may become unloading the treasure. That passage is quite small. And I do not relish bringing it in coin by coin. And if we block off the passage, how would we access it."

"This is where your able-bodied sailors come in."

"Do you propose they block and unblock it every time? That may draw more attention than we'd like."

"No, I do not. I propose something different entirely."

"Oh?"

"Come with me." She slipped into the main chamber and extinguished the lantern. They exited into the bright sunshine of the July day. Henrietta led him the short distance back to Whispering Manor. They pushed in through the front door.

"Ah, Mother!" Henrietta greeted her.

"Henrietta, how lovely to see you up and about."

"Clifton took me for a walk to breathe the fresh sea air. It has helped tremendously."

Miriam smiled at them. "I hoped to catch sight of William's ship returning, but alas, no luck. Maybe tomorrow."

Miriam's shoulders sagged at the mention of Henrietta's late husband. "Are you, Father, and Carolina off to enjoy the town? It is rather lovely in the summer months, though dreadfully cold and dreary in the winter. Oh, I do hope William returns in time for us to travel to a warmer climate for the winter."

"Henrietta…" her mother began when Clifton squeezed her arm.

"Mother, perhaps you should be going before you miss more of the day," he said.

Miriam eyed him, her eyes flitting to Henrietta with a worried glance.

"Clif's right, Mother. You really should go on ahead. I'll fetch Carolina!" Henrietta climbed the stairs in search of her sister.

"I am not certain we should leave given her mindset," Miriam whispered to Clifton.

He shook his head at the statement. "She is fine. She is grieving in her own way."

"Is it healthy to continue to allow her to ignore his death?"

"She will come to it in her own time. For now, what is the harm in it?"

"The realization may kill her when she makes it. And there are things that must be attended to. His will, his assets…" She lowered her voice. "The debts."

"Mother," Clifton said as he squeezed her arms, "you

worry too much. I have already taken care of all the necessary arrangements with his debts and his assets."

Miriam's brow furrowed. Clifton explained, "I have paid the debts."

"That was very kind of you, Clif," Miriam said. "But what of her home? What of Whispering Manor?"

"Whispering Manor belongs to me. Henrietta may live here for as long as she chooses. And if she chooses to leave, we shall worry about it then."

Miriam sighed. "Oh, Clif, you are a darling boy and a wonderful brother. I hope she realizes one day what you have done for her."

"She realizes it now, Mother. Even if she will not say it aloud. She realizes."

Henrietta marched Carolina down the stairs, John trailed behind them. "Here we are. All ready!"

"Why not come with us, dear?" John suggested.

"Oh, no, I have just come from a long walk on the beach. I should very much like to rest while the house is quiet."

"If you insist," John said. "Come along, Carolina. Let us leave your sister to rest and explore town."

"May I go to the sweet shop?" the girl asked as they stepped out of the house.

Henrietta slammed the door shut behind them. Clifton raised his eyebrows at her. "Well?" she inquired. "Are my acting skills still up to par?"

"You may have laid it on a little thick, Ri. Mother is concerned about your state of mind."

"Why play a role if you plan to do it poorly? Now, come along."

She pulled him into the library, pulling the pocket doors closed behind them. After a glance out the window revealed no one approaching the house or lurking on the porch, she waved him across the room to a bookcase.

"William showed me this, in case of a terrible storm." She reached to the inside of one shelf and pressed a button and pulled. "Help me."

Clifton hurried to her side and tugged with her. The bookcase swung open, revealing a passage.

"It leads to a small chamber buried underground," she explained. "I propose your men dig a passage toward the cave and connect the two. Then we can access the treasure from the house and seal off the beach cave entrance. I have drawn a map." She pulled a paper from a desk drawer with a rough sketch. "Here, you see. 'X' marks the spot."

Clifton studied the bookcase. "We must secure this."

"And we will. I have studied a few schematics for securing hidden passages. We can install a keyless locking mechanism that opens with a password. We'll hide it with books."

He grinned at her. "Your books."

"If you'd like," she said.

"I would very much. Speaking of, I have something for you."

"Oh?"

"Just a moment," he said as he pushed the bookcase shut.

Henrietta eased into an armchair as he disappeared from the room. He returned with a handful of papers. A smile crossed his face as he looked at them.

"What is that?" she inquired.

He handed them to her. "*Over Land and Sea*. Your unfinished novel."

Henrietta stared down at the papers. "I read it. Well, what you've written of it. And I hope you'll finish it. I feel rather let down that Captain Kendrall is left twisting in the wind, quite literally, on the final page."

Henrietta ran her hand over the title page. "I stopped writing the night you…"

"Yes, I know. Regrettable, if you ask me."

"I didn't," she said. "My heart could not bear it."

"And now?"

"Well, now, I shall have the time and inclination, shan't I?"

He grinned at her. "I have one other thing, too."

She raised her eyebrows at him. He held the gold coin between his thumb and forefinger.

"My coin!" she said as she reached for it.

He pulled it back. "Remember it came with a promise?"

"I remember."

"It seems you have forgotten it for several years."

"I thought it forgotten by you."

"When I left that night," Clifton began.

"No. Let's not rehash it."

"We must, Ri."

She leapt from the chair and stalked to the window. Her eyes searched the landscape outside. "I do not wish to argue."

"Neither do I, but there are things I must say."

"And if I do not wish to hear them?"

He grasped her shoulders and spun her to face him. "You must." She crossed her arms, a pout on her face. "When I left that night, Ri, I had every intention of keeping my promise. If I had taken you with me, I could not have done that."

Henrietta stared at the floor, batting her eyelashes as he spoke. "It was my promise that caused me to leave you there. Where you would be safe and looked after. It broke my heart to leave you behind, Ri, but I could not make your life worse."

A tear rolled down her cheek. "But you did, Clif."

"I tried to return and stop you from this marriage, but you would not have it!"

"Why did you have to leave?" she said with a sniff.

"I had to leave so I could return and offer you the freedom I promised."

She bit her lower lip as she flicked a tear from her cheek. "It is over now."

"Is it?"

"Yes. I do not wish to continue to discuss that terrible night. I wish you would have stayed. I needed you."

He tilted his head as he stared into her eyes. "That is where you are wrong. You may have wished I stayed, but it was not out of need. You, Henrietta Nichols Blanchard, *need* no one."

Henrietta straightened her shoulders and raised her eyebrows. "A fact you shouldn't forget."

"A fact I have never forgotten. And why I sought you out regarding the little matter of my very large treasure." He held up the gold coin again.

Henrietta snatched it from his hands and pressed it into her palm. "We should continue our discussions for that whilst we have privacy. Now, how long will it take your men to dig the passage?"

* * *

Henrietta stood with her shawl clutched tightly around her shoulders. The large ship sailed through the fog under the full moon, easing to stop across from her. Its black sails fluttered in the breeze and the Jolly Roger whipped in the wind from high atop the middle mast.

Henrietta eyed the vessel as activity flurried across her decks. Soon, skiffs were lowered in the water. Men climbed into them and chests were dangled over the side and loaded. The first dinghy began its journey across the moonlight sea toward shore.

The small boat neared and a man jumped into the water, his boots splashing. Two others followed his lead and leapt from the boat to drag it ashore.

Clifton stalked toward his sister. "Hello, Ri," he said with a grin.

She eyed him tip to tail. "I've never seen you in your pirate regalia," she commented.

He tipped his tricorn at her, his sword swinging as he bowed. "And I've flown the flag for you." He motioned toward the ship.

"I noticed."

"Have I struck fear into your heart?"

"I am trembling. Though more from the chill in the night air than your Jolly Roger."

"A dagger to my heart. There are men who shrink with fear when *Neptune's Servant* overtakes them."

"I am not so faint of heart. Now, where is the treasure?"

Clifton's crew busily unloaded the chests from their skiff before shoving the small boat back into the water and rowing back to their ship.

Clifton gestured toward the chests on the beach. A few men had stayed behind to shuttle them to their new location. With his foot, he flipped open one lid. Under the white moonlight, gold glittered.

Henrietta's face lit up with a satisfied smile. He slammed the lid shut and nodded to his men who carried the chest away toward the sea cave.

"We shall slip the smaller items through the passage. A few of the larger chests will need to be unloaded piece by piece."

"Larger chests?" she inquired, her eyes wide. "Are there larger chests than those?"

Clifton let out a belly laugh. "Yes, those are the small ones!"

She raised her eyebrows. "I wasn't joking when I said I feared it may sink the ship."

"I am growing concerned we will not finish tonight."

"We will," Clifton assured her. "And we shall sail *Neptune's Servant* into port with her white sails like a normal merchant ship before dawn. Shall we head into the chamber?"

The pair oversaw the unloading of bounty through the wee hours of the morning. Larger chests were hauled into the first cavern, then emptied. The empty chests were taken to the house. The men had dug a passage leading to the hidden storm haven under Whispering Manor, but only Henrietta and Clifton knew how to enter the chamber through the hidden panel in the library.

"Excellent work, men," Clifton said as they finished. "Back to the ship, lower the black sails, and raise the white. We'll slip into Hideaway Bay before the sun rises."

Henrietta studied several of the chests as Clifton approached her. "Ri? Ready? The men will block the passage after we've gone through."

She pulled a ruby necklace from one chest. It dangled from her fingers as she studied it in the flickering torches' light. "May I keep this?" she inquired.

He raised his eyebrows at her. "It is yours. You do not need to ask. What is mine is also yours, Ri."

She smiled at the necklace and slipped it into her pocket. They slipped through the small fissure and into the chamber beyond. Only two men remained. They piled rocks into the crack until it filled.

"Care for a ride?" Clifton inquired.

"What, aboard your pirate ship?"

He shrugged and raised his eyebrows at her.

"You must be joking. I could walk to the house faster."

"But you could sail on a pirate ship. And the dock is not very far. You'll be home by dawn."

She stared at the ship in the distance. "Come on, Ri! Live!"

She chuckled. "All right."

Clifton helped her aboard the skiff and climbed in next to

her. One of the crewmen shoved the boat further into the water and hopped in. They rowed to the large ship. Clifton steadied Henrietta as she stood in the bobbing boat to climb aboard.

She stood on the dock as the crew prepared *Neptune's Servant* to sail south into the harbor. Clifton ordered the anchor pulled up and the helmsman spun the wheel to set their course. Henrietta clutched the railing as the breeze filled the sails and caressed her skin.

In the east, the sun, still hiding below the horizon, began to paint the sky a myriad of colors. The ship continued down the coastline toward the harbor.

Henrietta glanced up. White sails replaced the black sails Clifton had used to sail under the cover of night. She narrowed her eyes as she spotted the black flag flying atop the middle mast.

"Clif!" she shouted as he joined her on the deck. "You've left the Jolly Roger flying!"

He grinned at her. "Just for you, sister. Now you've sailed on a pirate ship."

They sailed into the harbor at Hideaway Bay and docked the ship. Clifton's men removed the Jolly Roger flag quickly as the ship came to a rest. Henrietta found the exit from the ship easier than her entrance from the skiff.

"Shall we return to Whispering Manor and ogle our fortune?" Clifton inquired.

"I'd like nothing better."

They returned to the quiet house as the sun began to peek over the horizon. Henrietta closed the pocket doors to the library.

She crossed to the bookshelf and pulled several books from the shelf. With a candle, she highlighted the new mechanism in the back of the bookcase.

Six bronze wheels with letters sat flush with the back. "What is the passcode?" Clifton questioned.

"HENTON," she said.

He raised his eyebrows. "HEN for the start of my name and TON for the end of yours," she explained.

"Clever."

"And," she continued, "the books that hide it."

He smiled at her. "Your books."

"I have had them bound."

"I am quite pleased."

With a smile, Henrietta spun the wheels to spell the keyword. The latch released and Clifton pulled the bookcase open. They entered the chamber. "Pull the door shut behind you," she instructed.

With her candle, she lit a lantern and handed it to Clifton. They descended further into the passage.

As the stone corridor opened into the cavernous space, the gold glinted in the flickering flames. Henrietta ran her fingers over the gold bars stacked near the entrance. The cool metal sent a shiver up her arm, turning it to gooseflesh.

 e've done it," she whispered.

1798

Clifton smiled. "We've done it," he repeated. He swept her off her feet and swung her around before setting her down. "Happy?"

"Very," she said as she eyed the fortune. "We shall want for nothing."

"Speaking of, are you certain you want that ruby necklace? There are many others to choose from."

She pulled it from her pocket. "I like this one."

"The choice is yours."

"Aren't they technically all at my disposal?"

"Indeed, they are."

Henrietta fell silent for a moment as she studied the array of items. "Have you heard from your friend?"

"Redbeard?"

Henrietta nodded.

"No. Though I have heard he continues to search for the treasure, so I am pleased to have moved it."

"Will he guess you've moved it here?"

"Perhaps. Though I trust you'd not share it with him."

"No, though…"

"Ri, I will protect you."

Henrietta smiled at him. "Thank you. Though I realized the treasure did not need to be guarded against the choirs of angels, brother."

"To that end, I shall leave you with a pistol."

She snapped her head to stare at him. "I will show you how to use it," he promised.

"Before you sail into the sunset?"

"I will not sail until you feel secure."

"Do you promise?"

"I do."

She narrowed her eyes at him. He held up his hands in surrender. "This time I will not leave you without notice."

She smiled and nodded at him.

* * *

Henrietta stood on her widow's walk. In the distance, *Neptune's Servant* sailed toward the darkening sky. Clifton had stayed for two months before sailing south to cruise the Caribbean waters. He would return in several months.

A chuckle escaped Henrietta's lips as she spotted the Jolly Roger being hoisted. The skull and bones waved at her, signaling Clifton's farewell.

She returned to her bedroom and sat at her writing desk. In the months that followed her husband's untimely death, she had spent a good bit of time detailing her experiences in her journal. She caressed the brown leather before she shoved it aside.

She'd spent much of the past few months writing. Her creative spark had reignited with her reconciliation with Clifton. She planned a new story in the days before his departure. She would begin writing tonight. With any luck, she'd have it penned by his return.

She dipped her quill into the inkwell and set the tip to paper.

The Adventures of Black Jack

A smile spread across her face as she blew on the ink to dry it before setting it aside. She bit her lower lip as she hurriedly scrawled words across the page.

1800

The bright Caribbean sun beat down on the ship's deck.

"Has she been spotted yet?" Clifton inquired as he climbed to the helm.

"Not a sign yet, Captain," the helmsman answered.

"Keep pushing."

"Aye, sir."

Clifton scanned the horizon before he descended the stairs and disappeared into his cabin. He slid into his desk chair and pulled the drawer open. A stack of papers tied with twine sat inside. He pulled them out and studied the writing. The book chronicled his adventures at sea. Henrietta had presented it to him when he'd visited last.

"Read it when you're bored of pirating," she'd said.

He set the manuscript on his desk. With any luck, she'd have more to add after this trip. He flipped the page and began to read when a knock sounded at his door. Johnson's head poked in. "Sir, we have her in our sights."

"Good," Clifton said as he collected the papers and shoved

them into the drawer again.

"As you suspected, she is sitting off-shore of our old island. It seems several skiffs have already crossed over."

"Prepare our skiffs. We'll be going ashore."

"Very good, sir."

Clifton emerged onto the deck. He extended his spyglass and eyed the ship in the distance. The *Scourge of the Seas* bobbed in the choppy waters off the island's coast. He smirked at the sight as his crew lowered the dinghies into the water.

He climbed aboard one and they rowed to shore.

Clifton wandered up the beach toward the tree line. He'd left a contingent of his men to guard their dinghies. The other crew members who had rowed to the island followed him. He led them to the island's center. The cave mouth near the river yawned.

Clifton ducked into the darkened space. The river cut through the cavern. Clifton and his men leapt into the water and approached the back of the cavern. With a gulp of breath, they descended under the water and swam forward under the cave's back wall into the second chamber.

Rising silently from the water, Clifton assessed the scene. A small contingent of men milled around as a tall man with fiery red hair knelt on the ground, studying the imprint of a trunk left in the dirt.

Clifton smirked at him as he climbed from the water. The men whipped around, several of them drawing their swords. Clifton and his men were quick to react, drawing their weapons in return.

"Now, now, gentlemen," Clifton said. "Is there really a need for such hostility?"

"Where is it, Jack?" Redbeard growled.

"Where is what?"

"You know damn well what."

Clifton puckered his lips. "Oh! Did you mean the treasure?"

Redbeard narrowed his eyes at Clifton. "Where is it, Jack?"

"Wouldn't you like to know?"

Redbeard thrust his sword forward toward Jack's chin. "Where?" he demanded.

"Somewhere you will never find it. It's not yours, Redbeard. Stay away from it."

"It wasn't yours either."

"But it is now. Stay away from it, Redbeard. Pursue your own goals."

"But yours are so much easier to pursue."

"Ready, sir," a man said from the back of the cavern.

Clifton smirked and backed toward the river. With his sword still drawn, he sank into the water and backed toward the cavern wall. "I warn you one last time, Redbeard. Stay away."

He ducked under the water and emerged on the other side. "Quickly," he said as he scrambled from the back wall. A charge burned down as the men raced toward the cave entrance. Clifton was the last to leave, leaping through the opening as the charge detonated.

A cloud of dust billowed from the cave. Clifton picked himself up off the ground, brushing dirt and sand from his jacket. "Well, that ought to slow them down," he said with a chuckle.

A laugh went up among the men. "Back to the ship, men. We have work to do."

* * *

Henrietta wandered down the street toward the post office. Several people greeted her along the way. She waved and smiled at all of them. Even with the winter months approaching, her mood was considerably better these days. Her writing had taken off. She spent hours of her day disappearing into worlds of her own creation.

She delivered her letters to the postmaster and stepped back into the bright sunshine. Despite the cheery weather, the sun did little to warm the air. Henrietta hurried toward Whispering Manor.

A man approached. Henrietta nearly stumbled over him as he darted from a side alley. "Mrs. Blanchard?" he questioned her.

"Yes?" she asked as she stumbled back a few steps. She studied the man in front of her, certain she had never met him. She would remember those fiery red curls and that pointed red beard.

He smiled graciously. "My name is Ronan O'Rourke." Henrietta narrowed her eyes at him. "Oh, forgive me, I was friends with your husband, prior to his passing. I thought, perhaps, you'd recognize my name."

"I am sorry, I do not. William passes very little information along to me about his colleagues."

He offered a consoling smile. "I just wanted to pass along my condolences over his loss."

Henrietta raised her eyebrows. "Loss? He is missing, not dead. Though thank you for your wishes."

She pushed past him. "Oh, Mrs. Blanchard," he called to her, "would it be all right to stop in for tea tomorrow afternoon?"

She narrowed her eyes at him. "I am quite sorry, my afternoon is full tomorrow."

He chuckled, though the annoyance on his face was plain. "Perhaps another time then."

Henrietta nodded and continued on her way to Whispering Manor. She climbed the porch stairs and pushed through the front door, slamming it behind her and collapsing against it.

Her jaw tensed as she shut her eyes after the encounter. She opened them, her lips still puckered, and climbed the stairs to the second story. She entered her bedroom, removing her hat. A figure climbed from the armchair near the fireplace.

She pressed her hand over her heart. "Oh, must you always startle me like that?" she questioned.

"It keeps you on your toes, Ri," Clifton said with a sideways grin.

She shook her head at him. "It will kill me one day."

"I should hope not," he said.

Silence fell between them for a few moments before they exchanged a glance.

"I think we have a problem," they said at the same time.

Clifton raised his eyebrows. "Oh. Hmm. You first."

"I believe your friend, Redbeard, is in town."

Clifton tilted his head, his brow knitting tightly. Henrietta continued, "As I walked home from dropping off the post, a gentleman approached me, claiming to have been a friend of William's. He wanted to pass along his condolences and invited himself to tea."

"And you believe him to be Redbeard? How did he introduce himself?"

"As Ronan O'Rourke. And, yes, I believe him to be your Redbeard. His fiery red curls, red beard, and hooked nose gave him away."

Clifton tightened his grip on the hat he clutched in his hand. His lips formed a grimace. "Damn him!"

"Never fear, I declined his offer for tea," Henrietta said.

Clifton shook his head. "It troubles me he is here. That was my problem. I'd heard rumors he planned to seek information here. That is why I came."

"You expect trouble?"

"Yes."

"What is to be done?"

"He must be removed."

"Is he really that much of a threat, Clif? He has found nothing."

"It is enough that he has approached you. He suspects something, and I fear he may use you to get it."

Henrietta raised her eyebrows. "Perhaps I should have taken him up on his offer for tea."

"To what end?"

"A dash of a deadly substance, and we are rid of him."

"I can handle my own problems, Ri."

"He is our problem, brother, not just yours. We are partners, are we not?"

"I will not allow my sister to do my dirty work. Besides, it takes the fun out of it, really."

"Fun?"

"Yes, I shall quite enjoy sinking his ship."

Henrietta raised her eyebrows. "What?" he questioned. "It can be quite fun blowing holes in things."

She offered him a wry glance. "How will you lure him away?"

Clifton pondered it. "He is not aware I have followed him. I docked *Neptune's Servant* several ports away and traveled by carriage. I will need to create a scenario alluring enough to prompt him to leave. I shall then ensnare him and defeat him at sea."

"You make it sound easy."

"It will be a battle, but a battle I can win if I plan it correctly."

"I quite prefer my plan."

"I do not wish you to be involved."

"And I do not wish you to risk being blown to bits, Clif."

"I will not be blown to bits. The question is what will pique his interest enough to leave Hideaway Bay." Clifton placed his finger on his chin as he pondered it.

"Precious gems," Henrietta suggested.

His brow furrowed. "Gems?"

"Gemstones are quite alluring. Particularly when there are many of them."

"What are you suggesting?"

"Let slip that there is a particularly lucrative shipment of precious gemstones coming from Africa and that you plan to raid the ship. That should send him scurrying down the coast to beat you to it."

"I imagine this could work. He'll be furious if I beat him to that bounty."

"How will you get word to him?"

"Do not worry. He has his eyes on my crew at all times. I shall simply let it slip in a tavern as I gather my men."

"How will you ensnare him in a trap?"

"That, dear sister, is my affair." He placed his hat on his head and offered a kiss on her cheek.

"Just a moment. I am not at all comfortable with this plan."

"It is the best plan. I do not want him anywhere near you, Ri."

"And I..."

Clifton held up his hand. "Ri, trust me. I shall return to you within the month."

"You had better."

He offered a grin. "Or?"

"Or I will seek you out and kill you again."

"A terrifying prospect. I should do well to win, then."

With a salute and a grin, he disappeared through the doorway, leaving Henrietta to wait for news of Redbeard's demise.

CHAPTER 23

1800

Clifton strolled into the small tavern. Several of his men relaxed in chairs, ales in their hands. He scanned the room, spotting who he wanted to see. A man sat in the back corner, the brim of his hat pulled low. A trusted member of Redbeard's crew. He'd been left here to keep an eye on Clifton's movements.

He turned his head and let his gaze rest on his Chief Mate, Johnson. Clifton bypassed the bar and walked directly to Johnson. "Johnson, a word in private."

"Now, sir?"

"Yes, it is quite urgent," he said.

He slid his eyes sideways to the man in the back corner. The subtle shift in the man's shoulders suggested he'd picked up on the conversation.

Johnson set his mug on the table and stood, following Clifton outside into the afternoon sun. Clifton rounded the corner of the tavern, ducking into a side alley. He pretended to glance around before leaning in to Johnson to speak. As he glanced toward the street, he saw a fleck of blue peek around the corner. Satisfied they had been followed, he launched into his conversation.

"Gather the men, quickly and quietly. We sail tonight."

"Sir?"

"I have received word of a large shipment of rather valuable items. Diamonds. We must make it past Prickly Pear Island within the week to catch them unaware."

"How valuable?" the man inquired.

"Very," Clifton said. "If we pull this off, it will be another impressive haul."

"I shall gather them at once, sir."

Clifton clapped the man on the shoulder as he departed. He glanced to the corner of the building. The other man was gone. No doubt racing to inform his captain of the *Neptune's* new plans.

It would be a glorious day at sea soon, he reflected.

Neptune's Servant hid behind the rise of East Seal Dog Island. The weather was on their side as a thick fog wafted above the water. He'd sent a crew to the island. They kept their eyes on the horizon to the west, expecting to see the *Scourge of the Seas* appear by day's end.

The ship would have had to fight hard to catch them, but Clifton did not expect Redbeard to be far behind him. His guns were readied and his men prepared to fight. If they succeeded, they would destroy both Redbeard and his ship. That would make his own pirating easier and eliminate an enemy searching to destroy his legacy.

A signal showed from the island. A glint of glass forewarned them of Redbeard's approach. "Ready yourselves, men. The battle is upon us," he called.

The men from the island rowed back to the ship. As they climbed aboard, they gave a full report. "*Scourge of the Seas* approaches," one man reported. "She is just on the other side of West Seal."

"Lift the anchor," Clifton instructed. "And prepare for battle."

The chains rattled as they pulled the anchor up and the ship slipped forward from the cover of the island. They remained hidden in the fog, their black sails invisible against the darkening sky.

"Steady, men," Clifton cautioned them. "Do not fire until given the order, lest you give us away. We do not wish to give them a chance to tuck tail and run."

Several tense moments passed as they waited for the ship to close in on their position. After several moments, the outline of *Scourge of the Seas* became visible through the fog.

"Sir?" Johnson said, shifting his weight from foot to foot.

"Hold."

Johnson licked his lips, his eyes sliding sideways toward Clifton.

The front of the ship poked toward them, the now-damaged mermaid carving that graced the front becoming visible.

"Sir…"

"Hold."

A cry sounded from the opposite ship. We've been spotted, Clifton realized with a smirk. *Scourge of the Seas* lurched as they put her hard to starboard to pull alongside this ship and not ram her. As the port side became visible, Clifton uttered one word. "Fire."

"Fire! Fire! Fire!" Johnson shouted.

The cannons roared under their feet, rocking the boat

with each dispatch. Cannonballs sailed across the water, cutting through the fog as they sought their target. The first sailed wide, but the next struck its mark. Wood exploded into the water as the cannonball smashed through the side of the *Scourge of the Seas*.

"Continue to fire upon them," Clifton said. "And ready the hooks to board."

"Aye, sir." Johnson hurried across the deck shouting orders. The other ship struggled to recover from the cannon fire. They hurried to ready their own cannons, but being ill-prepared for battle, they were slow to respond.

"Sir, we are ready to board."

Another cannonball struck the ship, disabling two cannons and blowing a hole through the side of the ship. Clifton watched as Redbeard's men scrambled backward from the blow, one man toppling into the waters below.

"Board her. Send Porter and Richards to disable the rudder. Fire chain shot to disable the mainmast."

"Yes, sir," Johnson answered with a nod before barking orders to the crew. Grappling hooks were tossed to the other ship and men swung over. Redbeard's crew drew weapons as the fight ensued. Some scrambled to launch skiffs to escape the dying ship.

"Captain," Johnson said, holding a rope toward him.

"Thank you, Johnson," Clifton said with a smirk and a salute. He grasped the rope and swung over the sea onto the deck of the other ship.

He drew his sword and sliced toward an attacker, sending him spiraling backward as he shredded his shirt. A man ran up from his left side. Clifton swung his elbow into the man's gut, doubling him over. He spun and knocked another off his feet with a sweep of his left leg. He thrust his sword at another's neck. The man's eyes went wide and he stumbled back several steps before he turned and ran, leaping off the boat.

A bullet whizzed past his head, striking the wooden mast behind him. Clifton snapped his head in the direction the bullet came. A man stood across the deck, frantically reloading his pistol. He pointed the reloaded gun at Clifton. Clifton drew his pistol from his belt and fired, striking the man in the arm and knocking the gun from his grasp. It skittered across the wooden deck. One of Clifton's crewmen scooped it up and saluted to his captain.

Clifton returned the gesture before continuing his quest aboard. He fought through several other men as he approached the helm area.

The red curls of *Scourge's* captain swung wildly as he barked orders to try to keep his ship afloat and turn the tides of the battle.

Redbeard glowered at Clifton as he approached, his sword drawn and ready.

"You tricked me," he growled.

Clifton raised an eyebrow. "And now I shall end you."

Redbeard drew his sword and lunged at Clifton. Their blades clinked together as they danced across the helm, slashing and parrying. Redbeard dove toward Clifton, pinning him against the railing. "You should not have boarded my ship. I will kill you and that pretty sister of yours. I'm fairly certain she knows the location of the treasure. Doesn't she?"

With a shove, Clifton drove him back several steps before slashing at him again. Clifton lunged forward with another swipe of his sword. Redbeard danced backward another few steps until his back bent over the railing. Redbeard swung his sword forward, but Clifton knocked it out of his hand. It flew over the edge of the ship and splashed into the water below.

Redbeard's eyes followed his lost sword. As he returned his eyes forward, Clifton landed a blow against his jaw, sending the man sprawling across the helm's deck. Clifton leveled the sword at his throat. "You should not have threatened my sister."

With a thrust forward, he pierced the man's chest. Red blood soaked the man's shirt. He groaned as Clifton withdrew the sword. A splintering crack deafened everyone in the vicinity. The mainmast, hit by a chain shot fractured. The top swayed for a moment before it began a slow slide toward the deck. Men screamed and scrambled from its path as it crashed to the deck below.

"And now I must bid you adieu," Clifton said with a salute.

He hurried down the stairs. "Men, return to the *Neptune*, this ship is not long for this world."

His crewmen scrambled to swing back to their own ship. Others rushed to abandon their disabled galleon.

Clifton slid across the deck of his ship along with several others. "Mr. Johnson," he said as he stepped to the rail to eye the sinking ship next to them. "Are all crew accounted for?"

"Not a soul lost, sir."

"And all have returned?"

"Yes, sir," he assured him.

"Set a course for Hideaway Bay."

"Yes, sir. Any last orders for the *Scourge of the Seas*, sir?"

Clifton glanced over to the ship. Black smoke curled from the rear to the sky. Splintered wood rose into the air where the mainmast stood. She listed to her port side as water spilled into the holes blasted by cannonballs.

"Fire one last volley as we pull away. Send her to the locker, Mr. Johnson."

"Aye aye, sir."

Clifton climbed to the helm. The last round of cannon volleys blasted through the air. Water exploded in a violent spray as the cannonballs struck their target. As *Neptune's*

Servant pulled away, the other ship slipped below the water with a quiet burble. The lifeless body of Redbeard slipped below the surface with it.

* * *

Clifton strolled down the path to Whispering Manor. He'd slipped into port in the wee hours of the morning. Under the cover of night, he'd directed his men to hide the bounty from *Scourge of the Seas* in the chamber before blocking the sea cave access again.

As the sun peeked over the horizon, he'd left the ship and made his way to his sister's home. He slipped in through the front door. Candlelight flickered from the library. He peeked inside, finding it empty.

He stepped into the foyer, his eyes floating up the stairs. Footsteps sounded above. Before he could mount the stairs, Henrietta appeared, a book in her hand. She read it as she walked, grasping the railing before her foot searched for the step below.

She glanced up as she approached the bottom of the staircase. "Clif!" she exclaimed, a broad grin on her face.

"Hello, Ri."

She stared at him for a moment. "Well? Do you have some news?" she asked.

"I thought you'd never ask, Ri," he said with a grin. "Redbeard is no longer a problem."

"Then we are free!"

1802

Clifton lounged at the tavern in Tortuga, his feet propped on the table in front of him and a mug of ale perched on his midriff. The rowdy crowd around him enjoyed their evening.

Many of them were his crewmen, returned from another successful run. They'd need to add more to their treasure trove when he returned to Hideaway Bay.

A man wandered in, scanning the crowd. Red hair cascaded from under his hat. Clifton had never seen him before at the tavern, though he looked oddly familiar. The man's eyes focused on Clifton. Fury burned in his eyes as he stormed toward him. As he approached, he drew his pistol from his belt and pointed it at Clifton's chest.

The din hushed to silence and several of Clifton's crew members hurried to arm themselves. Six pistols pointed toward the red-haired man. Six pistols pointed back toward them as others rushed to defend the newcomer.

"Stand up, sir," the young man said.

Clifton crinkled his brow and stared up at him. "Who are you?"

"I said stand up, sir," he repeated.

"You are a dead man if you pull that trigger. You may be a dead man if you do not. What do you want?"

The man's jaw quivered for a moment before he firmed it. "I am Ronan O'Rourke, Junior. Son of…"

Realization dawned on Clifton and he interrupted him. "Of Redbeard."

The man nodded. "Yes. And I am here to issue a warning."

"A warning?" Clifton questioned.

"You killed my father."

"Yes, I did."

"So you admit it freely?"

"I do."

The man's jaw tensed. Clifton rose from his chair. The man steadied his gun. Clifton held up his hands. "Your father threatened both my life and my sister's. He knew well the dangers of his lifestyle and of such a threat."

"As do you. So when I kill you and your family, I will be justified. I have come to give you the honor of a warning."

Clifton inhaled deeply. "Do not do something foolish, my boy."

"I am not your boy!" he snapped.

"I can best you. Go back home."

He lowered his weapon and smirked at Clifton. "I spent a decade with my father on his ship. I captain my own ship now. I have loyal men, too. I will hunt you to the ends of the earth, Black Jack. And I will destroy the lives of your sisters, too. Henrietta and Carolina, is it? You have started a war you will lose. You have been warned. Henrietta will be first. If you have not surrendered your treasure and your life, I will murder Carolina next."

With a snap of his fingers, the other men lowered their weapons and followed the man from the tavern.

Clifton sighed as they departed. He took another sip of his ale. "Sir, your orders?" Johnson asked.

"Gather the crew. We set sail for Hideaway Bay tonight."

* * *

Clifton slipped into Whispering Manor as the afternoon sun hung low in the sky. A maid crossed the foyer. She stopped as he entered. "My sister?" he inquired.

"Mrs. Blanchard is writing," the girl informed him.

He nodded and climbed the stairs to the second floor. He pushed the door open to Henrietta's bedroom. She hunched over her writing desk, her quill flying across the page.

He wrapped his knuckles on the jamb. Henrietta jolted and spun to face the doorway, anger on her features. It melted away as she spotted him. "Clif! This is a surprise."

She stood from her chair as he maintained his post. "What is it? What's wrong?"

He swallowed hard. "We have a problem."

* * *

Henrietta paced the floor of her bedroom, considering the tale Clifton detailed. "And he is more of a concern than his father?"

"He has amassed a following of loyal sailors. I fear he can make good on his promise."

Henrietta mulled the information. "Can he be dealt with as his father?"

"I am not certain we could make a similar stand. He will not be as easy to manipulate as Redbeard. He is savvier."

"And all the wiser after his father's demise."

"Indeed."

"And he has threatened Carolina?"

"He has."

"We must put an end to that."

"Short of killing him, or him killing us, I do not see how we can."

"Or giving him the treasure."

"Perhaps we should."

"No!" Henrietta objected.

"Ri, it is not worth your life. Or Carolina's."

"Do you believe he will stop even if he attains the treasure?"

Clifton considered it. "No," he answered. "His attack is motivated by revenge. I believe he will seek it even if we give him every cent."

"Then we need another plan."

"But what?" Clifton said.

Henrietta paced for a few moments, her finger pressed to her lips. "I may have one."

Clifton raised his eyebrows. "How do you feel about a new ship?"

* * *

Clifton paced the floor of Henrietta's bedroom. "That's quite a plan, Ri," he said.

She beamed at him. "And one that will work."

"Are you certain you're happy with it?"

"As long as Carolina is safe, yes."

"It would be quite a change for you."

"I like change."

"You don't. I fear you may regret this."

Henrietta shook her head. "I will not. I am certain. I am ready for adventure."

"I suppose I have some things to prepare then."

"Yes, you have your work cut out for you."

* * *

The door to Whispering Manor creaked open on its hinges. Carolina glanced around the silent space. The last time she'd visited, her sister had learned of her husband's death.

She stepped inside, her eyes flitting to the sitting room. She recalled the moment Henrietta learned of Captain William Blanchard's death. Her sister had refused to accept it. She'd railed against anyone who dared suggest he was dead. She'd even tipped over his coffin at the funeral service.

And now she was dead. Both of her siblings were dead. Henrietta had thrown herself from the widow's walk, suffering from a bout of depression in which she realized her husband would never return from sea.

Her brother, Clifton, rife with guilt over what he described as failing his older sister had set sail on a dangerous mission. In an ironic twist of fate, his ship had wrecked off the same coast as William Blanchard's. The remains of the wreckage were spotted by another ship. They searched the waters for survivors, but found none.

Several skiffs had suffered a similar fate on the rocks. Another had bobbed in the water, empty. In six months' time, she had lost both her siblings. She should have reached out to Clif, she ruminated. She had been so busy preparing for her wedding, she had not, assuming there would be another opportunity.

James approached Carolina and squeezed her shoulder.

"I cannot believe they are both gone," she said as she reached for her husband's hand.

He offered her a weak smile. "She was so strong. So full of life. And then William died and…" Carolina's voice trailed off. "Her mind snapped. Poor Henrietta. I cannot imagine what went through her mind before she threw herself from the balcony."

"She was terribly disturbed, dear. She is at peace now."

"And Clif. Her death wrecked him."

"His occupation put him in danger, Carolina."

She nodded and wiped a tear from her cheek. "At least Mother and Father are not here to witness this."

"Though it is a shame you are left to deal with it alone."

She smiled at him through her tears. "I am not alone."

"Where shall we start?"

"I suppose upstairs. The rest of the items can stay with the home when we sell it. We should deal with her personal things, though."

Carolina and James climbed the stairs, stepping into Henrietta's bedroom. Carolina wandered to her desk. Several papers were scattered across it along with a brown leather journal.

She picked up the papers. Fantastical writing filled them.

"What is all this?" James asked as Carolina flipped through the brown book.

"Stories," she answered, as she paused at a crudely drawn map with a large "X" on it. "Henrietta was a writer. I imagine this is all her work."

"Will you keep it?"

Carolina shook her head as she gathered up the papers and the book. She descended the stairs and shoved the book onto a bookcase in the library. "Leave them for someone else to enjoy."

EPILOGUE

Henrietta sat in the library chair with a book on her lap. She'd long since lost interest in the story. Clifton had returned earlier in the day. With preparations made, it was time to implement their plan to remove the threat looming from Redbeard's progeny.

Nervous energy coursed through Henrietta. She bit her lower lip as she stared out the window.

"Mrs. Blanchard?" a voice called from the doorway.

Henrietta turned her gaze toward the girl. "What is it, Jane?"

"Would you like your afternoon tea brought into the library or your bedroom?"

"Hmm," Henrietta murmured. She fiddled with the edge of the book. "Perhaps here. I should like to be downstairs if William returns today." She focused on Jane. "Has there been any correspondence from him I've missed? It is not like him not to write?"

Jane offered an awkward smile. "No, Mrs. Blanchard."

"How odd. Clifton brought no news either. I am beginning to think he may not return."

"I shall fetch the tea."

Jane returned in a few moments with the tea tray. Henrietta's brow furrowed as she grabbed the girl's arm. "Jane," she said, "my memory seems to be failing me. When is the last time we heard from William?"

The girl swallowed hard and her eyes widened. Her lower lip bobbed as she attempted to formulate a response. "I am not certain, Mrs. Blanchard. Though I believe it has been years."

"What?" Henrietta inquired, her face incredulous. "No! It cannot be. You lie!"

The color drained from Jane's face as Henrietta's behavior deteriorated. "Now, now, what's all the ruckus in here?" Clifton inquired from the doorway.

Jane wrangled her arm away from Henrietta. "Jane claims William has not written in years. That's not true, is it? It cannot be true."

Clifton offered a conciliatory smile toward Jane. "You may go. I'll handle this."

Jane nodded and hurried from the room.

"Is it true, Clif?" Henrietta asked as Jane crossed the room.

"Now, Ri, we've been through this. William is not coming home."

"No! No! He cannot be dead. No, it cannot be true!" Henrietta shouted.

Clifton drew the pocket doors closed and spun to face her. She settled back in her chair with a wink. "Was I convincing?"

"I dare say so. Poor Jane was white as a sheet."

"It is a shame to have used her like that, but it must be done."

"Are you ready?"

"Are you?"

"Of course. Not long now."

"No. And then the first part of our plan shall be achieved."

"Then on to part two. Which I am still uncertain over."

Henrietta rolled her eyes at him. "Oh, Clif, I have every faith that you shall recover from your efforts. Think of it as a challenge."

* * *

As nightfall approached, Henrietta descended into the secret chamber behind the bookcase. Thunder rumbled overhead, resounding as she descended, guided by the meager flame of the hurricane lamp.

The light danced off the treasure in the cavern below. Henrietta searched through the chests, pocketing various items. She held up a bejeweled necklace. The gems sparkled in the light from the lamp. She slid it into her pocket.

She made her way to the exit. Before leaving, she took another look over the chamber. A shiver went up her spine. It was almost time. She bit her lower lip before squaring her shoulders and heading back to the house.

After securing the bookcase and resetting the tumblers for the lock, Henrietta paraded to the foyer.

"Jane!" Henrietta called. "Jane!" She huffed when the woman failed to appear. "Jane!" she shouted again.

Jane appeared in the back of the space. "Yes, Mrs. Blanchard?"

"Where have you been? I've called three times."

"My apologies, Mrs. Blanchard, I was scrubbing in the kitchen. With Elsie sick, I…"

"I do not wish to hear your excuses. Tea, please."

"Yes, ma'am. Will you take it in the sitting room?"

"No, in my bedroom. I must write. I feel a case of depression coming on, and it will be all I can do to stave it off. I must pour out my emotions onto the page."

Jane nodded at her and spun to retrieve the tea. Henrietta climbed the large staircase. She veered left at the top and entered her bedroom. Seating herself at her writing desk which overlooked a window facing the ocean, she gazed outside. The ocean's waves churned and roiled, crashing against the beach with all the fury of the building storm.

Her mind, too, roiled, but not with the depression she'd confessed to Jane. No, she mused, that was merely a distraction. An act. She had fooled them all. And she would continue to do so.

With a half-smile, she focused her attention on her brown leather journal. It sat open to a blank page. She dipped her quill in ink and began to pen a journal entry.

She finished the entry, penning the last words

Tonight, I shall take the first steps in cementing my destiny.

As she set the quill down, a knock sounded at her door. Jane entered after she called to her.

"I am leaving for my walk, Mrs. Blanchard. Unless you need something," Jane said.

Henrietta arched an eyebrow and a smirk formed on her lips. Before she faced the girl, she let her features fall and slumped her shoulders. "Nothing else."

Jane nodded and departed from the room, pulling the door closed behind her. Henrietta stood and gazed at the stormy sea again. It was time. Time for death.

She left her room and climbed to the widow's walk. Beforehand, she had changed into her black dress. The dress she'd worn to her husband's funeral.

The black fabric rustled in the night breeze. Lightning

still flashed over the rocky sea. Henrietta allowed a tear to roll down her cheek as she stared over the horizon.

Out of the corner of her eye, she spotted Jane leaving through the rear door. The woman glanced up at her. Henrietta gripped the railing and grimaced. She kept her eyes trained on the horizon as the girl continued down the beach.

When Jane was no longer in sight, Henrietta glanced over the edge of the railing. The hard ground lay below her. The view was dizzying. She swallowed hard. She could not avoid this moment. This would be the moment Henrietta Blanchard died.

She inched to the corner and raised her foot up to the railing. Grasping the metal bar that formed a ladder leading to the spot, she pulled herself upright until she balanced on the railing's edge.

The ground below danced as a gust of wind whipped past her. She clung to the foothold with her hands before she lifted one foot from the railing.

She stepped forward, swinging herself onto the ladder rung and shimmied down to the first story roof. She inched across it and scrambled down the trellis on the side of the house to the ground below.

"Good thing I taught you that trick when we were children," Clifton said as he appeared from behind one of the bushes.

"Yes, I did not wish to be caught going through the house. Do you have it?"

"Of course." He lifted a bucket clutched in his hand.

"Come along," she instructed, drawing him around the corner of the house. She stood under the widow's walk and pointed to a spot on the ground. "Pour it here. Not too much, just enough to be convincing."

Clifton poured the thick red liquid from the bucket. Pig's blood oozed onto the ground in a puddle. Henrietta reached for his hand as she lowered herself to the ground. She lined herself up with the puddle and lay back, her head centered in the blood spot.

"How do I look?" she asked.

"Convincing," Clifton said with a nod. "See you later."

"Wait!" Henrietta whispered.

Clifton stopped. She dipped her finger into the bucket swinging near her head and touched it to the corner of her mouth. The blood droplet ran down her cheek.

Clifton grimaced. "That's gruesome, Ri."

"But effective," she assured him. "Now go." She flitted her hand at him to shoo him away. He rounded the corner of the house as Henrietta lay on the cold ground.

Within ten minutes, Clifton's voice whispered, "Here she comes."

Henrietta froze with her limbs sprawled. She twisted her right leg at an awkward angle and flailed her left arm out to the side. She parted her lips and stared ahead with a blank expression.

She was careful not to flinch when, within a few moments of Clifton's warning, a scream sounded. Footfalls pounded toward her. Another scream. As she stared at the side of the house, she wished she could move to take in the scene but she held her breath, her eyes fixed forward.

"Help! Someone!" Jane called.

Within seconds, Clifton raced toward her. "What is it?" he questioned as he rounded the corner of the house.

His jaw fell open and he halted for a moment before he choked out, "Oh, no! Ri!" He collapsed at her side and hauled her into his arms. Henrietta did her best to stay limp, letting her head bobble as he pulled her toward him. Her arms hung limply at her side.

"Oh, Ri," he continued, "what have you done?"

Henrietta took the opportunity as he buried her face in his chest to blink. "We must get her upstairs."

"Shall I call for a doctor, sir?" Jane inquired.

Clifton lowered Henrietta's body for a moment and stared at her blank face. He ran his hand over her eyes, closing them. "I do not see the sense in it. She is gone. Poor woman. I thought she'd accepted William's death. It must have proved too much for her to bear."

"I should have stayed with her. She complained of depression."

"It is not your fault, Jane. I was here and I could do nothing to stop her. I assumed she'd returned to her room to rest after we'd spoken last."

He lifted Henrietta into his arms and carried her into the house. He climbed the stairs and laid her on her bed, arranging her arms across her stomach.

"Poor Mrs. Blanchard," Jane said. "May I bring you anything, sir?"

Clifton waved his hand to dismiss her. "No, nothing, thank you, Jane." He pushed a lock of hair away from Henrietta's face and wiped the blood from her lip. "Rest now, dear sister," he said as Jane pulled the door closed behind her.

After a moment, he whispered, "She's gone."

Henrietta popped her eyes open. "It worked!" she said with a grin.

"Yes. By tomorrow, you will officially be dead."

"And you shall take my body to be buried at sea."

"Then, Henrietta Blanchard will be no more."

She offered an amused smirk and her eyes sparkled. "And it will be your turn to perish."

* * *

Clifton sipped his ale at the tavern in Tortuga. He'd finished his solemn duty of sending his sister to a watery grave. He'd written Carolina to inform her of Henrietta's death and his plans. After the job was complete, he sailed into Tortuga for a respite before continuing their plan.

The men were aware of what needed to be done. And they were in agreement. Those that were not were given a generous severance for their time served and released amicably.

Clifton ordered another ale and pretended to down it. "Bartender, another!" he shouted with words slurred.

With another ale in his hands, he leaned forward over the mug. His eyelids grew heavy as he sipped at it.

Johnson entered the tavern. "Ah! Johnson, my good man," Clifton slurred as he leapt to his feet. The quick movement sent him stumbling back a step before he caught him.

"Captain," Johnson greeted him.

"Johnson," he slurred again. "Gather the men. We shall set sail tonight."

"Tonight, sir?"

Clifton nodded, a move that made him stagger forward a step. He leaned against Johnson, nearly collapsing into him. "I've heard a rumor, and I want to determine its truth."

"What rumor, captain?"

"A rumor about a treasure accessible only after dark."

Johnson furrowed his brow and swallowed hard. "I am not following, sir."

"Gather the men and prepare to set sail, Johnson. We sail for the Isle of Denvia."

"Is this a wise pursuit, Captain? You are still grieving the loss of your sister, only a foolish man who wishes death attempts…"

"Gather the men and prepare to set sail," Clifton repeated.

"Aye, sir. Though some of the men are… unavailable."

Clifton's head swiveled as though he had trouble steadying it. "Then we sail without them."

Johnson nodded and departed to gather the crew. Clifton collapsed into the chair behind him. A man approached from the back of the tavern. His slight stature and frame made it easy for him to squeeze through the other men and approach Clifton.

"Excuse me," he said.

Clifton eyed him. "Yes?"

"Are you, by chance, Black Jack? The Captain of *Neptune's Servant?*"

"Who wants to know?"

"A sailor hoping to join your crew."

Clifton eyed the man and laughed. "A sailor hoping to join my crew? You? You wouldn't survive a journey at sea."

"I am tougher than I look," the man said, placing his hands on his hips in defiance.

Clifton narrowed his eyes at the man. "Why do you wish to join me?"

"I've heard a rumor that you pursue a nearly unattainable goal."

"Did you, now?"

"Yes. And I wish to be a part of it."

"I contend once again that you would not survive the journey."

"I assure you I will. If you'll give me the chance, I shall prove my worth on this journey. If I do not, you may discharge me."

Clifton considered it. "All right, boy. You may join. Present yourself to Mr. Johnson at the ship. We sail tonight."

The man nodded and offered a half-smile before spinning on his heel and striding from the tavern.

* * *

The crew of *Neptune's Servant* hoisted the anchor and set sail as the sun set behind them. Clifton's newest crew member stood atop the helm, his arms crossed as the ship slipped from the port of Tortuga.

Clifton climbed the steps to the perch. "Are you certain you'll survive the journey?" he inquired.

"Yes," the man answered.

Clifton offered a half-smile. "You know, I forgot to ask your name, sailor."

With a smirk, he answered, "I've gone by a few, though those closest to me call me 'Ri.'" He removed his hat, revealing long flowing dark curls. His sister smirked at him and raised her eyebrows.

Clifton smirked at her. "I think you are quite enjoying this."

"I am!" She spun in a circle. "How do I look? I've never worn trousers before though I must say, I quite like them."

"Well, you certainly cannot be a pirate in a dress."

"I'm certain I could if I tried, but I find this much more convenient."

Clifton stared out over the horizon. "Are you sad to leave this behind?"

"The *Neptune* has been a good ship. And Black Jack has been an excellent pirate."

Henrietta eyed him sideways. "But it is time for a new adventure."

Neptune's Servant glided through the darkened waters as the sun slipped below the horizon. "Ease her to a stop, Daniels," Clifton ordered as they approached the Isle of Denvia. "Not too close yet."

"Captain," Johnson reported, "we are ready to disembark."

"Good, lower the skiffs and begin to shuttle the men."

"Aye, sir!"

Johnson set to work barking orders to the crew members.

Clifton twisted to face Henrietta, who still stood on the helm. "You should go."

She knit her brows and cocked her head. "You must be joking."

"I am not. Go."

"No. You will need help to finish this."

"I will ask Johnson."

"No." She crossed her arms and stood firm. "I will see it through."

"Ri…"

"Don't. We do it together or we do not do it at all."

Clifton shook his head and puckered his lips. "I'm beginning to second-guess this partnership."

She offered him a coy glance as Johnson approached. "Sir, the final boat is ready."

"Launch it and wait in the waters nearby."

"What about you, captain. And…" He motioned to Henrietta. "Her."

"We will join you once the mission is finished."

"Aye, sir," he said. He disappeared from the helm, climbing into the final skiff. Clifton watched as they rowed away, bobbing in the water.

"Come, along, Ri. We have work to do." Together, they raised the anchor and climbed back to the helm. Clifton used the ship's wheel to guide the *Neptune* toward the rocky coast of the island.

Within minutes, the ship shuddered as the bottom of the sea closed toward it. Seconds after, they were knocked from their feet as the ship struck a large outcropping. Wood splintered and cracked against the pointed rocks.

"Come on, Ri, time to abandon ship," Clifton said as he offered her a hand to climb to her feet.

They approached the rear of the ship. Clifton climbed onto the side and hoisted Henrietta up next to him. "Ready?"

She nodded. "Let's go be pirates."

The two leapt from the sinking vessel and swam toward the waiting dinghy. They were hauled aboard, and the crewmen rowed at a safe distance around the island. As they rounded it, Henrietta grinned at the sight.

A large four-masted ship stood tall in the water.

"She's larger than your last ship," Henrietta noted.

"Aye. She'll need to be with her two captains," Clifton said with a wink.

"She's beautiful," Henrietta said. "What did you name her?"

Clifton grinned at her. "*The Henton.*"

* * *

Keep reading the series with *A Pirate's Life for Ri*, Book 2 in the Clif & Ri on the Sea series.

A NOTE FROM THE AUTHOR

Dear Reader,

Thank you for reading this book! *Rise of a Pirate* was a complete surprise to me! It began as a prequel novella to Book 1 of my cozy mystery series Lily & Cassie by the Sea and blossomed into its own series. I loved the characters of Clif & Ri!

I hope you enjoyed reading this book as much as I did writing it! If you loved it, please consider leaving a review and help get the book into the hands of other interested readers.

Book 2 in this series isn't available yet, but look for it coming in 2023! In the meantime, you can read more about Clif and Henrietta in the series that gave birth to their story. *Ghosts, Lore & a House by the Shore* is available now!

If you'd like to stay up to date with all my news, be the first to find out about new releases first, sales and get free offers, join the Nellie H. Steele's Mystery Readers' Group! Or sign up for my newsletter now!

All the best, Nellie

GHOSTS, LORE & A HOUSE BY THE SHORE SYNOPSIS

A new town. A haunting legend. New beginnings or the beginning of the end?

After Cassie MacGuire's husband dies in a plane crash along with her father, both her and her mother, Lily Bennett, are widowed. Looking to make a new start, they move together to the quiet seaside town of Hideaway Bay. But their new home, Whispering Manor, has a reputation stretching back centuries. Legends of ghosts, paranormal disturbances and pirate treasure are all associated with the former sea captain's mansion, starting with the death of its first mistress, Henrietta Blanchard.

When Cassie stumbles upon Henrietta's journal and Lily uncovers a more recent tragedy in the home, they begin to wonder if the stories may be fact instead of fiction. When the strange occurrences turn dangerous, Lily and Cassie will have to investigate to save their home and possibly even their very lives!

Ghosts, Lore & a House by the Shore is the charming first installment in this small, seaside town mother-daughter cozy mystery series by Nellie H. Steele.

Grab *Ghosts, Lore & a House by the Shore* today!

GHOSTS, LORE & A HOUSE BY THE SHORE EXCERPT

*L*ily pulled the door open. Two women stood on the porch. A tall, lithe woman with a chic blonde bob, dressed in a bright pink skirt suit with matching heels smiled widely. Next to her stood a shorter, round woman. Her brunette bob mimicked the blonde's though fell shorter on style. She wore a navy pantsuit and a sensible pair of flats. She clutched her purse in both hands as she eyed Cassie and Lily.

"Hello," Lily said. "Can I help you?"

"Hi!" the blonde said in a cheery voice. "You must be Lily and Cassie." She stuck her hand out. "I'm Tinsley Thompson, Hideaway Bay's mayor and president of the welcoming committee! I'm also your neighbor! Two houses down that way." She pointed south.

The woman continued, motioning toward her companion. "And this is Penny Whitlock. She's part of the town's commerce committee. She reviewed *Buy the Sea's* business proposal."

"Oh," Lily said as she shook their hands, followed by

Cassie, "nice to meet you both. Is there a problem with the business proposal?"

"No!" Tinsley answered with a laugh that bordered on cackle. "No, nothing like that. We're here to say a friendly Hideaway Bay hello to the two new gals!"

"How nice," Lily answered. "Won't you come in?"

"Oh, just for a few moments," Tinsley said, wrinkling her nose. "I'm sure you're busy getting settled."

The two women stepped into the foyer. "Oh, it's been so long since I've seen the inside of this old place," Tinsley babbled.

"Can I get anyone something to drink? Hot tea or lemonade?" Cassie offered.

"Oh, a hot tea would be lovely!" Tinsley answered. "Wouldn't it, Penny?" The short woman nodded, seemingly pulled along with whatever Tinsley decided.

Cassie disappeared toward the kitchen to fill the orders of tea as Lily settled into the sitting room with the two women.

Tinsley perched on the edge of her chair and offered a wide smile to Lily. "It's so nice to see Whispering Manor with life in it again."

"It had been on the market quite a while from what I understand," Lily answered.

Tinsley nodded her head. "Oh, yes, yes. Two years. Though no one has lived here for at least five."

"More than that," Penny interjected.

"Well, I said *at least*," Tinsley retorted.

"Either way," Lily interjected, "we're so glad Lucy showed it to us. We fell in love with the house and the town."

"That's wonderful to hear," Tinsley said with a demure smile as Cassie returned with a tray of mugs.

"We've only unpacked the mugs. Sorry, no fancy china."

"Oh, it's just fine," Penny answered with a genuine smile as she accepted a steaming mug from the tray.

"We'll just have to book another tea party with the china once you're settled in," Tinsley said as she offered a half-smile, half-frown at the bulldog mascot emblazoned on the mug.

"Your business proposal was one of the best I've ever read," Penny said as Cassie settled onto the sofa next to Lily.

"Oh, thank you," Cassie said with a large smile. "Owning a shop like this has always been something we've talked about."

Tinsley raised her eyebrows. "Oh? How interesting. I thought you were a librarian."

"Yes, I was," Cassie answered. "Though after my husband and father passed away, we decided we needed a change. We had always talked about owning a shop and decided maybe now was the time."

"Oh, yes," Tinsley said with an understanding nod and a pout on her face. "What a terrible tragedy. Such a shame." She shook her head and clicked her tongue.

"How is the work at the shop coming?" Penny inquired. "I saw the sign already hanging out front earlier today."

Cassie opened her mouth to answer but Tinsley beat her to it.

"Oh, Penny, let's not badger them about it their first day in town! I'm sure they have plenty of settling in to do here before they worry about the shop!"

"Well, we hope to be there..." Lily began as Tinsley shushed her and waved for her to stop.

"There's no need to explain at all. We understand." She took a sip of her tea as awkward silence fell over the room. "Speaking of signs, I noticed your Whispering Manor sign dangling sideways from the lamppost sideways. I'm not sure if you saw it."

"Yes," Lily answered. "We hung it just before lunch and

the chain snapped. We'll need to fix it later. I insisted we have some lunch before Cassie climbed that ladder again."

"Ah, yes. A faulty chain." Tinsley offered a knowing glance. "I'm glad to see you are both so level-headed and didn't give in to the lore."

"Lore?" Cassie inquired.

"Oh, yes," Tinsley said with a slow nod of her head. "I'm surprised Lucy didn't tell you. Though, then again, she wanted to make the deal, no doubt. And I suppose she's not really required to disclose it. It IS only a rumor. And technically the death wasn't IN the house."

"Death? Disclose what?" Cassie asked.

"Oh," Tinsley said flicking her hand at Cassie and shaking her head. She puckered her lips and narrowed her eyes. "Nothing, nothing. Just…" She paused and added a dramatic shrug. "Some people would have read the snapping sign as a harbinger of bad things to come because…"

Cassie raised her eyebrows and cocked her head.

Tinsley glanced side-to-side before leaning forward and pressing her hand to the side of her mouth. "The house is haunted," she whispered.

Want to read more? Buy *Ghosts, Lore & a House by the Shore* today!

OTHER SERIES BY NELLIE H. STEELE

<u>Cozy Mystery Series</u>

Cate Kensie Mysteries
Lily & Cassie by the Sea Mysteries
Pearl Party Mysteries
Middle Age is Murder Cozy Mysteries

<u>Supernatural Suspense/Urban Fantasy</u>

Shadow Slayers Stories
Duchess of Blackmoore Mysteries

<u>Adventure</u>

Maggie Edwards Adventures
Clif & Ri on the Sea

www.ingramcontent.com/pod-product-compliance
Lightning Source LLC
Chambersburg PA
CBHW060909210726
48293CB00006B/2025